A NEW START

OUTBACK QUEENSLAND ROMANCE
BOOK 4

RHONDA FORREST

Valeena Press

ALSO BY RHONDA FORREST

OUTBACK QUEENSLAND ROMANCE SERIES

With a cast of eclectic characters and set amidst the rugged outback of Australia, the **Outback Queensland Romance Series** will introduce you to stories of friendship, resilience, and loving relationships that come together to triumph over obstacles defined by the past.

Two Heartbeats (Book 1) is followed by the sequel, *Time Will Tell* (Book 2)

Turn Left (Book 3), *A New Start* (Book 4), *Outback Magic* (Book 5) and *Echoes of the Outback* (Book 6) are stand-alone books with some links to the other books in this series.

To my wonderful lifelong friends, Dawn, Denise, and Karen, and to all those who also took the leap and embarked on a new start.

A NEW START

1

Elsie peered over the top of her book to take a look at the young man sitting across from her. He had boarded several stops after her and had offered a distraction for the last ten minutes. Commuting to work each morning not only provided her with time to immerse herself in a book but also offered the opportunity for some people-watching. It was one of her favourite pastimes and she had even invented names for the regulars who often sought out their usual spots. She avoided conversation with most on the train, the commuters on either side of her an exception to her rule of keeping to herself.

Matilda as usual sat next to her, the middle-aged woman's ample hips pushed up against Elsie's. Today as she did every day, Matilda wore a light blue house-keeping uniform that came down to just below her knees. She was a cleaner at Southbank and spent her day picking up cigarette butts and other pieces of rubbish that, 'Those grubs who throw their trash on the ground, really, they're the unsung heroes keeping my cleaning job thriving—turning litterbugs into job security, one discarded sandwich wrapper at a time,' she told Elsie.

On the other side of Elsie was Maurie, his portly body clothed in neat black trousers and a white collared shirt. Maurie, who had just turned sixty, waited on tables at West End, his time spent chasing pigeons away from diner's meals, serving drinks, washing up dishes and cleaning.

On most mornings the three of them managed to sit side-by-side and over the past couple of years Matilda and Maurie had become what Elsie thought of as her 'train friends'. They shared their good times and their problems, offering a sense of camaraderie amid the struggles of life. Sometimes it helped to realise that she wasn't the only one fighting to make ends meet or trying to navigate the difficulties of family life.

However, she consciously talked in depth only to Matilda and Maurie, often finding comfort and useful advice in the familiarity of their conversations. There were other regular commuters she recognised who lived in her suburb or who she had crossed paths with over the years, however she limited her interactions to a friendly nod or smile. Talking to others would only complicate her daily journey to work. She had enough of her own problems to contend with.

Matilda had also noticed the man sitting opposite and nudged Elsie. The older woman's eyes looked over the top of her glasses and then back to the knitting in her hands as she leaned in and whispered, 'Bit posh that one.'

'Maybe an undercover cop or a lawyer,' Elsie replied softly, concealing her voice behind her book so only

Matilda could hear. She stole another glance at the man who was stylishly dressed and probably worked in one of the offices in town, his home no doubt one of the fancy sorts of residences they didn't usually get a glimpse of from the train line. Glancing down she noticed his distinctive footwear; tan shiny leather shoes, with neatly tied laces matched by plain brown socks peeking out from under the pressed formal trouser legs. His shoes stood out among the usual array of thongs, worn-out sneakers and practical closed-in shoes that were standard for most commuters this time of the morning.

She stared as he readjusted his tie, the stark black of the fabric, neat and crisp against a formal white long-sleeved shirt.

As Elsie observed him, she couldn't help but marvel at the seemingly effortless life he embodied. Her thoughts drifted, contemplating the simplicity that must accompany such an existence. Her gaze lingered on his clean-shaven cheeks and handsome face; even his neatly arranged brown hair seemed to tell a tale of a life well put together. The short, perfectly styled strands hinted at a level of grooming she could only imagine. The thought of being able to afford regular visits to the hairdresser or to purchase shoes as polished as he had, briefly flitted through her mind.

At that moment, a subtle pang of envy crept in, like a shadow cast by the disparity between their worlds. She sighed inwardly, reminded once again of the stark contrast between her own struggles and the perceived ease of his life. Blinking quickly, she drew her eyes away, attempting to mask her judgements. His gaze however had already captured hers and as she looked back at him their eyes met. A knowing look passed between them—a silent acknowledgment of the unspoken observation that had transpired.

Despite her attempt to divert her attention, she felt a flush of embarrassment. His prolonged gaze left her in a state of uncertainty, a lingering doubt that he might have detected her discreet scrutiny of his appearance. The air seemed charged with an unspoken tension, a delicate dance between curiosity and self-consciousness. Elsie couldn't help but wonder what perceptions he held of her, a resident of the less polished side of life, caught in the act of studying the finer details of his seemingly charmed existence.

When he shuffled in his seat she took one last look, curious that he had a large well-worn leather bag with him. Usually, office workers had a briefcase or a computer case, not a bag that would hold enough clothes for a week. Averting her gaze, she instead stared in the other direction, past Maurie, as she adjusted her hair. She looked at her reflection in the dividing barrier between theirs and the next lot of seats. Today she wore different clothes, because today was not just any usual work day. Her regular navy uniform—with the insignia of the hotel where she cleaned stitched onto the sleeve— and closed-in shoes, had been replaced by jeans and a t-shirt, strappy sandals on her feet and her hair loose and resting on her shoulders. Maurie turned to her. 'You look beautiful, love,' he said. 'They'll adore you.'

She pushed the brown curls back behind her ears. 'Do you think they will Maurie? I hope so. I want to do a great job.'

'Who wouldn't want you working for them,' he

replied. 'I'm proud of you. We've sat on this train for over two years and shared a lot of ups and downs. You've done all you can for your family. It's your turn now. Look at you, you're twenty-five and ready to take on the world.'

She placed her hand on his arm. 'Thank you. That means a lot to me.'

Matilda leaned over and pushed a brown paper bag towards her. 'Just a knitted beanie and a crocheted blanket for you, my love. Not that you'll probably need it where you're going, but surely they get some cold weather sometime.'

Elsie put her book down and leaned each way to give them both a hug. 'Thank you. I'll miss these train chats. It'll be strange not to see you each morning as I go to work.'

'Don't let anyone stand in your way. You deserve a break. Go get 'em!' Matilda grinned broadly as she clenched her fist and held it high.

'Don't miss that connecting train,' Maurie advised as he stood up, ready to get out at the next stop. 'Today is the first day of your new life.'

She gave them both another hug, their destination, Southbank Station, now visible through the windows. They had exchanged phone numbers with each other and she intended to keep in touch with them both and let them know how she was going. They had been a source of support and sound advice over the previous two years as she grappled with ensuring not only her own well-being but also that of her siblings.

Maurie and Matilda stood on the platform and waved to her as the train pulled slowly out of the station. A pang of nostalgia swept over her. It wasn't only her two train friends who she was leaving behind. Others had supported her where she lived in Logan, the place she had called home her entire life. The ladies at the food centre, a few close friends and her brother and sister had always been there for her. She bent down and pulled her bag in closer. However she was ready for a move and hopefully this new teaching position at Matfield State High School was going to be the start of an interesting and fulfilling career and the end of the life she had known for the past twenty-five years.

When she finally looked away from the window and turned back to face the middle of the train, she noticed the man opposite her staring. She glowered back at him, knowing that he would have heard everything that Maurie and Matilda had said. The last thing she needed was some rich fella listening to her conversation and judging her. She picked her book up and put it in front of her face. It was always a good way to avoid eye contact or conversation with anyone.

As the train gradually pulled away from the station, Elsie made a conscious effort to quell the nervous flutter in her stomach. The enormity of the move she was making loomed before her. Maurie's words echoed in her mind, affirming that this was the initial leap into her new life. Other sentiments from those who knew her well also reverberated. 'Good on you. You deserve this chance,' they had cheered, encouraging her to take the leap, urging her to escape the confines of her home and distance herself from the challenges posed by her mother and her dysfunctional family life. Maurie was right. Today was the first day of her new life.

2

———

Elsie's family situation wasn't the typical nuclear model that many would deem 'functional'. However, despite the run-down timber house on Resilience Street being anything but normal, it had always been home. While it often echoed with heated arguments and abusive tirades, with her mother hurling insults at one or all three of them, it had crazily enough served as a security blanket. Not of her own choice, but out of necessity, it was a place to come back to every night. Despite her mother's tendency to roam the country and come and go when she felt like it, with whichever man happened to catch her fancy, Elsie chose to stay. The house, with all its imperfections, was a constant in her life and up until now, all she had ever known.

Once she was old enough, she could have moved out and tried to rent somewhere else, however she had stayed living at home so she could complete her schooling and then after that, make her way through the arduous struggle of university. Often she could only manage one subject at a time as her cleaning job in the city had to take priority. Luckily they lived not that far away from a train line and the motel where she worked paid well, providing her with consistent work over the years. It did however mean that she had to juggle travelling into the city with home life and studying. This chaotic existence along with other issues that continually popped up made the process of becoming a qualified teacher lengthy. There hadn't been a choice though and the reason she stayed at home was so she could look after her two younger siblings. Elsie sacrificed everything to make sure they were cared for and finished their schooling.

Now her younger brother, Peter had turned twenty and her sister, Jane who had recently completed high school, celebrated her eighteenth birthday the week before. Although they had also pulled their weight when it came to bringing in money from part-time jobs she had continued to uphold the vow she made to herself. Even from a young age, she felt a commitment towards them and always made sure to look after them. As the eldest, it was her responsibility. She had taken on the role of mother and father. Not that there had ever been a father. Who knew where he was? 'Dead or in jail,' her mother, Peggie, told them. 'And if he isn't I wish he was.' But who could ever believe what Peggie said? None of them could remember him being around so perhaps he was dead. Sometimes she wished that her mother was also dead. Life was less complicated when she wasn't around.

Elsie was only been sixteen when Peggie started to leave them to fend for themselves. She had regularly flounced in, announcing she had met the perfect man— again— and she was just going away for a while, travelling with him. When her mother's absences from the house first started, Elsie's initial response had been to panic. The overwhelming dread of trying to manage the household while taking responsibility for the younger two, who were only at primary school at that stage, was exhausting and stressful. The hurdles were endless and all she could do was take each day as it came. Her priorities, apart from making sure there was enough food in the house, were not only to ensure that she got to school but that Peter and Jane also attended their lessons each day. There was also the responsibility of working part-time to make sure she could pay for what they needed. Her aim was to make sure they all stayed safe and not draw attention to the fact that there was no adult in the house.

The dread of trying to juggle all of these problems was however over time, replaced by a sense of relief. She soon discovered that even with all the responsibilities she took on, life was better when it was just them at home without their mother. Peggie had a major drinking problem and when she went on a bender, life became a living hell. Over the years they developed strategies to avoid their mother's outbursts. Like young animals learning survival tactics, they worked out several plans to keep their daily routines intact and as normal as possible. It was like a game, eluding the frenzied outbursts and irrational behaviour that their mother constantly displayed while the three of them continued to turn up at school, just like it was any other ordinary day.

If they remained at school as long as they could, by participating in sports or musical lessons after three o'clock, they could stay together and leave school at the same time. The charity drop-in centre wasn't far away and it was a reliable safe stop on the way home. The people who volunteered there gave out free food and cooked meals, and sometimes she had even been given pencil cases filled with pens, pencils and other stationery that was always needed for school. Elsie had become an expert in finding ways of obtaining other items they needed and a couple of the older ladies at the centre often had a bag of clothes and toiletry items ready to give her when she dropped in.

She also made sure that the three of them stuck together at night and on weekends. It wasn't safe walking the streets once it was dark or hanging out in the park with some of the kids in the neighbourhood. There were plenty of others out there who were quick to prey on the young and vulnerable and she made sure her family didn't draw attention to themselves or hang out with the wrong people.

Although there were certain people that Elsie had learned to avoid in the neighbourhood there were also plenty of other kids who lived near them who could be trusted. Those kids also came from 'dysfunctional' homes and struggled similarly, always looking out for free food and household items. It was helpful to support each other but the bottom line was that everyone was trying to fend for themselves and she had learned that she could manage better if she focused on Peter and Jane. At least they had a house to stay in at night which was more than some of the other kids at her school had. For many of them it was safer to sleep under someone else's house or join the campers who had a collection of tents and humpies hidden in the bushes down near the river.

There was no way her family were ever going to sleep at the river. If they started down that track there would be no going back. Even though she had occasionally seen some of the local kids just stay at the camp for a while and then return to their homes, the majority of those who slept there became long-termers. Over the years they became bedraggled, more down and out, and often started running jobs for the druggies or other unsavoury people who frequented the camp.

Even though there had been quite a few occasions when Elsie had needed to put emergency plans into action to get out of the house quickly, she stayed away from the group near the river. When Peggie had been violent or brought a couple of her so-called friends back to their place, Elsie had been prepared. When a situation looked like it was going to get out of hand she had acted before it was too late. Bundling Peter and Jane up along with a bag full of food and clothes she had taken them to sleep, or rather hide, in an abandoned shed that was on a large block of land next door to where they lived. Their mother would never think to look for them in there. The yard where their hideout was had a six-foot timber fence around it, with wire running around the top of it. It was an industrial block of land that had a couple of sheds on it used for storage, timber and furniture. Peggie didn't know that Elsie had ensured that boards could be easily removed from the timber fence on their side and the three of them could quickly go through the gap, into the safety of a bleak, but warm and dry sanctuary.

It was a safe place to curl up and sleep, or sit and talk. They had used it even when they had been little kids and

Elsie called it the safe shed. 'Do you think Mum knows this is where we come?' Peter asked.

'She knows we leave the house,' Jane added. 'She swore at me the other day because she said she'd looked for us to go and buy her some more smokes and none of us were there. That night when they were all doing drugs and the police ended up coming in the morning.'

'What did you tell her?' Elsie asked.

'I didn't swear at her —just told her that mothers shouldn't ask their kids to walk around the streets so late at night just to buy their filthy cigarettes. Mum said it was only midnight when she looked for us and the servo didn't shut until one in the morning. She thought we would've had time to get them for her.'

Peter added, 'She reckons if we'd been at home and helped her they wouldn't have got so messed up and then the cops wouldn't have come. She told me it was all your fault, Elsie. Said you took us down to the river camp to stay the night and that you thought you were smart but really you aren't.'

Elsie shook her head. 'She's getting worse. Those scummy friends of hers cleaned out the fridge and cupboard. They stole my clothes off the washing line.' Elsie sighed. 'The problem was that fella Bert wasn't there. She wouldn't have had all those others over if he'd been around. I don't think he likes Mum's friends that much.'

For the last few years, Peggie had been in an on-and-off relationship with Bert, who lived on the other side of Logan. 'On the posh side of the highway,' her mother would love to tell them. 'He's good to me. Buys me flowers and expensive wine.'

Elsie had only met Bert on a couple of occasions and although he looked much like her mother's past boyfriends, with a huge stomach, bowlegs like a horse had just walked out from underneath, and a long beard, he seemed half decent. 'He don't like my friends though and he asks too many questions. I told him your grandma stays with you kids when I'm not here and we go away in his van,' her mother said.

Peter had screwed up his face. 'We don't have a grandma.'

'Well, he don't know that, does he? Anyway, Elsie is old enough to look after you. You're at school all day anyway.'

Elsie gritted her teeth. It had been the way of life for as long as she could remember. But now there were changes in the wind. Not only had she somehow managed to get herself through high school and nearly through university but Peter had also worked hard and was in his third year of university. He was studying Veterinary Science and living in a shared house with some other students in Townsville. Jane had finished Year 12 a couple of months ago and worked hard to win a scholarship that included board and lodgings with the Medical Faculty at Townsville University. Elsie was pleased that Peter and Jane would be living in the same city. At least they had each other nearby if needed. The three of them were set in different directions, all on career paths that would hopefully allow them to never step foot on Resilience Street again.

The only good part about coming from where they did was that the guidance officer at school had easily been able to plead Peter and Jane's cause for special scholarships that recognised high-performing students who came from disadvantaged backgrounds. 'Easy to tick the box and I'll write a reference to explain the issues that you contend with. You Jackson kids have all been super smart and great kids. You'd get into university probably without this help but these scholarships will give you the financial support to let you finish your degrees more easily.'

As the train slowed and glided into Roma Street in Brisbane, Elsie silently expressed her gratitude to the teachers and staff who had consistently supported her. While she hadn't been fortunate enough to receive a scholarship like Jane and Peter, she had financed her education by working nights, stocking shelves, and taking on cleaning duties at the local library. One year she also managed to work as a teacher-aide, the experience reinforcing that teaching was what she wanted to do. Cleaning at the hotel in the city had been the best job for the last two years, but now she had left that one also. Now that her siblings had found their respective paths it was time to forge her own destiny. The days of residing at number ten Resilience Street were behind her; a one-year contract at Matfield School awaited, marking the beginning of her professional journey. Hopefully this year, the stars would align for her.

3

Now as she stood up and moved to the back of the carriage towards where she could get out, she watched others who were also getting ready to disembark. It was clear that the man who had sat opposite her and had eavesdropped on her conversations with Maurie and Ruby didn't catch trains that often. He stood in front of her with his bag in hand, looking for the button to push that would unlatch the door. She leaned across in front of him, then stepped back as the doors in front of them opened. She stepped off onto the platform and took a deep breath. The next train she caught would take her towards her destination.

The rest of her belongings, of which there were very few, were being transported to her residence by the department, which was also covering any costs incurred with the move. There was a shortage of teachers throughout the country and she was lucky that in Queensland they were so in need of teachers that they were offering one-year contracts for those about to finish university. *Complete your degree while you learn on the job and get paid*, the advertisement stated. The arrangement suited her perfectly as well as the bonus conditions that came with the contracts offered; extra mentoring, a lighter load of teaching and additional pay for country service. With Jane and Peter settled and no longer at home it had been an easy choice. It was her way of finishing a degree that had already been stretched out over seven years. Recently she had felt as if she was never going to graduate. All her spare time had been spent working and she was exhausted. After work she had studied sometimes until the sun came up. Now instead of juggling all of that, she could concentrate on teaching and completing just one subject. 'Matfield here I come,' she whispered to herself.

MATT MADE a conscious effort not to glance at the girl seated across from him on the train. She appeared to be a regular traveller, evident in the ease with which she engaged with those beside her. Her familiarity with fellow passengers was obvious, given the nods she exchanged as others disembarked. The train hosted its usual assortment of commuters, a diverse mix typical of the mid-morning schedule. With the school rush having concluded, the seats were now occupied predominantly by workers, interspersed with a few individuals who bore the worn expression of a night spent on the streets. Having lodged at a friend's residence the previous night, Matt found the train to be the quickest means of reaching the city. An early morning appointment with a solicitor, whose office operated from a modest space in a suburban shopping centre, coincided precisely with the departure schedule of the current train and the subsequent connection in Brisbane

Jamieson, the solicitor, had tidied up all the loose ends that would let Matt have custody and care for his younger brother, Ethan, the youngest of his siblings. At sixteen Ethan still had a year of high school to go and Matt was going to make sure that he not only completed it but was in a situation to give it his best. The kids in his family, the Maloney's, might not have had the best home life or money to buy sometimes even the necessities they needed, but they had all been blessed with brains. Not all of them had put the high intelligence to good use though and one of Matt's brothers, Frank, had ended up on the wrong side of the law, landing in jail for robbery and stealing cars. Once he was released, he had taken off to Western Australia, where another brother, Jamie had also soon followed. That was over five years ago now and with Matt working in a variety of places throughout Queensland, for a long while it had only been Ethan at home.

Matt had come and gone in between his work contracts; after all, his parents were there. Ethan should have been looked after. But their home life had never been good and his mother and father's drinking habits as well as their gambling addictions had gone from bad to worse. The lifestyle his parents led had been the reason Matt left home so young and probably why his older brothers had gone off the rails. It was why he had never fulfilled his dream of finishing high school and going on to university. Not that he was complaining though. There was always plenty of good paying work on the properties out west. Fencing, mustering and anything anyone wanted doing — he was their man.

As he hoisted his bag onto his shoulder and tried to work out how to get the doors open, he felt a sense of relief. Now he had proper legal custody and within the week, Ethan would be coming out west to live with him and finish his final year of schooling. He flinched and dragged his thoughts back to the present as the girl he had been observing reached over in front of him and pushed a button, the doors immediately opening. She didn't look his way and he admired how she carried herself. Confident, pretty, and also a 'don't mess with me' attitude.

4

A bench of metal seats was full of waiting passengers and Elsie perched on the end of one, tucking her bag in under her feet. The connecting train to Rockhampton was stationary on the railway line in front, workers completing the last of their cleaning before letting a new lot of passengers on. Many of those waiting were elderly, although there was a group of younger people standing down further. Elsie watched them, thinking how they reminded her of some of her mother's friends. Middle-aged, scruffy, and smoking as they stood talking. She grimaced as they began to hurl abuse at one of the station workers who asked them to put out their cigarettes. The worker pointed to an area way down the other end of the platform which was a designated smoking area. Elsie looked away and ignored the rough language that some of them used. Hopefully, they wouldn't be near her on the train. She only had a seat, not the luxury of a sleeper, but Rockhampton was an eight-hour journey and she hoped to catch some sleep while she travelled, albeit sitting up.

A woman who was part of the smokers' group jumped around and at one stage bent over the railway line as if she was going to fall over the edge. She had long straggling hair and a range of tattoos covering her arms and now she approached the windows of the stationary train. Her language was coarse and she banged on the sides of the train demanding to be let in. Another man joined her, his language just as foul-mouthed as he hopped around, his attitude jittery and abusive. Elsie drew her eyes away, aware that many people were staring at the group and talking amongst themselves.

An older man next to her muttered under his breath, 'Scum. Bloody get the train for free and they still carry on.'

She ignored the comment. Growing up where she had she was used to different types of people. The smartest approach was to mind your own business and not draw attention to yourself, unless it was absolutely necessary and you had no other option but to stick up for yourself. The best practice was not to make eye contact. Life skills. She had plenty of them and over the years they had been put to good use. Life was tough where she came from, and from an early age, she had become a good judge of character. Going to university and working in a range of part-time jobs over the years had added more practical skills. She soon discovered that just because someone dressed or spoke posh, or had plenty of money, didn't mean they were a good person. It was something she'd taught her younger siblings. Don't judge a book by its cover. Sometimes the roughest people have the biggest hearts.

Now however, she was not so sure of that belief. The group she had been observing, hustled up and down the platform and she watched a few of them who were unsteady on their legs. Thankfully the train doors opened and she stood back, letting those who were so impatient to get on, go first. The noisy group seemed to be on the carriage behind the one where her allocated seat was. At least her carriage might be quiet and hopefully full of the older people who stood waiting beside her.

Reaching into her bag she took her ticket out, walked inside the carriage and looked for her designated seat. There were no single seats, only two side by side, either side of the aisle. It was the first time she had caught the train further than Brisbane and she moved slowly behind the line of people looking for their place.

People were taking their seats and the carriage appeared full. She made her way down the aisle, her bag in front of her as she perused the seat numbers. Counting down she could see her number coming up. Hers was the seat nearest to the aisle. Beside where she was about to sit, already in his place was a very large man. Although there was an armrest between her seat and his, his body bulged under and above the armrest leaving her very little room to sit. Her eyes flitted around, as she tried to think quickly. Opposite where she was supposed to sit was a spare seat and with the platform now empty this seat appeared to be undesignated to a passenger. She placed her bag down on it, not even looking in the direction of the seat she was supposed to be in. A man sitting in the window seat next to where she had put her bag, turned back from looking out the window. It was the man in the white shirt from the previous train this morning.

'Sorry, but that seat is taken,' he said.

She raised her eyes. 'No one is sitting there.'

'What's the number on your ticket,' he replied, looking up at her and then across to the empty seat on the other side of the aisle.

'I'm not sure,' she said, 'but I think this is my seat.'

A uniformed train attendant walked up the aisle, stopping when she got to Elsie. 'Welcome to the Spirit of Queensland. Is there a problem with your ticket? We're just about to come around and check them.'

'No problem. This is my seat,' Elsie replied, still standing, but with her bag firmly planted on the empty seat.

'Can I please have a look at your ticket?' the attendant enquired. The man in the white shirt gave her a look as if to say, 'I told you so'.

Elsie fumbled with her ticket and handed it to the attendant, who smiled sweetly at her before giving her directions in a business-like voice just like a flight attendant on a plane would. She patted the back part of the chair next to the large man. 'Please take your seat, that is this one on the left-hand side of the train, thank you. Shortly we will be around with menus and anything else you might need once we depart the station. The drinks carriage doesn't open until we reach Caboolture.'

'So sorry,' Elsie said as she wrenched her bag up and dumped it down in front of her designated seat.

5

———————

The large man barely glanced in her direction which suited her fine. Sweat glistened on his forehead and he had terrible body odour. She wrinkled her nose and tried to sit as far to the right of the seat as she could. Out of the corner of her eye, the empty seat opposite mocked her. The man in the white shirt put his bag on the empty seat, smiling as the attendant checked his ticket. 'You have both seats booked?' she crooned.

He replied, 'Yes.'

She passed his ticket back, a sickly smile still plastered across her face. 'The movie program is in the pocket in the seat in front of you and you can find points to plug in your laptop or anything else you need. I hope you're comfortable.'

Elsie rolled her eyes as she watched the woman's body language and fluttering eyelashes. The attendant was openly flirting with him. 'Just let me know if you'd like a cold drink or a coffee. Please don't hesitate to ask if there is anything else I can do to help. Welcome aboard the Spirit of Queensland. It's a privilege to have you travelling with us.'

'Thank you,' he replied.

Typical, Elsie thought. So much money he had booked two seats. She threw him a look of disgust and he smiled back at her, before getting the menu out and scanning it. The man next to her coughed and she tried not to look down at his bare legs that were thrust into a huge pair of rubber thongs. Don't judge, she reminded herself.

THANK goodness he had booked two seats, Matt thought. He was starting at a new work location and the fella Patrick, who was his new overseer had advised him that if he was going to catch the train it was well worth the money to pay for the extra seat and have the comfort to stretch out without anyone next to you.

Matt had worked for the same company for many years and when he told them what Patrick said, they had agreed to pay for a double seat for him. Matt had been a loyal worker and in five years had never taken a sick day. He was good at fencing and never complained about the location, which over the years had typically been in the remote outback areas of Queensland. Usually, he flew when he came back from Brisbane. But it was the end of the school holidays and flights had been booked out. Patrick wanted him to pick up a ute in Rockhampton that the company had just purchased and drive it out to where he would be working and living. The company had a camp and living quarters on a property that was about ten kilometres out of town and Matt was looking forward to having Ethan live with him and the rest of the fencing gang. A school bus ran past the camp and the manager had given permission for Ethan to live there also.

Matt closed his eyes and tried not to listen to the large man opposite coughing and spluttering. He could have been nice and offered the brown-haired girl the seat next to him. But he didn't know her. She might be just as annoying and loud as some of the others who were in the carriage behind.

ELSIE HAD NEVER BEEN SO glad to get off a train. Never again, she thought. By the time she needed to travel next, hopefully she would have saved up and bought herself a car. The last one she owned had ended up at the wreckers. It had been too old to try and fix, and with very little savings she had managed to get by using public transport for the last couple of years. The only public transport in Matfield was a train that went through twice a week. She had been assured however that her apartment was within walking distance to the school.

Now as she stood up and got ready to depart, she looked at the man and woman who sat behind her, their conversation about what they had been up on charges for, the places they had lived and the hardships they had endured in their lives had been audible to everyone in the carriage the entire journey. Now they slept. What a luxury she thought. Peace compared to the few minutes she had managed to catch. Between waking up to the loud snoring of the man next to her and the interruption when the train stopped for a lengthy amount of time at Bundaberg so the police could board and arrest a woman from the carriage behind, there had been very little sleep. There hadn't been a dull moment and she wondered if this was a usual journey or just something special on a Friday afternoon.

Mr White Shirt opposite her looked very comfortable and well-rested. He had appeared to enjoy his meal when it was brought around and had sipped a glass of red wine, for all the world looking like he was in the lap of luxury as he gazed out the window. His body was stretched across both seats and he had rested and probably slept for much of the journey. Now as he also stood, she looked at his crushed white shirt, untucked and hanging over his trousers. His shoes were still shiny though and his hair neat as if he had just brushed it.

He smiled at her again as they stood next to each other waiting for the doors to open. Narrowing her eyes she glared back at him, using one of her hands to push her hair—which hadn't been brushed—out of her eyes.

His voice was deep when he spoke. 'Interesting journey,' he said as the train came to a jolting halt.

He had blue eyes that seemed to be laughing at her and there was no way she was going to give him the satisfaction of a reply. Turning her back to him she picked her bag up, making sure she was the first one out of the carriage. She made her way straight to the bathroom on the platform. There were quite a few hours between now and the departure of the connecting train that would take her to Matfield. One more part of the journey to go. Hopefully, this part of her travels would be quieter and more comfortable.

6

Matt also made his way to the bathroom at the train station. He couldn't wait to get out of the formal clothes he had worn to the solicitors that morning. Once he was changed into his work shorts and fluoro shirt, along with thick socks and work boots, he felt at ease. There had certainly been some interesting characters on the train and thank goodness he had taken his earplugs to block out the noise. The conversation of a few people sitting nearby and the snoring of the large man opposite had been distracting and he was thankful now to be picking up his own vehicle. Matfield here I come, he thought.

BY THE TIME Elsie arrived at Matfield Station, she felt like she had been travelling for days. Three trains and now a walk in the hot morning sun were starting to take a toll on her. She walked slowly, wishing she wore a hat to guard against the heat of the sun. Her bag was heavy and she changed hands now and again as she trudged along the main street and towards where she was going to live.

In the other hand she held a piece of paper with the address on it; the key to the apartment would be under the mat.

Leaving a key out was a strange concept. There obviously wasn't much crime in these parts. This was her first time in the 'outback' and she looked in awe at her surroundings as she walked. The train station was only a short distance from the centre of town but it was also one of the last buildings on the western side. Behind it as far as she could see were paddocks, the grass in them tinged with green as the morning sunlight cast a golden glow over the top. Flat land stretched out before her and she held her hand over her eyes, shielding them against the sun as she looked at a range of mountains that ran along the horizon. Smaller hills rose in the foreground, a line of trees designating the end of the far-reaching paddocks. Standing near a large tree to shelter in the shade, she put her bag down on the ground and turned a full circle, watching as a flock of brightly coloured galahs squawked and flew overhead.

The bird calls echoed as she approached the main street and turned her gaze to the buildings that lined either side. The scene was different to the sprawling suburbs and large shopping malls that she was used to and she walked slower, looking with interest at each business as she passed. Cafes, gift shops and a clothing store, all had large glass windows at the front, their wares displayed for shoppers to look at.

A large double-storey pub on the corner had intricate

fretwork railings. with matching brackets either side of the timber posts. A red tin roof glimmered in the morning light and similar coloured awnings protected the leadlight windows that ran down one side of the pub. It was a beautiful building and she stared at the wide verandahs. A lady hanging over the railing as she smoked a cigarette gave her a friendly wave. At the same time, three old men sitting on a low brick wall on the corner outside the pub all lifted their hands in greeting. She tentatively waved back. The department had told her that she would find the small outback town full of friendly people. Someone opened the doors of the pub and started putting blackboards out, the day's special meals creatively written and promoted in thick colourful chalk. There was so much character in the old building and now as she gazed further up the street she could see other interesting businesses on either side of the main street.

Back home in the suburbs, the pubs were ugly concrete buildings, with cold brick pillars and large automatic glass doors. Huge signs with flashing lights advertising the pokies or whatever was on special that week, lured patrons in to waste any money they might have. The local pub near to where she had lived was the biggest eyesore she had ever seen. The large building stuck out like a sore thumb from the hodgepodge collection of smaller equally ugly mismatched shops, offices and other establishments that surrounded it. The few times she had been there, usually to pick her mother up, she had found the interior to be distasteful, the stale smell of beer, flashing lights and noises of the poker machines making her want to get out of there as quickly as possible.

Here in this little town, there wasn't a concrete carpark to be seen and she admired the heritage style that had been retained. Someone shook out a floormat as they stood in one of the wide pub doorways. They looked her way as she picked up her bag and made her way up the street, their call cheery and loud. 'Morning, young lady. I bet you're the new teacher. We heard you were coming.'

She waved back, surprised that someone would know who she was. She passed a newsagency that had a stack of newspapers piled up outside of it. A lady who had just started moving the papers greeted her. 'Good morning. It's going to be a warm one,' she said. 'You're new to town. Got off the morning train, did ya? Are you chasing a job?'

Elsie smiled back. 'Thank you, but no. I'm starting at the high school.'

The lady looked surprised. 'That's great. You look young enough to be a student. Good luck with that. You've come at a good time. We've had rain. The paddocks are green and the farmers are happy. All the best with your new job.'

She thanked the lady and kept walking. This was certainly going to be different from home.

The high school soon appeared on her right and she stopped, gazing up at the sign above the gates. *Matfield State High School*, the sign proudly proclaimed. *Respect. Responsibility. Resilience.* Next to the high school was the primary school and from the directions she had been given, not too far down the road was where she was going to live.

She moved over onto the footpath. A large truck appeared behind her and she stood still, watching it pass by. Three stock carriages full of cattle rattled past, the driver of the large blue truck towing them giving her a salute as he passed. The dust took a long while to settle and she held her breath until the lingering smell of the cattle dissipated. New sights. New sounds. New smells, all unfolding before her, bringing a sense of independence and the promise of a fresh start.

Encouraged by this newfound feeling she quickened her pace. It was January and she could feel the heat of the sun on her shoulders. She checked the address she had been given and stopped on the footpath outside a modest block of brick apartments. The single-storey complex housed ten separate living quarters and boasted ample parking—a welcome prospect for when she purchased a car in the future. The sun was starting to get to her and she put her bag on her head, trying to stop her face from getting burnt. Looking up she observed the weathered red tiles adorning the roof of the apartment block, the faded style matching the old-style red bricks and the peeling paint on the doors. Scanning the row, she identified the apartment marked with the number seven, her cherished lucky number.

It was still early in the morning and there was no one around. The key was under the mat as promised, and she opened the door and let herself in. The department had supplied her with a small lounge and coffee table. She put her bag down and then wandered through an adjacent doorway that led to the bedroom. 'Yay!' she exclaimed, unable to contain her excitement. True to their word, the department had also had a bed delivered, its new mattress still encased in plastic. Overwhelmed by the sudden rush of emotion, she ventured further into the room. Not only was there a bed but a dressing table with a small mirror on top. She opened the built-in cupboards. Plenty of room to hang her clothes and best of all, an upright row of drawers. More room than she had ever had. It was all hers. Her own personal haven.

The kitchen was basic but still big enough for what she needed. Although the tiles in the bathroom were cracked and the light didn't work when she turned it on, she decided that overall the apartment was satisfactory. Thet had even supplied a washing machine. Once she started earning, she could buy some extra items to make the place more homely. For the first time in her life she had somewhere to call her own.

She walked back into the loungeroom and opened one of the boxes that had come from home. They would have been delivered the previous week and she had been told someone would make sure they were put inside, ready for when she arrived. She had bought some sheets and other linen from an op shop near home and now she pulled them out of a box. Her priority was to make the bed. She didn't have a pillow yet but she rolled up a towel she had brought with her to put under her head. When she lay down, she sighed deeply and closed her eyes. She was here. Her new home.

7

The last few weeks and three train rides had caught up with Elsie and she must have slept for three or more hours. When she started to stir, it took a while to work out where she was; her eyes opened and then closed a few times before she remembered that she was on a new bed in her new bedroom.

The room looked like it had been freshly painted and maybe they had even hung new curtains. It was a small space but it was hers. Lying on her back she thought about the trip to get here. She was a long way from home, a long way from the suburbs of Logan and a long way from her family. Kicking her legs up in the air she decided that, apart from not being close to her brother and sister, the *long way from everything* was a good thing.

THE NEXT FEW days were spent getting the place in order. With only a week left before school started, there were a few items she needed to purchase. A two-hundred-dollar advance had been deposited into her bank account— a starting bonus, they had called it. Bribery, she thought. No one wanted to come to these outback towns. Most of the graduates she'd met at university were aiming for the coastal areas. Somewhere where there was a bit of nightlife, decent shops and not so much dust and dry. Still, she had taken the advance with gratitude and an electric frying pan, a jug and a toaster as well as a couple of towels were added to her belongings. The rest of the money she spent on groceries. She had a small amount of savings in the bank after most of her money had previously gone on food and helping her sister finish school. At least before she left she had been able to buy some clothes from the op shops. Starting a new job, it was important to make a good impression.

THE FIRST WEEK she was in Matfield she cleaned the apartment and sorted out her belongings. So far she hadn't met many people and there didn't seem to be any other tenants in the other apartments, although it was obvious someone lived next door, judging by a couple of chairs and a small table with a pot plant on it placed near their front door. They were probably away on school holidays she thought. When she wandered into town she had talked to a few of the local shop owners who seemed friendly and interested in her new job. 'Make sure you settle in and don't put up with anything from that principal,' the lady at the corner store told her. 'He's known as a bully around here. Half the reason we never seem to keep teachers. I hope you're going to stay.'

'I have no choice,' Elsie told her. 'I'm on contract for a year while I finish my last subject at university. It's a new scheme to get graduates like me to come to somewhere regional like Matfield.'

She thanked the lady for the milk and bread, keeping her advice in mind. She would have to watch herself as a new teacher and take everything slowly. She was used to not trusting anyone. That was par for the course where she came from. Head down, mouth shut, and just do the job. She would have plenty enough to think about, just learning the routines of being a teacher.

BY THE TIME the first day of school came around, she felt she was ready to begin and keen to get started with her classes. The apartment still felt a bit empty, the walls blank and the bookshelves bare, apart from a few favourite books she had brought with her. Yesterday when she came back from walking around town, she encountered the lady next door. It would be nice to have someone nearby and she hoped that perhaps this might be the first friend she would make.

'Eliza Tuls is my name,' the woman said as she poked her head out through her doorway. 'I'm a senior experienced teacher at the high school.'

'Nice to meet you,' Elsie replied, holding her hand out for Eliza to shake. The older woman looked her up and down, her lips pursed, her eyes narrowing. 'The last teacher in your apartment played her music too loud and at very inappropriate times. Make sure you don't.'

Elsie was taken aback. It wasn't the response she was expecting and she drew her hand back. 'Righto. See you around,' she quickly said, retreating inside. Someone to avoid she thought to herself. Forget about the friend prospect. Hopefully, others at the school would be more welcoming.

And they were. By the time her first day ended at her new school, she had shaken hands and been welcomed by a group of teachers who seemed very pleasant and supportive. Samson, an older man who was the PE teacher and had been at Matfield High for years gave her a tour of the school. He had a laid-back personality and put her at ease. 'Luckily we have a student-free day today. You can settle in before the kids get back. There's a group of us who stick together here at school and we'll support you however we can. We've been through a long run of young teachers and we've vowed to make sure you don't go the same way as the others. That is, out the door and back to greener pastures.'

'I intend to stay,' Elsie answered, immediately drawn to the honest nature of Samson. 'Everything will be new to me but I've studied for a long time and now I only have one subject to go. I feel very lucky to be in this new scheme where I can work and study at the same time. I'm looking forward to having classes of my own.'

'What do you teach again?'

'English.'

'Perfect. There are three other English teachers in your staff room and you'll find them all helpful.' He bent down and spoke quietly. 'It's the ones up at the office you have to be wary of. Watch out for the admin staff; from the principal down. Not all of them mind you. Just be careful who you trust.'

'Thanks for the heads up, Samson. I'll be careful.'

Samson was not the only one who warned her about the principal and by the time she met Mr Gantarro that afternoon she was prepared.

'I'VE HAD a run of useless young teachers over the past couple of years,' was how he greeted her.

She held her breath, shocked at his unwelcoming words.

'I've asked time and time again for more experienced teachers but to no avail. Now they give me one who hasn't even graduated.' He made a strange huffing noise and she made sure to keep the same interested look on her face. She didn't want to get on the wrong side of him right from the start. She was as good at pretending as anyone. 'Words of advice, girlie. Do your job and do as you're asked. Is that clear?'

'I'm happy to be here. Thank you,' she replied. He glared hard at her from behind his large wooden desk, and she tried not to stare at his unfriendly face.

Broken veins ran across his cheeks and his mean little eyes flitted back and forth as he berated her. A shudder ran through her body as she noticed spit forming in the corner of his mouth and she looked instead through a window on the side wall. She could see a group of cleaners talking, one of them throwing her arms in the air as if she were angry about something. It was strange.

She felt like she should be down there with the cleaning crew, working out whatever the problem was, instead of biting her tongue and pretending to be confident in the art of teaching. Maybe she had bitten off more than she could chew. At least when she was working in a cleaning job she was confident and knew what was required. Garranto's scraping voice brought her attention back. 'Don't think just because the department has given you extra money to come out here and thrown in a few freebies that you'll get any consideration from me. You need to work and make sure you do everything I ask of you.'

She sat silently. The others had been right. He was a bully. She had seen and heard it all before. But he didn't intimidate her. She was a lot smarter than he was and could play the game as well as anyone. He ran his hand through his thinning hair which looked like it was slicked back with oil. She waited for him to continue.

'Please ensure that you get to your classes on time and your discipline is tight. You're not here to make friends with the students. Do I make myself clear?'

She nodded.

'Secondly, don't fraternise with any of the parents. In the past, teachers have been sacked because of their inappropriate behaviour. Do you understand?'

She nodded again.

'Lastly, attend all meetings and check your emails frequently. I run a tight establishment here and young teachers need to fall into line.'

When he leaned over the desk and gave her a steely glare, she had the urge to laugh. But she held her emotions in check and simply nodded again. 'Is that all

Mr Gantarro? I'd like to fix up a few things in my classroom.'

His head tilted to the side and he looked at her for a long while. 'Good day, Miss Jackson.'

With that, he proceeded to shuffle papers around on his desk. She stood up and left, closing the door firmly behind her.

8

The first month of school was overwhelming and she put in long hours both at work and once she got home. Everything had to be the way she wanted and she needed full lessons to keep the students focused and engaged. She found if she hesitated for even a moment or had to look for what she was teaching next, they nearly ate her alive. It only took a few moments of distraction for them to start talking or call out and become unruly. She needed to learn behaviour management skills where she could reign them in quickly, otherwise, like on a few occasions, the entire class became out of control.

Thankfully a teacher called Penny taught in the classroom beside her. Penny was thirty-six and had been teaching for fifteen years. To Elsie, she was the perfect picture of what a teacher should look like. She wore straight skirts that came to above her knee and a collared blouse that fitted firmly over her slim figure. Her glasses were colourful and modern and her hair, makeup and jewellery were immaculately matching. Elsie admired her style and the firm way she talked to the students. There was a lot she could learn from Penny from just observing her in the classroom. Penny had taught in remote areas and a range of low socio-economic schools. She had also lived and worked on Torres Strait Island, was a wealth of information and took Elsie under her wing from the first day.

'I took a job here because my partner works in the mines further out. This was the closest school to work at. It saves him flying in and flying out and now that we're settled we're thinking about starting a family this year.'

Penny was that person who every new teacher needed. She went out of her way to help and nothing was ever too much trouble. Elsie felt like she could ask her anything. 'I don't know what I would have done without you this last month, Penny. You've saved my life.'

'I was warned about the principal here by a friend who used to work here. But I came prepared with experience and skin as thick as a bullock's. Garranto doesn't intimidate me and I won't let him bully new teachers either. We lost a good music teacher last year. She was in another staff room, and being the only music teacher, I don't think others around her realised how bad it was for her. By the time they did it was too late and she'd decided to leave. I've already heard the way he talks to you. I must say though you seem to know the right way to steer around him. You'll find some of the ladies who work in the office will help you out. They work closely with him and always know the inside information. They've saved me a few times.'

Elsie sat on one of the desks in Penny's classroom, her

legs swinging in front. 'I've worked with a variety of people. Some good, others not. Where I come from it's survival of the fittest. He won't worry me.'

'How are your classes going?' Penny asked as she roamed around the room picking up rubbish on the floor —a couple of water bottles and, she held them in the air, empty chips packets. 'Sneaky lot. I missed that obviously. Must have been when I was sitting with some of the kids who needed extra help.' She threw the rubbish in the bin. 'There is such a wide range of academic abilities in these classes. Breaks my heart that I can't get to all of them in the time we have.'

'I'm so glad you said that. That is my biggest problem at the moment and I lie awake at night worrying about it. I was nearly in tears the other day because some of them are just so low in their literacy levels. There are thirty kids in the class and only an hour for each lesson. How are you supposed to help them?'

'You learn to live with it. If you let it worry you, you won't last. It's the same most places I've been. Some schools might have more teacher aides to help than they do here. Garranto pushes that money elsewhere, because I've never had a teacher aide in to help. Just do the best you can.'

She nodded. Every bit of advice was filed away, adding to the experiences and knowledge she was gaining every day. 'I do have a few behaviour problems. Nothing I didn't expect. I think I've sorted them out though and the advice you gave me works. I feel lucky to have you next to me.'

'Yes, any trouble you can't deal with, just send them to me. Although, you have a very firm grasp from what I can see. Especially for a new teacher, and you haven't even finished your studies yet. I take my hat off to you.'

Elsie didn't usually make friends quickly but there was something about Penny that she admired. She had a wealth of experience and had been friendly right from the start. A few of the other teachers from her staff room had also been helpful and she was starting to feel like part of a team. It was also a team that stuck together against the nature of Mr Garranto and his crew of disciples. She had picked up from the start who was closest to him and avoided those particular people. She also made sure she didn't go to the office unless it was absolutely essential. That way she didn't run the risk of running into him. Not that he would stop and talk to her. He had made it very clear that she was at the bottom of the list for consideration.

Penny pushed the chairs in and neatened the rows of desks. 'Make sure you get to the pub on time this Friday. You can sit next to me. I'll save you a seat. It's a big fundraiser for the primary school and everyone will be there. There are raffles, prizes and even an auction.'

'Jees, what do I wear?' Elsie asked. Her wardrobe was still very limited, although now that she had finished buying the few bits of furniture she needed from the second-hand shop in town, she could work her budget out a bit better and spend a little on herself. Her sister Jane was doing okay with the scholarship money she received and had also picked up some tutoring work. When they last talked, she had told Elsie not to send her any more money. 'Look after yourself, Elsie. I owe you. Don't you dare send me any more.'

'You don't owe me anything. We got through. You, me

and Peter. I don't know how, but we all made it to the other side.'

'Have you talked to Mum lately?' Jane asked.

'A few weeks after I left, she rang me. She wanted to tell me she was subletting the house and had moved in with Bert. She never even asked how I was going. All she did was talk about herself and of course, ask if I had any spare money.'

'Typical,' Jane said, a hint of annoyance in her voice. 'Never did put us first. Are you allowed to sub-let a government house? You didn't give her any money, did you?'

'I don't have any to give and I've drawn a line with that in regard to Mum. She only spends it on cigarettes or grog. I'd say she'll have a group of her friends living in the house paying her cash while she's away. I think if we want to live a good life, the three of us need to have as little to do with her as possible. We need to move on and make better lives for ourselves.'

ELSIE FOUND it challenging to release the maternal role she had assumed for Jane and Peter. Despite the physical distance, she made a concerted effort to maintain a strong connection with them, ensuring to call each week to check on their wellbeing. Beyond the routine check-ins, there were instances when Jane and Peter reached out to her, seeking guidance or eager to share exciting developments in their lives. The bond they enjoyed was unbreakable, a testament to the closeness they had formed over the years. It wasn't merely a family connection, it was a tight-knit unit, forged through the trials and tribulations they had faced together; the challenges of their childhood that they had overcome.

Now however she needed to focus on her own challenges at work.

That week at school, one of the girls in her class had whispered to Elsie that her hem had come undone at the back of her skirt. 'It's okay Miss, but the hem is undone and it looks a bit untidy. One side is longer than the other.'

She thanked the girl, whose name was Belinda, and together they found some safety pins and fixed it for the day. Belinda lingered and when Elsie asked if there was anything she wanted to talk about, the young girl had opened up. 'Miss, you sort of wear the same clothes each week. You should go online and buy new ones. I can give you the names of some good sites.'

Elsie smiled as she regarded Belinda, a tenth-grade student in her class. Like many of the girls initially, Belinda too, had tested the waters with a bit of misbehaviour during the early weeks. However, much like her peers, she swiftly fell in line as soon as she grasped the firm expectations that Elsie established in her classroom. Elsie's approach left no room for those who dared to talk back or disrupt the class with unnecessary chatter. Her rules were explicit and she had no tolerance for those who didn't follow her expectations. Even the most defiant boys had been unable to find loopholes in her stringent system.

As the term started to near the end she experienced a sense of accomplishment, feeling that she had successfully steered everyone onto the path she deemed fit. The classroom now resonated with a disciplined harmony, a testament to her unwavering commitment to maintaining order and having a calm and structured learning environment.

Of course, some chose not to work or were sulky and non-responsive. But overall, her classes were working well and she felt like she was starting to get some good results. One boy in particular stood out. He was a friendly boy who seemed like he was a bit rough around the edges, much like she had been as a teenager, she thought. At first he had been quiet and kept his head down, not mixing with any of the others. He had caught her attention when he started falling asleep in class, and one day she kept him behind to question him. 'Why are you so tired, Ethan?' she asked as she sat behind her desk, looking up at him where he stood in front of her. He shuffled from foot to foot, readjusting his school bag on his back.

'Just tired, Miss. That's all.'

'What did you have to eat this morning, before school?'

'Nothing.'

'What about today? What did you have for lunch?'

'Nothing.'

'Why not?'

'Nothing in the fridge at home.'

It was hard to get any further information from him and she opened a cupboard behind where she sat. She kept some packets of chips and muesli bars in there for this very reason. The schools where she had done her practicums all had breakfast clubs. Many of the students came from homes where there was no food, so the school supplied it. More than anyone else Elsie understood the challenges of learning on an empty stomach.

'Take a couple of packets of these and here's a few muesli bars,' she offered.

'Thanks, Miss.'

'You know, Ethan, your marks are some of the highest in the class.'

His eyes lit up and he looked straight at her. 'Thank you.'

'Are you doing as well in your other subjects?'

'I am, although English is always my best. I want to be a speech therapist. It's something I've always wanted to do.'

'Wow. Good on you. Well, anything you need help with, you come and see me.'

'Thanks. I've started looking at universities to go to.' He hesitated and she could tell he was unsure whether to keep talking.

'I understand if you're coming from a tricky background or if you need help with looking into where and how to go.'

He relaxed and sat down in a chair in front of her desk. 'I do need help. I don't know how to even start looking at where to go. I sit up all night looking on the internet at the different options. It's confusing.'

She looked at the clock on the wall and stood up. 'I have to go to a meeting, Ethan, but can we chat about this another time? I'll get some booklets and ideas for you. Do you have support at home? Anyone you can talk to about what you want?'

He stood also and she thought what an intelligent and likeable boy he was. His brown hair was wavy and short, his face tanned. Intense blue eyes looked at her. 'Not really. You probably wouldn't understand but I don't come from an ordinary family.'

She laughed loudly. 'What's ordinary? I'd love to help you. I worked out similar study paths for my younger siblings as well as myself.'

'Really? I'd love that. Seeya, Miss.' With that, he turned and walked out. She looked at the clock again. She was five minutes late for the meeting.

9

———

Thankfully Mr Garranto and his group of disciples, as Penny called them, were in deep discussion at the front of the room. The teachers seated in front of them chatted and Penny waved to her, gesturing to a spare seat beside her. 'I kept one for you. Something important going on out the front there with the powers that be.'

Nodding at some of the teachers who said hello, Elsie sat down. Meetings were something she was trying to get used to. It seemed like there was one every second day. Another teacher, Gus, leaned over her and spoke to Penny. 'Probably trying to work out when to schedule the meetings for the next ten years. You know how important the sharing of their wisdom is to that lot.'

Elsie stifled a giggle. It hadn't taken her long to work out how the place ran and who was in the know. Gus who had been quick to introduce himself to her when she arrived at the school was always a source of valuable information. He was good friends with one of the helpful office ladies, Bron, who always knew exactly what was going on and often gave him a heads-up about any trouble that was brewing. 'I'm always here if you need someone,' he told her right from day one. 'Been around the traps for years and right now we need to keep you young teachers. It's what we need; vitality, energy and youth.'

She had taken to Gus immediately and had already asked him for help with some of the technology devices she used in her classroom. Not only had he come one afternoon and spent time helping her set up her white-board and projector, but he had also sat there while she practised using the devices. His approach reminded her of some of the teachers she had when she went to school and she gave silent thanks for such good people around her.

Penny was the same. So many of the staff had gone out of their way to support her. Now Penny whispered to Gus and Elsie. 'They love drama that lot out the front,' she said. 'Here we go. What wonderful things will we hear about today?'

Elsie sat in silence through the meeting, observing the teachers who all looked as bored as she was. The staff members ranged in age and there seemed to be as many men as women. The important people seated in special seats at the front were the ones she had learned to be wary of. Luckily, she knew how to keep her mouth shut because even a small complaint, not meant to be taken seriously, usually found its way to the office.

'Head down, mouth shut,' Gus warned re-iterating Penny's advice.

As she filed out with the other teachers, she thought

about what she was going to wear tonight. Penny had brought in a bag of clothes that she said no longer fitted her. 'Take what you want, but if they don't fit just give them to the op shop. Some of them are fairly new. They must have shrunk because they're tight on me.'

The bag Penny had gifted Elsie contained a selection of clothes that effortlessly complemented her figure. Her wardrobe now housed a fresh array of size eight attire, courtesy of Penny's recent weight gain. Despite the prospect of going out that evening, Elsie harboured a reluctance, aware that a pile of schoolwork awaited her attention. It would have been easier to stay at home, the solace of her private space free from the concerns of others being an indulgence she had grown to love. However, Penny and the others had been friendly and insisted she celebrate with them.

A tight pair of jeans that looked brand new and a floral blouse that showed off her figure had been her top pick out of the bag of clothes. Turning around in front of the full-length mirror she brushed her hair again. She wore only a touch of makeup. Makeup that was so old she couldn't even remember when she had bought it. Her brown eyes looked darker tonight and she ran her finger over her eyebrow, flattening it down and pushing it up in the middle. Dressing up made her nervous and as she slipped strappy sandals on—the same ones she wore to school every day—she felt butterflies in her stomach. Over the years she hadn't gone out very often, instead keeping to herself. That way life was easier with fewer complications.

Now as she entered the pub, she took a deep breath and reminded herself to look confident. She was no timid wallflower; it was just that large groups and socialising were not in her normal routine.

The pub was brimming with people. Fundraising events were a major call to get together in a small town and she said hello to some of the teachers as she approached the group. They were a friendly lot and the girls from her staffroom had made sure to save her a bar stool next to Penny. They sat around a high bench, most of them dressed casually and similarly to how she was. The teachers greeted her, putting her at ease. Brett, a science teacher who often left a chocolate on her desk in the staffroom, handed her a glass of wine from a tray he was passing around. 'Here you go, love. This one's on me. Congratulations on surviving a term.'

'We're not there yet,' Liam, another science teacher called out. 'Don't jinx her.'

She settled in amongst the group. Although she had only been at the school for eight weeks some of the teachers had become firm friends. Not that she had let any get too close or ask too many questions about her past life. But they seemed to take her for who she was and treated her with respect. Even though she was technically still a university student and not fully qualified, they had always included her and often asked for her opinion on something they were working on.

One of the older English teachers, Elizabeth threw a beautiful smile Elsie's way. Not only did Elizabeth know everything there was to know about the subject, but she made sure to check on Elsie every day and always had some extra lessons up her sleeve that she shared. The support and care that had been given by the teachers around her made starting at the school so much easier and Elsie reminded herself to never forget how kind they had been. 'You've got a great way with the kids,' Elizabeth said. 'You're firm but fair.'

'The kids love you,' Penny added. 'It's also because you have the knowledge. Those kids can sense a fraud or someone who doesn't care or know their stuff from a mile away. They're not stupid.'

'Empathy, rapport, and knowledge. In that order,' Paul another teacher added in. 'And you've got it. We can all see it. Keep up the good work and don't let those bastards up in the office tell you any different.'

She had been appreciative of all the advice she had been given, and the praise. Not that she needed praise or was used to it, but it helped to know she was on the right track. Particularly as there was nothing at all coming from anyone higher up that led her to believe she was doing a good job.

The group all raised their glasses and beers in the air and Elsie joined with them. 'Here's to nearly the end of term one,' Paul said. They clinked their glasses together and she laughed along with them. 'Now, remember no shop talk here at the pub,' he added. 'Forget about school and all the shit that goes with it.'

Liam leaned over the bench table. 'So, young Elsie. Tell us your story. Are you single? Are you looking for someone? I've got a son about your age. Tall, good-looking, intelligent, single. Just like his father, well not the single part.'

Everyone stopped talking and she felt her face redden, unused to so much attention. 'I come from south of Brisbane and this is my first time to the outback. I'm loving it so far.'

Liam raised his eyebrows. When she first met him she thought he was stern and not as friendly as the other teachers. Over the term however, he had become one of her favourites. He had a wicked sense of humour and told great jokes that kept everyone in his staffroom amused. He was also known for having stand up arguments with Garranto, who so far, as much as he had tried, so far hadn't been able to transfer Liam out of the school. Now he pushed her for an answer. 'You didn't answer my question.'

Penny elbowed her in the ribs, remarking, 'You won't be able to do anything in a small town like this anyway, so you might as well give them something.'

She took a sip of her wine. 'I am single but definitely not looking for anyone. I've always lived at home so I'm enjoying being by myself.'

Elizabeth chuckled and then tut-tutted. 'Oh dear. You're probably missing living at home. No one to do your washing or cooking. My boys stayed at home until I kicked them out in their thirties. It will do you good to stand on your own two feet. Well done for taking up the challenge of coming here. I raise my glass to Elsie. Good luck!'

A table next to them that was full of noisy young men joined in the chorus and to Elsie's dismay they too raised their glasses in unison. 'To Elsie,' they all roared before turning back to their own discussions.

She wished she could disappear and the conversation move on to something or somebody else. For a moment she thought that would happen as the music started playing and the noise surrounding them increased. There was a lot of loud cheering and wolf whistles as the first event started up on the small stage at the front of the room. After a while the room quietened and a row of men filed up onto the stage.

'They're all dressed up for tonight,' Penny said to her. 'They always start and finish with this event. It's the most popular one of the night.'

Elsie swivelled on her stool so she could get a better view of the stage. The lights were bright and focused on the men on stage and a bright spotlight scanned across the audience. A few people yelled out to 'turn the bloody spotlight off' and 'we can't see.'

When the cheering and comments ceased, she looked up to the stage where ten men were standing in a row. They were all dressed in jeans and collared shirts, their row of leather boots causing more comments and calls from the audience. 'Go for the one with the shiniest boots,' someone near them yelled.

'I'll have the one with the dusty ones,' a lady at the front screamed out.

There was more laughter and lots of noise as the spotlight once again scanned across the audience. She shielded her eyes with her hands. 'I can't see them properly,' she said to Penny. 'What happens now?'

'Whoever is working that spotlight is either already full of beer or doesn't know what they're doing. They'll auction off half of the men to start the show. Then they'll auction the others at the close. All the money raised goes to the primary school. It's our biggest fundraising event of the year.'

'What do you mean, auction them off?'

'People will bid to have dates with them?'

Elsie watched the crowd as some of the women on the

side of the room, stood up to ensure they had a good view. A portly man who was also dressed in jeans, a collared shirt and leather boots held a microphone in his hand and the bidding started.

'He's the cattle auctioneer.' Penny said. 'Best caller in the west.'

The auctioneer's voice rattled off information quickly, as the first man stepped forward.

'Ladies and gentlemen, gather 'round. You better be prepared to be swept off your feet by this young man who is not only strikingly handsome but also embodies the essence of charm and charisma. It's time to introduce, Matfield's very own bachelor boy, Mr Cowboy.'

The excitement built in the room and Elsie was enjoying watching everyone having so much fun. Her eyes were fixed on the auctioneer who talked so quickly she had to listen hard to understand what he said.

He picked up his pace even more. 'This young man boasts a fit young body, and thick black hair as smooth and shiny as a prize bull's rump. He's not just easy on the eye, folks, he's the best bull, or should I say, man, in town. He's single, ready to date and will make one lucky lady's night one to remember. Don't forget, this isn't just about the quality of the stock, agh should I say, the character of the beast, it's all about raising funds for the primary school. So, get those raised hands ready and call out your winning bids for – put your hands together for Mr Cowboy!'

The auctioneer waited until the applause and cat whistles calmed down. 'Let's start the bid for this handsome bull at ten dollars. Someone give me ten dollars. Am I bid ten dollars? I have twenty dollars over here to the gentleman in the blue shirt. Thirty to the lady with the gorgeous red hat on. Forty, here we go folks. Do I hear fifty?'

The crowd went wild as the bids started flowing, the auctioneer and the crowd picking up the pace until the last bid was drowned by a roaring crescendo of yelling and whistling. The woman who stood over to the side had been intent on winning and she waved and called out to Mr Cowboy as the bidding concluded.

The auctioneer slammed his hammer down, his words slowing as he held his hand in the air and pointed to the winning bidder. 'Sold to the highest bidder. We have three hundred and thirty dollars for Mr Cowboy from the lady in the red hat. Congratulations on winning a date with our charming bachelor!'

Paul turned around and got the attention of the other teachers. 'I think we should bid on the next fella for young Elsie here. What better way to become familiar with the locals. He looks like a nice young man.'

Elsie nearly spat her drink out, horrified at the thought. 'Oh please no. Don't do that. No.

Liam laughed. 'Brilliant! It's for a good cause. We'll all put in. Good idea, Paul. Hang on, the next young man has just stepped out. Let me check he's okay.'

Elsie turned her back to the stage and put her hands over her face. She focused her stare on the back wall of the room, feeling like she wanted to sink into the floor. Surely, they wouldn't. They couldn't. She would die of embarrassment. The auctioneer introduced the next man and she turned back to the group she was with, sending glaring looks at Paul and Liam, and all the others around the bench table who all seemed to think this was a good idea. Penny put her arm around her shoulders. 'Relax. It's just a bit of fun and a way to raise funds.'

She took a deep breath. It was too late to get up and walk out. She was trapped. In the background she could hear the auctioneer's voice. The bids started and once the audience realised that the group bidding was the teachers from the high school, all eyes cast their way. Paul started the bidding, which had drawn loud comments from the crowd. 'I don't think you're his type,' someone called out. 'He's too young for you.'

The auctioneer paused and then continued. Do I hear eighty? Ninety over there. One hundred from the teachers. How could you resist this fine specimen? Mr Blue Eyes. Single. Fit. Fun-loving and might I say encouraged and coerced up here tonight by his workmates. Maybe he's a bit shy.'

The comments were met with loud laughter and Elsie shrunk down in her seat, her hands over her face. 'One hundred and fifty.' She peeped through her fingers, growling at Paul whose hand was up in the air.

The auctioneer stopped and asked, 'Two hundred and might I ask who are you bidding on behalf of Sir?'

Paul stood up as the crowd quietened, his teacher's voice coming in handy as he loudly declared, 'We're bidding on behalf of a new colleague. The amazing Elsie Jackson.'

Elsie put her head down on the bench. How more embarrassing could this get? The crowd cheered and she didn't dare to look up as the bidding continued. Paul jumped up and down and clapped his hands when his winning bid of three hundred dollars was accepted. The crowd had gone crazy and their calls were accompanied by the loud tune of 'You're the One that I Want' belting out from the speakers.

Penny, who was laughing and seemed delighted at the result grabbed Elsie's arm and led her through the maze of people up onto the stage. 'You just have to shake his hand and look like you're excited. It's all about the money raised. This is an annual event and we usually bid for someone. You're not the first newbie we've done this to.'

As the cheering increased Elsie wished once again that she could vanish. But that was not going to happen. There were a few stairs to walk up and then before she knew it the auctioneer grabbed her arm and led her over to the row of men. The man she had just 'won' smiled broadly and held his hand out for her to shake. For the first time, she looked up, straight into the eyes of the white-shirted man who had been on the train. She blinked rapidly, remembering Penny's instructions. She didn't want to appear snobby or ungrateful. It was all just a bit of fun. 'It's you,' she said.

'Wow,' the man replied. 'The name's Matt. Pleased to meet you. It's a small world.'

She shook her head as she grabbed his hand. 'This was not my idea,' she said.

He grinned broadly, his grip firm. 'Mine neither.'

10

———

The group around the table clapped as she returned to them. She scowled at them all, her eyes moving from one to the next. Paul squirmed in his chair and Brett rolled his eyes around, refusing to look her in the eye. She made a growling noise and then shook her head. A few minutes of silence came between them before she playfully punched Paul on the arm, her face breaking into a wide smile. 'Thank you all so much for this special night that I will never forget. I will at some stage pay each and every one of you back for making me the centre of attention. Something I spent my entire life avoiding. When you're least expecting it, watch out. Because I will get you back.'

They all took a collective sigh of relief. 'Have another wine,' Paul said as he passed her a drink. 'This could be your lucky night.'

～

THANK goodness the attention that had been on her, now reverted to the remaining men on the stage. As the bidding continued the crowd got rowdier and louder and the last man, who seemed very uncomfortable with being on stage, had a bidding war going on between two women who shouted their bids out loudly. In the end, the women conferred with the auctioneer. 'The two lovely ladies here have decided to both pay four hundred dollars each and that means, Errol here, will get to go on two dates.'

The audience roared and the women stood either side of Errol, both pressing their lips to either side of his face as the local photographer took a photo of the three of them.

'Something for the front page of the newspaper,' Penny said. 'Be thankful yours was the second date to be auctioned. The night will get livelier as we go on.'

THE NIGHT BECAME MORE raucous as everyone continued to drink. Elsie ordered a cheap meal and was ravenous by the time it was served. She'd had two wines already and she opted for a soft drink, rather than become tipsy.

'You need to loosen up, Elsie,' one of the younger teachers, Rachel, said. 'Let your hair down.'

'I'm fine. I enjoy watching everyone have a good time. I'm not really a party girl and...' she lost her last words as Rachel pulled her up onto the dance floor. She yelled in Rachel's ear as she was led to an area that was now full of mostly women. 'I don't dance.'

'Now you do,' Rachel said as she held Elsie's hands and started spinning around her.'

There hadn't been much time for night clubbing or dancing in the past. Sometimes at parties she had joined in, but she had been with school friends, girls she had grown up with. Occasionally she danced with some of the boys, but not many had ever interested her enough to go on a date with. There had been a boy she was keen on at school, Elias. A friendly, intelligent boy who was the captain of the football team. They were an item for a while, but he'd left school early and moved to Sydney to pursue his football career. He promised to keep in touch but the next she saw him was on the social pages of a newspaper that one of her friends showed her. It seemed like he had moved on and found another girlfriend, one who was very glamorous and hung off his arm like she was an ornament.

Elsie's heart had been broken for a while but she had focused on her schoolwork and promised herself never to fall in love again. Keep it simple, she reminded herself. Now as Rachel pulled her around the floor, swirling around her she lost track of what she was reminiscing about. Elias. School. Home. Family. One of her favourite songs was playing. Her feet started to move to the beat and her arms soon followed. If she closed her eyes and listened to the music, her body moved naturally. 'Woo hoo!' Rachel called out to her. 'You can move.'

As the song came to an end she was glad that Rachel pulled her hand and guided her off the floor. The dancing had been more than enjoyable; it had been invigorating and felt good. Really good. Matfield was showing her new experiences. As she passed the table of men near to where she had been sitting, she drew her breath in sharply. Matt, the man she had won the date with was among them. He looked up at her and smiled warmly, the other men erupting in cheering noises as Rachel and she made their way past. She might embrace the refreshing feeling of dancing at the local pub, but dating a stranger, or for that matter, any man, was not a new experience she was looking forward to.

11

———————

Matt had found himself entangled in a situation he had never intended to be a part of. 'Come on,' his boss, Patrick, cajoled. 'It's for a good cause, and you're single. Most of the other workers have partners. If I can get up there, so can you.'

Reluctantly, he joined his colleagues at the pub. It was just over eight weeks since Ethan, his younger brother, had come to live with him. Despite Matt's efforts, Ethan, now sixteen, insisted on being treated like an adult. He felt like he was constantly nagging his younger brother. 'I will treat you like an adult if you start to pick up after yourself and put your dirty dishes in the sink. This is a small space for the two of us and it has to be kept tidy.'

'You're bloody fussy,' Ethan said as he laid back on his bed, as usual a book in front of his face. 'I don't know why you won't let me do the grocery shopping or get a part-time job in town.'

'I told you when you arrived, the main idea of this living arrangement is that you finish school. I want you to focus on your schoolwork, not some part-time job. We have enough money with my wage.'

Matt had to concede that organisation was not his forte. After a day working in the paddocks under the scorching summer sun, his body exhausted and dust-covered, he preferred to shower, relax, and watch television. His cooking skills were basic, and their food supply often ran low, not due to lack of money but rather his lack of budgeting skills. However, he was unwilling to let his younger brother handle those responsibilities; Ethan needed to concentrate on school. At least someone in the family would make it to university and that would be the youngest, Ethan.

Despite the decent pay, fencing wasn't the career Matt had envisioned in school. From a young age his heart had been set on becoming a vet. Growing up he had taken in every stray animal that came his way. His bedroom had often sheltered a bird with a broken wing, a lorikeet that had fallen out of the nest or a pup that someone had given him. Once he left home he usually had a dog. This year was the first time in as long as he could remember that he didn't have one by his side. His old blue cattle dog, Archie, had died just over three months ago and he decided that where he was living and his lifestyle with the fencing job wasn't the best mixture for having a dog.

He dreamt about one day being surrounded by animals. Maybe he would live somewhere where he could bring home every stray he wanted to and he would know how to fix their broken bones or how to treat them when they were sick. A vet. Since he was a kid he had dreamt about it. But, that hadn't been his lot in life. Fencing was a far cry from working in a veterinary clinic.

Nevertheless, over the years he had accepted that it was his reality.

ONSTAGE AT THE PUB, amid the swirling bids, Matt felt a discomfort he hadn't experienced in a while. Being the centre of attention and the prospect of going on a date was unnerving. Although he'd had several girlfriends and a couple of long-term relationships, his nomadic job choices had put an end to those.

When he was on the stage and looked into the eyes of the girl from the train, he had laughed at the situation. What a coincidence. She seemed as uneasy as he felt. Perhaps they could forego the date altogether. But now as she passed by and he offered her a smile, he berated himself for being a coward. If he backed out she might think he wasn't interested or that he considered himself superior. Surely, he could spend a couple of hours with someone unfamiliar. The auctioneer had made it clear: he needed to talk to her tonight and set up a dinner date or the bid would be invalid, and the school would lose out on the money.

Elsie, now seated safely back with Penny and Rachel, felt a tap on her shoulder. 'Excuse me, um, I don't even know your name.'

'Her name's Elsie,' Penny chimed in.

Turning around, Elsie found Matt standing behind her, looking embarrassed. He ran his hands through his hair, stumbling over his words. 'The auctioneer said I need to get a contact number or something like that. You know, so we can arrange a date.'

Rachel produced a piece of paper, and Liam handed over a pen. 'Always have one in my pocket,' he quipped with a smirk on his face. Elsie shot him a glare. She wrote her name and phone number on the paper. 'I can only go out on a Saturday night.'

He took the paper. 'Right. Where would you like to go?'

'She's new to town,' Elizabeth said. 'Why don't you take her to the fancy restaurant up on the hill? *The Fortress*. It opened recently.'

Elsie gulped; she didn't have that much money for an expensive meal. She had already spent more than planned tonight. Had that thought been evident on her face? 'I'll pay,' Matt said. 'I'll message you and pick you up, say around six.'

She nodded, lost for words, wondering how she had ended up in this predicament. Glancing around at her friends, she waited until Matt was back at his table. 'I don't go on dates. What if he isn't nice?'

'Well, you can ring one of us, and we'll pick you up,' Paul assured her.

'He's really cute,' Rachel added. 'That rugged look.'

Elsie refrained from mentioning she had seen him before, dressed formally. He likely worked in one of the offices in town. No doubt she'd find out on Saturday.

12

———

It had been difficult to concentrate at school that week. The air-conditioning in her room was not working properly and was difficult to regulate. Like the students, she became frazzled and cranky. Although she was on a special contract where she was supposed to get extra time off, Mr Garranto had given her an additional subject. This meant she had no spare lessons. Teachers were entitled to a couple of spares a week. That promised time was meant for studying and also getting lessons ready. Although she was organised and competent, as a new teacher everything took twice as long as it did for someone more experienced.

Bron, the lady at the office had made an appointment for her to see the principal, although she had tried to talk Elsie out of meeting with him. 'Are you sure, love, that you need to talk to him? Maybe try and talk to Penny or Elizabeth. You'll find them way more helpful.'

'Thanks, Bron. I appreciate your advice but I do need to talk to him directly.' She whispered her last word, 'unfortunately.' As she knocked on his door, she straightened her blouse and pulled her shoulders back. She had the written agreement with the department in her hand. Penny and a couple of the others had advised not to antagonise anyone in a higher position. But she wasn't going to be pushed around. She had kept her mouth shut about enough things already here at the school that were totally unethical and unfair. This was about her, not anyone else. If she just went by herself she wouldn't be dragging anyone else into what she thought would probably end up in an argument.

Mr Garranto's personal assistant, Gwen, sat in a chair in the corner of the room. She had a notebook and pen in hand and peered over the top of her glasses at Elsie as she entered the room. Elsie knew enough from what everyone had told her, that this woman was not to be trusted. Apparently she was as nasty as Garranto and loved nothing more than to repeat gossip or spy on the teachers. She was as Gus said, a direct link back to the boss. A rat who loved nothing more than to observe and report on anything she deemed ,'inappropriate.'

At the time Elsie thought that Gus was being a bit harsh. As Gwen sniffed and gave her a sneering look she realised he had not been exaggerating.

She waited for Mr Garranto to ask her to sit down, but he also peered over the top of his glasses at her, his fingers crossed as he rested his hands on the desk.'

'You wanted to ask something, Miss Jackson?' he enquired.

'Yes. May I sit down?'

'If you have to.'

'Thank you,' she said as she positioned herself in the

chair in front of him. 'I've come to talk about the extra lesson I've been given. The music class. I was told when I accepted this position that because I was working within the guidelines of this new program, I would be given a spare each day and extra time off for my studies. This latest timetable does not give me that.'

He chuckled, a wheezy sound that antagonised her more than his patronising glare. 'It doesn't always work how you think it might. We're short on staff. There isn't a music teacher here anymore and you will learn to teach whatever I give you.'

'I know you're understaffed but that isn't my problem and it's also why I've come here. To help fill a shortage of teachers in regional areas. I'll need to have the spares to complete my studies, otherwise the position isn't tenable for me. It won't help anyone if I don't pass my final semester at university.'

'I repeat myself. You will take lessons as directed. Your study is not my concern.'

She stood up. 'And I will repeat myself. The contract states a spare a day and I will take that spare. If needed I will ring the department and ensure it happens.'

Mr Garranto's face went red and he also stood up. 'You aren't the boss here, girlie, I am.'

'I know that and as the boss you need to ensure I get my spares.' She thought quickly. She had no intentions of moving to any other school but the man in front of her was an idiot and underneath his bluff he was spineless. 'Many other areas are after teachers and the program I am on enables me to move to anywhere I want that is regional. I will need a new timetable by tomorrow otherwise I will put different plans into place. Thank you for your time.'

With that, she walked briskly to the door and closed it firmly behind her. She hadn't looked at Gwen who had started to say something but hadn't been quick enough. Taking a deep breath Elsie saved her best smile for Bron as she walked past her. Elsie was sure she heard Bron giggle, before offering Elsie a thumbs up as she continued back to her classroom. No one was going to push her around. You could take the girl out of Logan but you couldn't take Logan out of the girl.

13

That afternoon when the bell had gone, Ethan lingered until everyone was gone. Penny was busy marking in the room next door and Elsie pulled the divider back so that the rooms were as one. She waved to Penny who was sipping a large cup of coffee. 'Bloody hell. I have one million drafts to mark,' Penny called out. 'Most of them hopeless. These kids couldn't care less. So tempted to write WTF next to some of their sentences.'

Elsie laughed. 'I have a student here to talk to,' she tilted her head towards Ethan who sat patiently in front of her desk.

'You didn't hear that,' Penny yelled out to him.

'I heard nothing.' He grinned back at her.

Ethan had only been at Matfield High for the first term but he was already a favourite with many of the teachers. They had discussed him in the staff room. 'Comes from a rough background, I'd say,' Elizabeth said, 'but my God, the boy's smart. Topping every class he's in.'

'Pity he's not getting fed at home,' Rachel added. 'I keep extra food for him. He's in my form class.'

'I feed him in Science,' Brett said.

'Me too,' someone else added.

Elsie thought of the food conversation as she pulled out a bag of chips from her cupboard. He certainly didn't look like he was fading away. That wasn't likely when every teacher he had was feeding him.

'Hungry?' she asked.

'Always. Thanks, Miss.'

She had meant to look up his personal information to see what the home situation was. Maybe he had a single mum or a large family with lots of kids. She must remember to have a look. There didn't seem to be time for anything and with the end of the term looming and that stupid date on Saturday night, at the moment she felt like life was a blurry rollercoaster. 'I have something for you,' she said. 'I found them in one of the staffrooms. These booklets will give you information about every course at all the different universities. Take them and have a look over the holidays and then we can talk about your options next term.'

He took them from her, his mouth full of chips. She waited until he finished eating.

'If you're busy over the holidays or going away don't worry if you don't have time because there's a lot in there to read. You'll see courses you wouldn't even know existed.'

'I'm set on speech pathology,' he said. 'A kid next door to where I used to live needed that sort of help and I looked up info on the internet. His name was Benny and I used to help him every afternoon by using everything I could find on websites. I know I wasn't an expert but no one else cared about him. And besides, it worked. What we did together was amazing and his speech became so improved that you could hardly tell he had problems. I kept it up for three years, three afternoons a week. He lived next door to me so he would come over after school. He was a great kid who wanted to improve his speech.'

'I can see you working with kids like that. There's a lot of students out there who don't get help and need it so badly.'

'You wouldn't believe it, Miss. The school I came from was in one of the roughest areas and a lot of kids had a bad home life. The teachers saved them. If it wasn't for them we all would have left school and ended up on the streets.'

She was about to add to the conversation when the classroom door flung open. It was Rachel and in her hand she held a sheet of paper. 'Hey, Elsie. Sorry to interrupt.'

Ethan stood up. 'I gotta go. I'm getting picked up soon. Thanks, Miss. I'll read the booklet over the holidays. Not going anywhere, so nothing to do but read. See ya round.'

Rachel passed the paper to Elsie as Ethan closed the door behind him. 'This was in your pigeonhole. Thought I'd bring it directly to you.' Rachel looked at the back of Ethan as he jumped down the set of stairs and started jogging along the path that led to the front of the school. 'I reckon every teacher in this school is keeping him alive with food,' Rachel said. 'I wonder what his story is?'

'I keep meaning to have a look at his home details,' Elsie sighed. 'There is just never enough time to do anything though. Sometimes I feel, or actually I often feel like I'm only doing half a job. Although I have my doubts about young Ethan. I have a feeling he's stringing us along with the food issue. He doesn't look like he's starving. Perhaps he's just smart and loves food.' Elsie took the paper which was a copy of her new timetable from Rachel's outstretched hand. She smirked. 'Thank you, Mr Garranto,' she said. 'A spare each day. Exactly what I'm entitled to.'

14

___

Now that she had overcome the first hurdle on her list, her focus turned to the next big one. The date. In less than twenty-four hours she would have to get in a car with a stranger and sit and talk for at least two hours about .... what?

Penny had saved her from the dilemma of what to wear with another hand-me-down dress. 'This will look gorgeous on you. It was my sister's and then mine. I reckon it's only been worn half a dozen times though.'

Elsie loved Penny. They had become best friends and she couldn't remember the last time she had trusted or liked someone so much. She had even met Penny's husband, Ian, and he seemed lovely also. In direct contrast to Penny, who spoke with lovely pronunciation and elegant words, Ian spoke like he was at the pub or out working with his mining crew. He had grown up in the Northern Territory on a sprawling cattle station and there were no airs and graces about him. Where Penny was stylish and well-dressed, Ian wore casual shorts and a T-shirt that had a funny saying on it. Penny had already warned him to watch his language although all he had said was, 'bloody.' It was obvious that he adored, 'his Penny', as he called her and when they invited Elsie around for dinner one night, she had enjoyed watching the two of them together. 'Maybe I should come as a chaperone on your date,' Ian said as he placed a large bowl of curry and rice in front of her.

'She'll be fine, Ian. Elsie is good at sticking up for herself. She's sorted Mr Garranto out better than anyone else has been able to.'

'He's a slime bag,' Ian said. 'He's having an affair with the woman who lives in the apartment next to you. You know he owns those buildings as well.'

'I didn't know that,' Elsie replied. 'That's Eliza Tuls who lives next door to me. It always amuses me, her surname that is.'

'Why is that?' Penny asked.

'Spell it backwards.'

They were all quiet for a moment and then Ian laughed loudly. 'Apt name for her. You know he's married. Word is his wife knows about his extra-marital affairs.'

'I don't know how she puts up with him,' Penny said.

They talked and laughed together and a warmth wrapped around Elsie. These were good people and this had been a special night. A sense of belonging swept over her. Ian and Penny always fussed over her and they were becoming like family. She had even shared some of her stories about her own family; concerns about Peter and Jane, who were always in her thoughts. Her mother rarely came to her mind though and that information she didn't share with anyone. She had rung Elsie a couple of times and then hadn't bothered once she realised her eldest daughter was not going to part with any of her hard-earned money. At least when Peter or Jane rang Elsie, they had something positive to tell her; a high mark for an assessment, selection for a special program or another scholarship for further study. They were both doing so well and she was filled with pride whenever she talked to them. They were also interested in how she was going and they'd cheered when she told them about her win with her latest timetable.

'Don't push a Logan gal around,' Peter had said.

They also laughed and took great delight when she filled them in about her 'hot' date, as Penny liked to call it. Now she wished one of them was here to give the tick of approval to her outfit. The dress from Penny was shorter than what she usually wore and she rubbed some moisturiser on her bare arms that were tanned from walking to and from school each day. Running her hands over the fabric, she admired the patterns, the subdued paisley design of pinks and oranges sitting firmly against her slim waist.

Slipping her sandals on she thought ahead to holidays. The two weeks would be a good time to not only get a load of schoolwork done and everything ready for term two, but she also planned to look online and order some new shoes and perhaps even some new underwear.

She had never earned so much money in her life and each fortnight she stashed most of it away. Her skimpy budget and the little rent she had to pay left a large amount to save. Her bank account was growing steadily and hopefully by the end of the year, she would have enough money to buy a small second-hand car. That was another reason she was staying at home for the holidays. She couldn't travel anywhere even if she wanted to. If she caught the train back to one of the larger towns she would have to pay for accommodation and her ticket. Not that she minded; two weeks would fly past and with a couple of good books from the library she was set. All she had to do was get this terrible date out of the way.

15

———

Matt had also dithered about what to wear. He only had one good outfit that he kept for special occasions, like going to the solicitors. Apart from that he had two good pairs of jeans and the shirt he had already worn to the pub.

When he picked Ethan up from school on Friday afternoon he asked him to come with him to the clothes shop in town. 'I have to go on a date. I got dragged into this auction thing at the pub. It's all about raising money for the primary school and the boss made me take part.'

'Holey, dooley. You, go on a date? What are you going to wear?'

'That's where you come in. I have jeans and boots but I can't wear the same shirt I had on that night.'

'Who's the girl?'

'I don't know. Some girl I've never met before, whose friends also pushed her into taking part. I don't think she was keen either.'

'What's she look like?'

'Cute. Really pretty. Way too pretty for me.' He didn't add that she was a teacher. He wasn't sure if she was from the high school or the primary school. It wouldn't matter, because after tonight he didn't need to see her again.

For once Matt let Ethan take control of the situation. He'd tried on a few different shirts but Ethan had chosen a light blue one and said without a doubt it looked the best on him. 'You should get new jeans also. Look at these.' He held them up and Matt agreed he did like them. 'Just try them on,' Ethan said as he bundled a few different outfits into Matt's arms, 'and if they look good, buy them. When's the last time you bought new clothes?'

The jeans had fitted perfectly and with the shirt Ethan had chosen the outfit was very smart. By the time they left the store, Matt had two new shirts and a pair of jeans. He also bought the same for Ethan. 'You need new clothes too. Here, chose some shorts and a new T-shirt. Grab whatever jeans you want.'

It had been fun and for once Matt felt a closeness to his brother that wasn't always there. At home they spent so much time arguing and getting in each other's way that there hadn't been many occasions when they laughed or had fun together.

It was hard not to be serious. His responsibility to Ethan was a big task and he wanted to make sure he got it right. The only way out of the circumstances they had grown up in was to gain an education. That way you weren't limited in what you wanted to do. You had choices.

His brother must have also enjoyed the shopping time together because afterwards there was a difference in the way he spoke to Matt. The mood was lighter and more amicable and when they got home Ethan helped tidy up. He put all the new clothes away and even volunteered to help cook a meal. As the two of them sat and ate they chatted. Matt relaxed and thought life wasn't too bad. All he needed to do was to get this stupid date out of the way.

16

Ethan helped Matt get ready late on Saturday afternoon. His new shirt was ironed, his jeans crisp and stylish and his leather boots shone with fresh polish. He had combed his hair that he'd made sure to get cut during the week and his face was clean-shaven.

'You're going to a lot of trouble,' Ethan quipped. 'You look hot.'

'Jees, that's the last thing I reckon I look. Do you think my hair looks okay?'

'Perfect. How come you don't have a girlfriend? I remember a couple of them from years ago but that's a long time ago.'

Matt combed his hair again. 'Never worked out. I move around with work too much. And the last girl was full-on and all she wanted was to get married and have kids. I'm only twenty-seven and that was three years ago. Maybe I'll think about a girlfriend once you go to uni.'

Ethan grabbed his phone. 'Stand outside and I'll take

a photo of you. The other blokes are around the firepit having a beer already. They'll want to see how fancy you look.'

Some of the other workers were already sitting down, relaxing after a hard week of work. Beyond where they sat, the sun was sinking in the western sky and a flock of cockatoos squawked as they flew overhead. Matt watched them, following their path of flight. His eyes were drawn to the golden paddocks, a track of dark red dirt winding through the thick grass. A line of cattle followed the well-trod path, the dust kicking up behind them as the last of the sun's rays filtered across the space. Although they had decent rainfall in the previous months, it didn't take long for the ground to dry out. Beneath the new shoots of green grass, small trees and shrubs that had come back to life after the wet, was dusty red soil; a powdery fine dirt that seemed to get into everything. Growing up in the suburbs of Brisbane, the changing landscape of the outback never ceased to amaze him. What was dried and parched for months, sometimes years on end, could miraculously transform into green paddocks with water-holes and creeks filled with water. It was an ever-changing countryside and he had grown to love it.

'Bit different than home, Ethan said, his hand held above his eyes as he watched the setting sun. 'Stand here and I'll take a photo of you. Maybe after that, the boys will take one of us together.'

The camp where Matt called home consisted of a cluster of dongas that the fencing gang lived in. Some other temporary buildings operated as admin spaces and kitchens. It was a remote existence but one he had grown used to and over the years some of the men he worked with had become like family.

Rusty, a burly foreman, called out to him. 'Oye, give us a look at you. Not every day we see you in all your finery.'

'Stone the crows,' Pedro, an elderly fencer added in, 'You scrub up alright.'

Both men had been in the same work gang as Matt for the last five years. When he was younger they had taken him under their wing, making sure he stayed out of trouble and was looked after. Together they went where the work was and these men were some of the reasons why he stayed with the company. Rusty had a wife and grown-up kids who all lived in Cairns. He worked one month on and one month off. 'Wifey loves it. Fusses over me when I'm there, cries when I leave and then doesn't stop smiling for a month. No cooking, cleaning or looking after me. Spends all her time with the grandkids and sipping lattes at those posh cafes on the esplanade in Cairns. What a life!'

Pedro's family lived closer. He was the eldest of the work group and they had celebrated his sixtieth birthday at the pub a couple of weeks ago. 'Wife still works cleaning at the local school. She loves her job. God knows why. Kids are all grown up and one of them and her family live in a second house down the back of our block. Always someone there with her. It's worked out well for us. Don't know what I'll do if I have to retire.'

Pedro pulled out a chair for Ethan. 'Come and sit young man. Come and listen to our Saturday afternoon bullshit. You never know what you'll learn.'

Ethan passed Matt the car keys. 'Have fun. We'll want to hear all about it when you get home.'

Pedro passed Ethan a plate of stew and a large chunk of damper he had cooked in the fire. 'This poor boy. Anyone would think you never fed him, Matt. Always hungry. We keep all our leftovers for him.'

Matt shook his head. 'Never stops eating. Our fridge is always stocked up. I'd better go. I tell you though I'd rather spend the night sitting here with you lot.'

'Mind your manners and don't forget to open the car door for her. Girls like that sort of thing,' Rusty said.

'I'm not aiming to impress, but thank you, I'll remember to do that.'

WHEN HE PULLED into the carpark of the apartment building Matt took one last look at himself in the rear-view mirror. His hair had a habit of falling over his forehead and he pushed it back, cursing the long fringe. He wasn't sure why he felt so nervous, although it had been a long time since he had been on a date and he'd never taken anyone out who he didn't know as a friend beforehand. Just get it over with, he reminded himself.

Parking outside the apartment he waited to see if she would appear. 'Elsie,' he said aloud. Her name was Elsie. Remember it. Checking the time, he got out of the car and looked at the number on the doors. Number seven. He knocked softly and then louder when no one appeared. Perhaps she had forgotten and he could go home instead and sit around the fire.

Just as he was about to turn and leave, the door

opened and she stood in front of him. 'Sorry, I had the noisy washing machine on. It jumps around and bangs into the wall. I barely heard you knock.'

'No worries. I thought you might have forgotten.'

'Hang on. I'll just grab my bag.'

He stood on the doorstep, watching as she disappeared into a room off the lounge room. The apartment was sparsely furnished and he remembered that these places were mainly used to accommodate teachers. He could see a round wooden table with two chairs, the top of the table covered in books and papers. It was the start of the school holidays and he wondered if she was going away. That could be something they could talk about. The thought of what the conversation might be made him nervous and he wrung his hands together, stepping back as she re-emerged. She was pretty. Prettier than he remembered and he was glad that Ethan had made him buy new clothes. 'I'll just lock the door,' she said, as she turned the key and came to stand beside him. 'Right. I'm ready.'

He nodded and she followed him to his car. When he went to step in front of her and open the car door she laughed and grabbed it herself. 'I can open a door. Thank you.'

Shit, he thought to himself. This was not going to be easy.

For some reason, her seatbelt wouldn't work and he had to get out of the car and come back around to her side. They both jiggled with it and eventually the strap came free and he passed it to her. 'I'll let you do it up,' he said. 'I meant to clean that side out. Excuse the mess on the floor.'

She screwed up her face as she shuffled her feet in between the chip packets and empty cans of coke that littered the floor of the car. 'I don't like mess.'

In front of them, the door to the neighbouring apartment opened and a woman stood with folded arms glaring at them both. Matt started the car as Elsie put down her window and very clearly stuck her middle finger up in the air, aiming her gesture at the woman who now stood wide-mouthed. The woman promptly twirled around and headed back inside, slamming her door behind her.

'She's a bitch. A constant thorn in my side.' Elsie said. 'I'm sorry you had to witness that, but I've had enough of her.'

Matt didn't know which way to look. There was a strong antagonism in Elsie's voice and he wasn't sure if it was because of the mess at her feet or the woman from next door who she obviously did not like. He took a deep breath before pulling out of the driveway. 'Look. I don't think either you or I are keen on going on this date. We both seem to have been dragged into a situation that I must admit is foreign to me. So if you like we can just call it quits and go our separate ways right here. I can tell you're unhappy.' He nearly said cranky but then thought better of it. 'And I'm sorry about the mess. What do you say? Forget the date?'

She also took a deep breath and he noticed her chest rise up and down. For a while she didn't speak.

He looked at her again. Her face was stony and she looked every which way except at him. Perhaps he needed to say more, to see if she did really want to cancel the date. 'I mean, I don't mind going out for dinner if you still want to, but I don't want to force you to go.'

She eventually turned to look at him and he noticed her dark broody eyes. He thought she was going to apologise for her unhappy attitude. But she didn't.

'We have to go out otherwise the money that the teachers so kindly bid for you won't get donated. I'm hungry. Let's just go and eat, and get the date over and done with.'

He swung out of the driveway onto the main street. 'Sounds good. I'm also hungry.' Perhaps he should have added that it had been a long hot day at work and he'd gone to a lot of trouble to dress up, but he could tell she wasn't up for conversation. That suited him fine.

ELSIE HADN'T MEANT to snap or sound angry. But for goodness sakes. How much trouble could it have been to at least clean the car floor where her feet were going to go? The seat also seemed dusty and she wondered when the last time was the car had been washed. Then there was also the added problem of Eliza Tuls. The woman had become unbearable, banging on the wall as soon as Elsie started to play her music or if the television was even remotely loud. Sometimes she turned the music up just to annoy Eliza. The antagonising woman was also always at the window watching every move Elsie made. Every time she saw Eliza peering through the curtains or standing in the doorway, unashamedly spying on her, she always thought about how this woman was having an affair with Garranto. Ughh. Who would want either of them?

Now she had to spend time with this Matt fellow. He must have been knocking for a while because by the time she realised someone was there, he was five minutes late. At least he had made an effort with his clothes and she had to admit he was very good-looking. Blue eyes, a chiselled face and brown hair that always seemed to sit in a perfect position. If she didn't know better, she would suspect he'd had it recently cut. It was just as she had assumed from the start. He had money. Maybe he was from one of the wealthy cattle farmer dynasties that she had quickly learned held a lot of sway in the community. Many of them had been here for generations and there were several kids in her classes who were from those families.

They were great kids who didn't want for anything, vastly different from those she had grown up with. It was interesting to hear about what they did in their spare time and she loved how they talked to her about their lives. Most of them swore like troopers and on weekends they rode motorbikes and horses, went to sporting carnivals and rodeos, mustered cattle and did camp drafts. Mostly though they spent time with their families which included a multitude of cousins, aunties, and uncles.

That could be a topic she could talk about tonight. If she got him talking about his family and their cattle property, that would fill in some of the time.

17

─────────

The restaurant called *The Fortress* was new. A couple from the coast had recently opened it and it boasted the best Italian food in the district. That wouldn't be hard as there weren't any other Italian eateries within three hundred kilometres. At first the locals had been wary of the foreign food and the newcomers. They were worried it would take business away from other eateries and it was hard enough as it was to get staff. Al and Anita had brought some of their extended family with them though, so there was always enough staff to help run the restaurant.

Although they had only been in the town for six months all of them had quickly become part of the community. They joined committees at the school where their young children went and talked one of their cousins into moving from Sydney so she could work at the local kindy. Sometimes if there was a large function at the pub they helped out with the food or offered extra accommodation if there was a big event in town. Now they welcomed Matt and Elsie like they were royalty.

'Welcome. Welcome. You are our special guests for the night. Come. Come.'

Anita led them to a secluded corner of the restaurant, next to a large window. 'The best view in the house. Look. The moon is just there and the stars, the stars, they are coming.'

Al pulled their chairs out and Elsie jumped as he flicked her serviette and placed it on her lap. 'Thank you,' she said, smiling at him. Who wouldn't be charmed by the couple's accent and gracious warm welcome? As she looked around, she had to agree they had been seated at the best table in the restaurant.

Outside, flares lit the way through a garden that led to the main house where the couple lived. Further down there were a couple of cabins that were let out for accommodation and some other outbuildings where other members of their family lived. The couple had brought the garden back to life. A bore that had been unused for years had been re-established and now the garden grew all the greens and herbs, not only for *The Fortress* but also for many of the shops and eateries in town. Anita's parents had planted other trees and vegetables and some of the kids from Elsie's classes had come out to the property during the term to do work experience.

Matt was also now seated and she stared straight across the table at him, both in awkward silence as they looked at each other. Al bustled back and forth. 'So, here is a complimentary bottle of the most famous Italian wine for you.' He chuckled. 'Whoops. I tell a little lie.

Maybe not so famous really and from South Australia. It is a good one though.'

Matt found his voice. 'Thank you so much, Al. I'm sure it'll be perfect.'

They watched as he expertly poured them both a glass, a crisp white serviette draped over his arm, his hand twisting dramatically as he finished filling their glasses. He leaned over and spoke quietly. His words were silken and they both sat enthralled by Al speaking in Italian. 'È una serata romantica. It is a night for romance,' he declared.

Elsie looked down in her glass as Al continued talking. He took out his phone. 'I have been directed by the organiser of the auction that a photo must be taken. The local paper will love it. Now lean over the table so your heads are together and hold your glasses high. Salute!'

Both managed a smile for the photo and Al was delighted with the result. 'Bella. Godere.' Matt and Elsie looked at each other as Al popped his phone back into his pocket and made his way back to the kitchen. They both took a large gulp from their drinks.

There was an awkward silence as Matt took another large sip from his wine and Elsie followed suit. 'You have to admit. This is pretty funny,' Matt finally said. 'Both of us here, neither wanting to be and everyone making such a fuss over us.'

The wine was warm on Elsie's throat and she enjoyed the taste and effect. She felt her tension loosen. 'Small towns,' she said. 'I was warned about how everyone knows everything about everyone.' She relaxed a little more, the cool rich wine hitting the spot and calming her nerves a little. 'I guess you've lived here for a long while and you're used to it. The farming families in the area all seem to know everyone.'

He threw a quizzical look her way and she noticed that the corners of his mouth twisted up in a cute sort of half smile as he spoke. 'Not me. I've only lived here for about six months.'

'Oh, I assumed you had lived here forever. Does your family own a property or do you work in one of the offices in town?'

He put his head back and laughed, pushing his hair back from his forehead. 'Me? Work in an office? Why would you think that?'

She was intrigued and didn't want to reveal her judgements based on the clothing she had originally seen him wearing on the train. 'What do you do then?'

'Guess.'

'Um, work for the council. Lawyer. Accountant.'

He took another long sip of his wine, his blue eyes looking over the top of his glass, a look of amusement on his face. 'Do you really think that's what I look like I do for a job?'

'I don't know. When I first saw you on the train you were dressed like you worked in the city.' She screwed her face up and scanned his face. Perhaps she had read him wrong. He was tanned and his body was strong. Maybe he did work outside.

Anita appeared with some garlic bread and the entrees. She placed them carefully in front of them. 'I see you two getting along. It is a special night. The stars are out and it is a night for romance.'

There was no use trying to tell her they were just trying to get through the dinner and do the right thing by the fundraising committee. Let them all think the date was going as they wanted.

As she munched on the delicious bread Elsie asked Matt, 'Do you work on the roads?'

'Nope.'

'Drive trucks?'

'No.'

'Work at the medical centre? Doctor? Dentist?'

'No, you couldn't be further from what I do.'

'Come on, just tell me. I'm never going to guess.'

Now he seemed hesitant to tell her. Perhaps she shouldn't have built up the expectation of what he did so much. It didn't matter anyway.

'It's nothing special, but you're way off track. I'm a fencing contractor. I build and fix fences, do a bit of mustering and pretty much a Jack of all trades.'

'Wow. I never would have guessed that. Are you sure? You looked like you worked in one of the big law firms in town or one of the banks. I never took you for just a labourer.' Her last words hadn't come out how she wanted them to and she wanted to take them back as soon as she said them. It was obvious that Matt was insulted and she noted the change of tone in his voice. 'There's nothing wrong with working with your hands. I wouldn't have taken you for a teacher when I first saw you either.' His last remark was rude. Almost like a tit-for-tat. She didn't want to ask him any more questions and she concentrated on her food as Anita reappeared with their main meals. The date was not off to a good start and she tried to think of other conversations to have. Waiting until he had finished his meal, she poured them both another glass of wine. She couldn't stand to sit in silence. 'What did you think of the train trip? The one that boarded in Brisbane.'

Matt wiped his mouth with the serviette. 'What a trip. I don't think I'll do that one again. I had to pick up a company ute in one of the small towns so that's why I railed it instead of flying. It was certainly interesting.'

'I think you might have been more comfortable than I was. I suppose it could have been worse. Imagine being seated in the carriage behind where we were.'

They had talked for a while, laughing about the antics of some of the other passengers and the fact that someone had been arrested and carted off. 'Takes all types,' she said. 'It did make for an interesting trip though.'

'I probably should have been a bit friendlier and let you sit next to me.' He looked at her and for the first time she felt a sense of camaraderie between them.

'No way. How were you to know who I was? I could have been just as noisy and annoying as some of the other people on there.'

They had laughed and she sensed that he relaxed a little. Perhaps she had been a bit harsh. He was probably just as uncomfortable and nervous as she was. When he asked her about her job as a teacher, she'd described some of the antics that happened at the school, as well as the bullying nature of the principal and some of the others. He wiped his mouth with his serviette. Anita had lit a candle on their table and his blue eyes sparkled in the light reflected from it. 'I know they've gone through a few different teachers in the past year or so. Some of the fellas at work have told me about it.'

'I intend to stay. Mr Garranto, or dickhead, as I like to

think of him, won't get the better of me. I've worked with his type before.'

'Sounds like you know what you're doing.' He held his hands up like he was surrendering. 'I reckon you could take him on. Doesn't sound like too much gets past you.'

'You have to stick up for yourself. Where I come from it's survival of the fittest.'

'I know what that's like,' he replied.

She doubted that he did really know, but at least he was being amicable and she was able to make conversation with him. They had talked about his job then and she'd asked questions. She had never met a fencer or musterer before and she was intrigued by how he had got into the business of fencing. However, he became a bit guarded about what he had done before this job and she backed off a bit with the questions. She also didn't like to reveal too much about herself. Keep things simple she reminded herself.

By the time the dinner was finished, she decided that Matt was not such a bad fella. He had been interesting to talk to, intelligent with what he spoke about, and seemed like he had a placid nature. Not that you could ever tell from just a few hours of chatting but first impressions were usually right with her and she got a good feeling about him. Fortunately, there had been ample topics to talk about concerning their respective jobs. When he dropped her home, they shook hands. 'Guess I'll see us in the paper,' he said, giving her a wave as he walked back to his car.

'Guess so. See you around, Matt.'

Eliza had not bothered to come to the window this time and Elsie noticed that her car was also missing. Maybe she was out with Mr Garranto somewhere. The thought made her grimace. As she drew the curtains and sank into the single lounge chair that she had picked up at the op shop, she thought about Matt. There was something about him that intrigued her. Something she couldn't exactly put her finger on, but an aspect of him that made him interesting. It was a small town. How long would it be until she ran into him again?

18

Matt had also thought about the date as he drove back home. In his mind he pictured Elsie's shiny brown hair, the way it curled a little and sat neatly on her shoulders. She was a contradiction in terms. One minute she was polite and asked appropriate questions but the next minute she was guarded and avoided revealing aspects of her life before she came to Matfield. Fair enough, he thought. He was similar. It appeared though that she had lived with her family until she arrived here at the start of the year. She probably had lived at home with her parents, like a lot of people who went to university did. Parents who paid the bills and charged no rent or board, making sure their kids got through the years of study with the least number of difficulties.

A full moon hung languidly over the hills, and the paddocks that he drove through were lit up like it was daytime. Living in the middle of nowhere suited him, although it wasn't as easy now Ethan had joined him.

Perhaps he was, as Ethan said, too serious. There hadn't been a lot of fun in his life over the last couple of years. Living with the other men suited him, but the question that so often rattled in his mind plagued him again. Was fencing what he wanted to do for the rest of his life? Did he always want to live out in remote areas and mix mainly with other men? Ethan was going to study at university. He would take the opportunity that Matt never had. He looked up at the moon again. Life was sometimes plotted for you. Pre-destined. Sometimes the choices were taken out of your hands. It was best to be happy with what you had and not dream about something unattainable.

When he pulled up at the campsite, Pedro and Rusty were still sitting around the campfire. They waved and he walked towards them. 'How did you go, Romeo?' Pedro asked as Matt sat down on a chair beside them.

'It was a nice night. It went okay. We got through it.'

'Was she lovely?' Rusty leaned towards him, the wrinkles around his eyes widening as he grinned at Matt.

'Pretty. Intelligent. A bit feisty.'

'What did you talk about?'

'Just the usual. Jobs. The town. You know.'

'Did you ask for a second date?' Pedro was curious and Matt could tell both men were fishing for details and further information. 'You didn't, did you? You wasted an opportunity. What's wrong with you boy?'

'She's in a different league than I am.'

'That's bullshit.' Rusty slapped his hand on his knee. My wife came from one of the wealthiest families in our town. I came from the poorest. Nothing stopped us being together.'

'I'm not chasing anyone, Pedro. It was just a date.'

Ethan had also been awake when he went inside the donga. He was reading as well as listening to music, his earplugs as usual fixed in his ears. It always amazed Matt how he could do both at once.

He pulled his earplugs out and asked Matt, 'How'd you go? Was she nice?'

'She was. Very nice.'

'Did you kiss her?'

'Good God no. We shook hands.'

'You should have at least kissed her goodnight.'

'You need to get your head out of those stupid books you read. That's not how it works in the real world. She's out of my league and I reckon if I had kissed her she would have taken me out. Lovely girl, but not one to be messed with.'

Ethan rolled over and looked at the ceiling. 'Do you reckon we'll always have a chip on our shoulder that we're not good enough? Because of where we come from?'

'Probably. I know where I belong.'

'What? Fencing? Stuck out here?'

'It's all I've got.'

'Bullshit. It's all you think you've got.'

19

The holidays had come and gone and Elsie was surprised how quickly the two weeks passed. Most of the time she had stayed in the apartment and studied or did her schoolwork. She had a couple of exams coming up; her final ones. There was light at the end of the tunnel; she just needed to pass the exams and she would be finished. Fully qualified.

Surprisingly she hadn't run into Matt since their date. Matfield was only a small place and she had been into town a few times to get small amounts of groceries. Without a car, she had to make sure to pick up a few items every few days. However, that problem was made a little easier when Penny called around and dropped off a second-hand pushbike with a large wicker basket on the back of it. 'I spotted this at the dump,' she declared proudly. 'Someone had left it to the side. You know where everyone leaves anything that's any good, hoping that someone takes it and uses it.'

'Oh, my goodness. It's perfect. That will make my life a little easier until I get my car.'

'Ian fixed it and painted it for you.'

'He's very kind. Tell him I said thank you.'

The bike had given her a new sense of freedom and she'd ridden around every street in town as well as out on some of the backroads. Often she'd stop and stand for a while, enjoying the scenery. In the late afternoons there were spectacular sunsets that filled the western sky and when the sun lowered further the hazy light turned the green tips of the grass in the endless paddocks to a golden hue. It would be a vastly different scene when there was no rain, and she was glad that she was seeing the countryside in its best light.

The sides of the road however still carried that fine dust that she had become used to. Whenever she came back from her ride she was covered in it, usually from a large cattle truck coming the other way, coating her and the bike in a thick layer of red particles. Just like the dust, there were so many unfamiliar things to get used to.

One afternoon, after a lengthy ride, Elsie parked her bike against the wall by her front door. Dusting off the dirt from her clothes and hair, she observed a four-wheel drive pull into the space in front of her. Stepping out was a well-dressed middle-aged woman, impeccably put together with a pleated skirt, a well-fitted blouse, and short blonde hair that was perfectly styled. Approaching Elsie, she exuded an air of refinement. With a well-educated tone, she inquired, 'Hello. I was wondering if you could inform me which apartment Eliza Tuls resides in.'

Elsie, who had been trying to fix a part on her pedal,

looked up. She knew straight away who the woman was. Penny had pointed her out one day when they sat having coffee in the café together. Elsie looked towards the door on the other side of where they stood. 'She lives in there but she's away at the moment.'

The woman looked surprised. 'Is she now? Do you know how long she's been away for?'

'A couple of weeks.'

'I don't suppose you know where she's gone.'

'No. I don't.' Even if she had known there was no way she was going to tell. She'd already said enough but she hadn't been able to help herself. Not only had she seen her at the café, but Penny had also pointed her out a couple of times when she had been playing bridge with some of the other ladies in the lounge room of the pub. The lady who now thanked her and went back to her car was Mr Garranto's wife. Penelope Garranto.

Hosing the dust off her legs Elsie watched the car as it sped out of the carpark and onto the main road. Trouble was brewing for sure. Everyone in town knew what was going on between Garranto and Eliza. Surely his wife did too.

20

Term two passed much the same as the first one and Elsie felt like she had really settled in. There had been the usual run-ins with the principal and a few social afternoons at the pub with the others from work. Mostly though the days consisted of teaching, meetings and preparation. Work, work and more work. A set of holidays had come and gone and now she was swinging into the first day of another new term; term three, the one everyone promised was the busiest one of the year. Elsie needed to stay on top of her work and out of the way of Garranto if she was going to make it to the end of the term, never mind the end of the year.

The term had started well and she slid back into the routine like she had been there for years. A couple of times she had gone with some of the others on a Friday afternoon to the pub, even dancing with Rachel on a couple of occasions. Everyone at work was keen to try and get her to go out more, but she was happy by herself.

'Don't drown in school work,' Elizabeth advised. 'You'll burn out if you keep going the way you are. A girl your age should be going out and having fun.'

Now as she got her room ready for teacher-parent interviews, she did wonder why she was still at school and probably would be there until eight o'clock. At least this afternoon she had made sure to eat something and have a cup of coffee. The last thing she wanted was to look tired or appear as if she wasn't coping with everything. However, her final exams were next week and she had been up until all hours studying. Her eyes were sore and felt heavy. Often when she went home in the afternoon she'd have a nap, sometimes waking up well into the night. Maybe Elizabeth was right that she was doing too much. She walked around the classroom, making sure she had everything ready to talk to parents. Workbooks. Marks. Reports. Concerns. Everything was in order. Keep walking, she told herself. If she sat down and relaxed for a moment, chances were she might go to sleep. That would not be a great example, with her first parent interview about to begin.

AFTER TWO HOURS of talking to parents, she was completely worn out. Only one more to go and then she could go home. Penny's room was in darkness and when she looked across to some of the classrooms opposite her it appeared that those teachers had also packed up and gone home. She must have one of the latest interviews. When she looked outside most of the other lights were off and she told herself to make this interview a quick one and get out and back home as fast as she could. She still had some study to finish tonight and more work to get ready for lessons tomorrow. Today she had walked instead of riding to school so there was also the walk home in the dark to add to her day. The small town was fairly safe but she was always wary about the dark streets, since many of the street lights were not working. Without a moon there would be very little light.

Her thoughts were interrupted as a man walked up the path. To her surprise it was Matt and her heart leapt as she recognised him. He seemed lost and she called out and waved to him. 'Matt. How are you? It's Elsie. Remember me?'

He looked up and walked towards her. A wide smile crossed his face. 'Remember you? Of course, I do. How many dates do you think I go on?'

She couldn't help but smile, his familiar face a pleasant distraction from her long day at work. 'You look lost,' she quipped.

'I am. I need room EN7. Miss Jackson. I think that's the teacher I'm looking for.'

She was confused. 'That's me. I only have one interview left and that's with Ethan's dad. That can't be you. Can it?'

He laughed, that deep sound that felt familiar. 'I'm not that old. I'm actually Ethan's brother. His legal guardian. My interview must be with you, his English teacher.'

'You never told me you had a brother here at school and Ethan never said he lived with his brother. That's crazy.'

'Well, it's a fact. We live together. I'm his guardian and

I'm here to talk about how he's going and if there are any concerns.'

She shook her head and laughed. 'Come in. Come in.'

~

HER HEAD WAS STILL SPINNING as she sat down. 'I can't believe it. Who would have ever thought.'

'Like you said, it's crazy. I never mentioned your name to Ethan when we went on the date so he wouldn't have known who it was I was taking to dinner. He's probably talked about you at home but I never made a connection. The thought never even crossed my mind.'

She shook her head and arranged the papers she had in front of her. Not that she needed to look at anything to talk about Ethan. Much like with all her students, she possessed a deep understanding of both his challenges and strengths.

Matt reached into his backpack. 'I hope you don't mind but I haven't had dinner yet. You look tired. Have you eaten?'

She thought how the comment about looking tired could really be interpreted as, 'You look like shit. But now wasn't the time to be worried about how she looked, and she pushed his remark to the side. 'No, I haven't. It's been one of those days.'

He pulled out a white paper parcel, the smell of hot chips wafting through the classroom. When she picked up her papers and moved them out of the way, he spread the chips out in front of them. 'Sauce?' he asked, squeezing some out when she nodded. 'I must have known something because I bought way too many chips. Dig in. We can talk about Ethan as we eat.'

With Matt being the last interview and after a long day, Elsie felt like all her energy was sapped. Before he had walked in she didn't feel like she had anything more to give. It was like the parents and students had sucked any last vestige of vitality from her. Was their daughter doing enough homework? Was she behaving in class and was she hanging around the girl they had separated her from in other classes? Was their son spending enough time on his schoolwork or was his entire focus on his football? Was Lucy on her laptop too much? Did Neville try and use his phone in class? And did she think Ben was taking drugs? The questions had been endless and she had quickly learned that as a teacher she was also expected to be a counsellor and informant.

Now as she tucked into the chips, thinking that they tasted like the best meal in the world, she was re-invigorated and the past interviews were pushed to the back of her mind. Even when Mr Garranto stuck his head in through the doorway and questioned how much longer she was going to be, she didn't care about the angry look on his face. She could tell that he was not impressed, his brow furrowing, his eyes scrunching up in disgust. However, he didn't get a chance to say anything because Matt raised a chip in the air and pointed it in his direction. 'Cheers, Mr Garranto. How are you? I'm here to discuss young Ethan and I'm having my dinner as we talk. Ethan's a lucky kid to have Miss Jackson as his teacher. He says she's the best teacher in the school. For that matter the best teacher he's ever had.'

Garranto scowled and muttered under his breath, his

eyes narrowing even more. 'You're the last one here, Miss Jackson. Make sure you turn all the lights off and lock up. The alarm for this section is your responsibility. Make sure it's turned on.'

She nodded as she ate, throwing Matt a look as the surly principal stomped down the stairs and along the pathway. 'Nice of him to wait around until I'm finished. You can see what his attitude is like. He's a regular pain in the butt.'

Matt squeezed some more sauce out and pushed a pile of chips in her direction. 'What a pleasure that man is and what happened to looking after your staff? Someone should report him. I'll wait around until you leave and make sure you're okay. It's dark out there tonight. No moon.'

They talked for a bit longer and finished the chips. She even found a coffee cup and accepted half of his can of Coke. 'I think I would have passed out if you hadn't come along. I haven't eaten since morning tea.'

'I'm sorry, but you look really tired. You have black circles under your eyes.'

'Thanks for your honesty,' she said with a wry smile. 'I'm completing my last subject at uni and also trying to keep up with the work here. It has been a bit full-on, but nothing I can't handle. Now let's talk about Ethan.'

She had been surprised at how anxious Matt was about Ethan's progress, considering he was topping all his subjects and there had been no concerns.

'I've had interviews with all his teachers tonight and they all say the same thing,' he said. 'I just want to make sure he gets high enough marks to get into uni. It's vital that he goes. And just for the record, those compliments I said about you to that principal were all true. Ethan told me what he thought of you when I said I was coming for these interviews.' He laughed. 'Imagine when I tell him you were my date.'

She felt her face redden and knew she was blushing. Compliments didn't come her way that often and what Matt had said meant a lot. 'Thank you. I am enjoying teaching and I love the kids. They're great. Now back to Ethan. Of course, it's important that he goes on to do further study and he'll have no trouble getting into whatever he wants with the marks he's getting. I gave him some books with all the courses in it.'

'He's had his head in those books all holidays.'

She sat up straight. 'I think, considering what you have told me about being his guardian and that you're probably a sole supporter, that he should apply for a disadvantaged background scholarship. He will most likely get in without one, but if he can win a scholarship, he will receive a large amount of money and that might make it easier on you and him.'

Matt screwed up his face. 'I don't know about that. We're not in a disadvantaged situation and we don't take handouts. We're doing okay and I make good money.'

'He may choose to study for several years. The scholarships are big if he can win one. Thirty thousand dollars big.'

'What? How much?'

'Thirty thousand. They pay it over a few years, but it would make a huge difference. I'm sure he'd fit the category for the ones I'm thinking of, going by what you've told me about his situation.' She could tell he was unsure. 'I know it might seem strange getting help but those scholarships are there for kids like Ethan.' She hesitated. 'Both my sister and brother won similar ones and they're both studying at uni now, all of it paid for by the scholarships. Like Ethan, they were top of their classes and worked really hard so that helps a lot.'

'Yeah, but you're not talking about an academic scholarship for Ethan, you're talking that we'plead that we are poor and disadvantaged.'

'It's not about being poor, it's about ensuring that every student regardless of their background has the opportunity to pursue their educational goals. The scholarships provide financial aid, mentorship, and guidance. That is exactly what my siblings received.' She said it slowly so he fully understood. 'A disadvantaged background scholarship. My sister does medicine and my brother is doing Vet Science.'

'Your siblings? They got those sorts of scholarships?'

'Yes. Unfortunately, I missed out. I worked for six months after school and I wasn't aware of what I could have applied for. Hence, it has taken me over seven years to complete a four-year course. I've had to work as well as study because of the money situation.'

He gazed at her intently and swung back in his chair.

'Don't swing,' she reprimanded, her voice stern.

'Sorry. I'm in shock.'

'Why?'

'I thought you came from a wealthy family. You said you lived at home before coming here.'

She had told him enough. 'Well, your assumptions were wrong. And, I asked you to stop swinging.'

THANK goodness he had stayed with her until she packed up. He was still in shock that firstly she was Ethan's teacher and secondly, she also seemed to come from a dysfunctional background. He had stopped asking her questions when he noticed she had clammed up, clearly deciding that she had told him enough. Fair enough. Not fair enough though that the principal had left her here in the dark and to lock up. Using his phone light Matt walked with her through the deserted school and to the front gate.

The school ground were empty. 'I can't believe he was going to leave you here by yourself. It's really dark and a bit strange seeing it so deserted.'

She walked closely to him. 'It's so different when it's not filled with noisy kids. Thank you, I'm grateful that you waited.' When they got to the carpark, he noticed there were no other vehicles except his ute. 'Where is your car?'

'I don't have one. I walked to school today. Sometimes I ride my bicycle, but mostly I walk. It's not far although I should have remembered that my interviews went until late. It would have been better to ride my bike.'

'Well, I can tell you right now, you're not walking home. I'll drive you.'

She was too tired to argue and besides it was dark and windy, the trees blowing beside his car creeping her out, not to mention the huge bats that flew above, their wings making a flapping noise that made her jump. 'Thank you. It's not far and I don't feel like walking by myself. There aren't many streetlights. It's probably safer here than where I've come from, but still, I accept your offer.'

'Oh, so you do sometimes accept help?' he said as he smiled at her.

She tried not to notice his straight white teeth and full lips. For the first time in as long as she could remember she allowed someone else to take charge. She let him take her books from her and place them in the back seat, as well as fixing her seat belt and shutting her car door. Sometimes it was just too hard to argue. Tonight, she was too tired. Now all she had to do was stay awake for the short trip home.

When they reached her apartment she felt rude not inviting him in for a cup of tea or coffee but he also seemed keen to get home. 'I start at four in the morning so I'll get going. It'll be a long day tomorrow. Your neighbour is peering through her window at us. Shall I wave? How annoying.'

She looked in the direction of the window next door. 'Tonight, I'm too tired to care. Thank you and good night, Matt. We'll talk again soon and I'll get some paperwork sorted to show you.'

His voice was soft when he answered. 'Good night, and see you soon.'

21

———

The following day Elsie was still tired. She needed to get some sleep and fit in just a bit more study before sitting for her final exams. The university had rung her and also contacted the primary school. 'We tried to reach your principal at the high school but he never returned our emails and we were unable to get past the secretary to talk to him on the phone. Someone in the office here knows the principal, Mrs Berry, at the primary school. She has agreed to oversee your exams. There needs to be another teacher in attendance and she has also agreed for that to happen. They get paid for supervising you, but it still means they have to come in on Saturday so you can do one exam in the morning and one in the afternoon. I hope that suits you.'

A wave of relief filled her. Sometimes exams had to be taken at one of the universities or often in one of the larger towns. The arrangements they had so kindly made would save her catching a train into one of the cities on the coast and then paying for accommodation. 'You have no idea how much that helps me. I can't thank you enough.'

'No worries. Just make sure you get in contact with Mrs Berry and she'll give you the details of when and where you have to go. Good luck!'

Elsie was overwhelmed. Recently, so many people had gone out of their way to help her. For once she felt that the odds against her weren't insurmountable. There were a lot of good people around and she needed to remind herself about that and not be so distrustful.

Ethan was waiting for her at the school gate the next morning. 'I can't believe it. It was you who my brother, Matt, took out.'

'Small world, hey,' she answered, trying not to make a big deal out of it. Her personal life was better left out of the school, but living and working in such a small town and with such unexpected coincidences occurring there wasn't really much she could do about it. Word soon got around the school about the auction and the date between Ethan's brother and Miss Jackson. The kids made jokes about her falling in love and getting married. She smiled and said nothing, hoping they'd soon forget about it and move on to the next piece of town gossip.

Mr Garranto had also been keen to talk to her and as soon as she opened her laptop the nauseating pinging sound of incoming emails sounded. As usual, his words of communication were short and abrupt. *You will need to attend a meeting in my office this afternoon. 3.30 sharp. Be on time.*

It was her last afternoon before sitting for her final exams and she had counted on getting everything in order and reading over her notes. No doubt the meeting would be short. Who knew what he was upset about this time? Probably that she had been eating hot chips in the classroom, and doing so with a parent, or rather a guardian, she thought. She was not in the mood for an argument with him and she'd need to remain calm. Tired and cranky were not good combinations for her.

Garranto's interview would be in stark contrast to the conversation she had with the primary principal earlier in the day. Mrs Berry had talked to her in a professional respectful way and left Elsie in no doubt that she was happy to supervise her two exams the next day. 'I'm at the school working anyway and so is the other teacher. We just have to hand out your exams and supervise you. I've done it many times before. Now make sure to get a good night's sleep. Good luck and we'll see you in the morning!'

When she got off the phone the thought crossed her mind that perhaps she would have been better being a primary school teacher and having Mrs Berry as her principal rather than the surly and nasty Garranto. Now she thought of that same option again as she faced him, his glare cutting as he stared down his nose at her.

'I'll make this quick,' he said as he looked at his watch. Once again he didn't offer for her to sit down and she stood in front of him, a bundle of books in her arms.

'That would be nice,' she replied. 'I have another appointment at four and I need to get these books back to the library.'

He made a funny huffing noise and she noticed the red spider veins that ran across his face, darkening. 'I have put in a complaint to the Code of Ethics Department about your behaviour.'

'Really?' she said. 'And what is the complaint?'

'You have been fraternising with a parent or guardian of one of our students. It is against my regulations and I made that very clear to you when you started here. I have the photo that appeared yesterday in the local newspaper to prove it. This man in the photo is not only the same man I saw you fraternising with last night on school grounds, but he is also the guardian of one of our students.'

She laughed which seemed to infuriate him further. 'The photo was taken when I went on a date that was organised by the primary school. The entire event was organised by the school and was for fundraising. Complain to whoever you want. I couldn't care less. Now, I really do have a lot to do this afternoon. Is that all?'

He snarled at her response and she thought how his appearance was like that of an ill-tempered bull-dog about to attack. 'How dare you speak to me like that? I am your principal and you will go by my rules.'

She put on her best nonchalant, *I don't give a shit*, voice. 'Whatever.'

'I beg your pardon,' he stammered, his entire face now a dark red colour.

This time she spoke slowly. 'I said, what...ever.'

By now she had suffered enough of him and his bullying nature. She gave him a little smile before turning and walking out the door. He called out after her but she ignored whatever he said as she smiled at the secretary behind the desk and continued walking out through the front door.

***

For the first time she was annoyed she had to walk home. The sun was blazing and her bag and books were heavy. Perhaps it was for the best though. If she had a car to drive off in, she may have been tempted to do a small burnout, or squeal the brakes, just to annoy him. Hoisting the books on her hip she set off down the street, breathing in the dust and smell of a cattle truck that had ambled past just before her. She didn't mind. The smell was better than the stench of Garranto and his office. He could report her or do whatever he wanted to. For now, all she cared about was the exam tomorrow. She needed dinner, a shower, and sleep.

When she opened her front door she noticed an envelope that someone had slid under the door. Placing her books down on the table she leaned down to pick it up. There was a card inside and she opened it, the colourful galahs on the front making her smile. Inside were some beautifully written words and it took her a while to read what it said and realise who it was from. She glanced at the signatures down the bottom. Matt and Ethan.

She read aloud, amazed at the neat handwriting that must belong to Matt. Ethan's was never that tidy.

We just wanted to wish you all the best for your exams tomorrow.

You have worked so hard and deserve the best.

Rest up tonight and give it all you have.

We are proud of you.

From Matt and Ethan

Tears welled in her eyes and she fought to hold them back. So much kindness in such a short letter. She couldn't remember the last time she had cried. Only a few simple words but they meant so much.

22

By Saturday night she was exhausted. She felt that the exams had gone well but the entire day of concentrating had drained any energy she had. Mrs Berry had sent the other teacher, Viviane, into town for coffee and sandwiches and the three of them had sat and eaten lunch together in between the exams. Viviane had been excited to find out that Elsie had grown up in the same neighbourhood as she had, and they compared stories about the school they both went to. Viviane was five years older but there were a few family names and teachers they both knew. 'Tough place to grow up,' Viviane said, 'but I've never forgotten where I come from. Lots of good people in those areas.'

'I feel the same. Although I don't miss it. It's good to get out of the suburbs and become your own person. It's like writing your own story. The way you want it.'

That night she'd thought about the conversation before she fell asleep. The small town of Matfield and the people who lived in it were something special. Well, most of them anyway.

SHE'D SLEPT MOST of Sunday and only dragged herself out of bed when someone knocked on her door. Wearing an old t-shirt and pyjama shorts she pushed her hair back from her face and tied it back in a ponytail. She opened the door cautiously. It was Matt and he had a bunch of flowers in his hand. 'Oh, my goodness. I just got out of bed,' she said. 'I've nearly slept the entire day and I'm still in my pyjamas.'

He pushed the flowers towards her. 'I wanted to give you these.'

She took them from him, noting that he was also in casual clothes. Maybe not as casual as her pyjamas but he wore a faded t-shirt and an old pair of shorts. She beckoned for him to come in. 'I'll put the jug on. Do you want a cuppa?' she asked.

'I'd love one.'

Pushing her nose into the flowers she inhaled their scent. 'Thank you so much. I've never had someone buy me flowers before.'

He laughed. 'It's the first time I've ever bought flowers. Congratulations on finishing your study.'

As she filled the jug up, they talked. 'I don't know if I've passed yet, but I feel like I did okay. I just have to wait a few weeks and then I get the results.'

'That's a big achievement. You said it's taken a lot longer than usual.'

'This has been a long time coming. There were plenty

of times when I thought I wasn't going to get to the end. It's definitely the culmination of a very long process and I can tell you I won't miss the late nights or the assignments.'

They had talked about her study and then she asked about his job. His descriptions of the hot and dusty conditions as well as the hours and physical workload, explained why he was so fit and tanned. Long days out in the paddocks in the sun was sometimes a lonely job but it seemed like he got on well with the men he worked with and enjoyed what he did.

He helped her find an empty jar to put the flowers in and they joked as she arranged them so that the coloured roses were at the front. She had even managed to find some biscuits to have with their tea and he didn't seem to mind that his cup had a chip out of it or that the chair he sat on was a bit wonky. It was heartening to have someone to talk to and she was sorry when he said it was time for him to get going.

'I'll let you get some more rest,' he said as he picked up his hat and placed it back on his head. 'I want to make an appointment to see you about Ethan and this scholarship thing. I don't want to talk about it today. It's your weekend.'

'Sure. Just ring the office and they'll make an interview time after school. We should do it through the proper channels. I'm already in trouble with Garranto because of the photo in the paper. He's made a complaint to the Code of Ethics Department. Watch him, because he might make trouble for you and Ethan. He's furious and I only worsened the situation with my response when he called me up to the office. I wasn't very apologetic and I walked out before he had finished. He was still yelling as I went out through the front doors of the Admin block. I'm not putting up with him anymore. I've had enough.'

Matt looked annoyed. 'Reported it? Has he now? Well, I might have something to say to him about his code of ethics if he wants to pursue the matter. Maybe I might have to raise the problem about how he conducts himself as a married man. Code of ethics! What a hypocrite. I hope he does come for me. Bring it on.'

23

Elsie arrived at school early on Monday morning. With the exams over and some extra sleep, she felt a bit more like herself. The term was reaching its busiest time though and this morning she planned on getting more lessons prepared and completing her marking before the classes started.

Penny had also been in her classroom and they sat and talked for a while as they both enjoyed a coffee. 'Matt is coming in this afternoon to talk about Ethan and the scholarships he might be able to apply for. I don't think he's that keen for Ethan to apply for the disadvantaged background one,' Elsie stated.

'I can understand why,' Penny concluded. 'He's probably not used to accepting help. He could have let the school know from the start that he was only a young guardian and they weren't receiving any help from their parents regarding Ethan's education. But he's obviously chosen to work everything out himself. None of Ethan's teachers knew anything about his background. I'd say they decided to keep the arrangements quiet and not ask for any help.'

'I know. Matt's doing a great job, but sometimes you just have to take advantage of disadvantage. If the universities are offering scholarships, why not go for them?'

'I know. I'm with you, but I've seen plenty of others decline similar offers. Pride. Independence. Maybe Matt feels there might be some stigma attached.'

'Well, I won't back down. I'll tell him what he should do.'

'Go steady. You know you're pretty forceful when you set your mind on something. Don't forget he's Ethan's guardian. Maybe let him decide.'

'I think students and parents should take every opportunity they can. Especially when you're talking about someone's future.'

'Wait and see what he says and don't forget to fill me in when he lets you know what he's doing.' She looked curiously at Elsie. 'Are you falling for this guy? You said you were never going to see him again after the first date.'

Elsie made a funny snorting noise; as if Penny had said something far from the truth. 'Matt is nice. But we're friends. That's all.'

MATT HAD SIGNED in through the office in the afternoon and he met Elsie in one of the library conference rooms. 'Bit official,' he said, as he sat down in one of the large office chairs.

He had come straight from work and wore his work

clothes and boots. 'Didn't have time to change,' he told her. 'Excuse the dirty work clothes.'

Seeing him in his work gear for the first time, she observed how different he appeared from their initial encounter on the train. Her earlier assumptions about his profession now seemed entirely off the mark. He looked good, even if he did have some dirt marks on his shirt and his socks were stained from the red dust. 'That's fine,' she replied. 'Did you want to discuss the scholarship?'

'I did. I've had a good look and talked about this with Ethan also. There are a range of academic scholarships he could go for that would give him the same amount of money as the disadvantaged one you talked about. We have decided that he should apply for one of them. The straight academic ones, that is. If he's good enough to get one, he will.'

Elsie sat up straight. 'But the other one is surer. With the academic ones he'll be up against way more students and they'll all be the top academic kids in the state. I'm not sure he'll get it. I can check with the guidance officer at one of the other schools; the woman who does that job here isn't qualified and is useless. She's just some friend of Gwen's. I've been down this track before and I feel sure you should go for the one I talked about. I've even rung the unis to make sure he would have a good chance. They also recommended he go for that one. They're called equity scholarships in some places. Think of it as equity, rather than disadvantaged.'

'I know you've done your research and put a lot of time into finding out information for us. We appreciate your help. Ethan and I have discussed this at length. But we've made our minds up. He can go for one of the regular academic ones.'

'And what's your plan if he doesn't get one? What do you think he'll do if he misses out, just go and work with you?'

Matt visibly stiffened. 'And would there be anything wrong with that?'

'You know I don't mean there is anything wrong with that. It's just you said it was important that he go to uni.'

'I did say that and he will go. I just can't fill in all those forms for something neither of us feels right about. I earn good money and we do okay. I don't consider that we're disadvantaged.'

By now Elsie had heard enough. All the time she had spent gathering information. All the knowledge she had from going through this process twice before. Matt had not been listening to her. She had the forms here ready for him to fill out. 'What, you do so well that your brother comes to school hungry every day.' She tried to keep her voice even but her words came out louder than she wanted. 'We all feed him. All the teachers do. You have so much money yet you don't buy enough food for him to have proper meals.'

'What the hell are you talking about? You have no idea what our life is like. There's plenty of food in our house. Sure, sometimes it gets low but that's only because he eats so much. If he's telling you he's hungry then you've all been fooled.' He stood up. 'I can't believe you've all been talking about me behind my back. Why didn't someone mention this at one of the meetings I had? Do you really think I'm that poor I can't afford food?' He laughed, a fake chuckle filled with sarcasm.

Her voice, filled with anger, reverberated within the confined room. Though there were others nearby, the closed door thankfully provided a barrier, containing their escalating argument to just the two of them. Her tone echoed the frustration that she could no longer hold in. 'Don't tell me I have no idea. I came here today to try and help but if you don't want assistance then forget it. I'm sorry I even tried.'

'Good. I don't need your help. I've managed to get him this far by myself. I can certainly get him the rest of the way. Good day, Miss Jackson.'

With that, he pushed his chair back, strode to the door and walked out through the library. She had stood up when he had, but now she slumped back in her chair. What had just happened? This was supposed to be a meeting for some papers to get signed and sent away. Instead, she had let her temper get the better of her and argued with someone who wasn't thinking rationally. In less than five minutes their interactions had gone from friendly banter to an antagonistic exchange of words. Breathing heavily she bit her lip. If Matt didn't want help for Ethan, then the two of them could work out his future by themselves. Right now, she wished she had never gone to the bother of talking to him about the best direction for Ethan to go, and more than that she wished she had never met him or gone on that stupid date.

24

Ethan was quiet the next morning at school and in the afternoon she took her time packing up the classroom, waiting until the other students had left. She had a fair idea that he would stay behind to talk to her. Perhaps he would go behind his brother's back and make his own decision. Surely, he could see the value of going for the scholarship she recommended.

'I know you talked to Matt yesterday,' he said, scuffing his shoe on the carpet.

'I did.'

'He said you disagreed about which scholarship I should go for.'

'I'm only recommending what I know is the best. Like I said both my siblings got into university through similar pathways. Once you're in, it doesn't matter how you got there. You still have to prove yourself and if you can't keep up you won't pass. It doesn't mean you're less smart than the other students, it's just another way of getting in.'

'I'm sorry, Miss Jackson, but I'm with Matt on this one.

If I can't get one of the other scholarships on my merit then I'll just go in through the usual way. I can always get a part-time job, or work in the holidays with Matt to support myself. It'll be okay.'

'I have no doubt you'll get in, but those scholarships are worth a lot of money.'

'You did it the hard way. You survived.'

'I have, but it's been very difficult and I haven't had much of a life because I've spent most of the time working to pay the bills to get me through. Please think about it.'

'We've, well I've, made up my mind. I don't want you to think I don't appreciate the help you've given me. You've been the best teacher I've ever had and what you've done is an inspiration to me. I just don't want that 'disadvantaged' tag hanging over my head. There are plenty of others worse off than me. Probably like your brother and sister were.'

Her emotions were becoming harder to keep in check and she struggled to keep her voice steady. Was she getting too involved in her students' lives? Should she back off and not care so much? Penny had warned her to not take over and that sometimes you couldn't solve everyone's problems. She waited until she was sure her voice was even. 'Do what you think is best. I will help you, whichever way you decide to go.'

25

———

The term rolled on and she managed to stay out of trouble with Garranto. Nothing had come of his threats to report her to the Code of Ethics Departmentand she revelled in the fact that she had let him know without a doubt, that she was not scared of him or cared what he thought. Her final university results had come in and Penny had taken her to the pub with some of the others to celebrate. She had achieved high marks and, finally, she was a qualified teacher. It had been refreshing to go out with the others and let her hair down a bit. This term she had hardly left the apartment, except to go to school or to go walking on the weekend. The others had tried to get her to join in with some of the social events throughout the term, but since arguing with Matt she felt despondent, angry, and like something was missing in her life.

'Something is missing alright,' Elizabeth leaned over and stroked her arm. 'All you do is work and then go home and work some more. Talk to us. That's what we're here for. We're your family now.'

Sometimes Elsie let down her guard with the other teachers and Elizabeth, who was like a mother figure to her, had managed to get some details of her childhood out of her. It had been good to offload some of the hurts of the past and although Elizabeth's childhood had been the complete opposite, she understood. 'I've been teaching for many years in many different places,' she told Elsie. 'I've seen it all. Not much you can tell me that will surprise me. Family life can be terrible for many.'

Rachel passed her a wine. 'You're doing such a great job with your students. But maybe you do need to get a hobby or find something other than work to do on the weekend. You don't want to turn into one of those boring teachers who talk about nothing else except work and have no other interest in their life.'

Elizabeth patted her on the arm, her reassuring touch the only physical contact Elsie had felt in a very long time. The older woman spoke directly to her, her eyes full of sadness as she recalled experiences over the years. 'I've seen kids who come from families like yours try and get through school. At night they sit up with mothers with mental health conditions or stay awake to protect them from violent partners. As experienced teachers who've worked in different places, many of us understand how difficult it can be. It breaks our hearts when we can't fix all the wrongs that kids have to deal with. It sounds to me like you've had a tough time over the years. Now you need to look after yourself more. Give yourself a break. We all care about you.'

Elsie had trouble speaking, and she tried to keep her

emotions in check. 'Thanks, Elizabeth. That means a lot to me. I'm fine though. I'm used to looking after myself. In a few weeks, my sister and brother are coming to visit for the weekend. I'm really looking forward to that. We are very close the three of us.'

'Not your mum or dad?' Rachel asked.

'No. I don't have a dad and Mum, well ....' She took a long sip of her wine. 'Well, Mum's not interested in any of us. She has her own life and to tell you the truth it's less complicated when none of us have to deal with her problems or have her near us. All she does is bring us down.'

'Ah, you poor lassie,' Paul said as he put his arm around her shoulders. 'Think of us as your kin. One day you'll get married and have kids of your own. Then you'll have a family to call your own.'

She laughed and felt a weight lift from her shoulders. It did help to talk to the others. She had become part of their tight-knit group and she valued this new feeling of belonging and the camaraderie between them. 'I very much doubt that, Paul. After what I've seen there's no way I'm having kids or getting married. Misery and trouble. That's all it seems to be.'

'Oh no. Family life can be wonderful.' Elizabeth looked shocked, her eyes wide. 'My husband and I have been together for over forty years and are more in love than ever. We brought up five children who are now lovely happy adults, some with families of their own. You've only seen the bad side of it. Lots of people have great families around them and relationships that are amazing and last the distance.'

'Well, I haven't seen too many. Nearly all the kids who lived around us growing up were in similar circumstances to what we were. Some of them were even worse off than we were.'

Liam thumped his fist down on the bench, making everyone sit up straight. He was a man of few words and when he spoke everyone listened. 'You need a man, my love. A good man. That'll fix your problems.'

'I don't need anyone, thank you Liam for your concern and I don't have any problems. Everything is fine, I'm just a bit tired. Elizabeth is probably right. I need a hobby or something else to do on the weekends other than schoolwork.'

Penny leaned over and whispered in her ear. 'Talking about a man. Here comes your hot date, Mr Blue-Eyes. Don't look now but he's coming this way.'

Elsie's body stiffened and she kept her eyes down. Hopefully, he would pass without noticing her. 'Good afternoon, ladies,' a deep voice behind them said. 'Good to see you relaxing after putting up with those kids all week. How are you going Penny, Elizabeth, Rachel and ....' The man who Elsie didn't know, put his hand out and she looked up at him. Beside him stood Matt, who nodded politely at everyone. The man spoke again. 'Oh, hello, you're Matt's date from the charity auction. I saw your photo in the newspaper. Pleased to meet you. I'm Damon. Father of Jeremy, but don't hold that against me. He's in Penny's class.'

Elsie turned in her chair and averted Matt's gaze. 'Pleased to meet you. I know Jeremy quite well. He's good friends with one of the girls in my class.'

'Oh, that would be his girlfriend, Elaine. Lovely girl,' Damon said.

Elizabeth piped up. 'We're here to celebrate Elsie's

completion of her study. She's now a fully qualified teacher. Top marks also.'

'Congratulations. Clever girl,' Damon said, casting a wide smile her way. 'Not sure why anyone would want to be a teacher but I take my hat off to you.'

'Thank you,' she managed to say.

For a moment Elsie was worried the two men were going to sit down next to them. But Matt must have also had the same concerns and he nodded politely and walked around Damon, continuing to the bar.

'Right,' Damon said. 'Someone's in a hurry for a drink.' He tipped his hat at them. 'Have a good afternoon, all.'

26

Matt had not expected to see Elsie at the pub or imagined that Damon would stop to have a chat with her and the others. Since their argument at the school he had been unable to get her out of his mind and now the sight of her made his heart thump hard. He ran his hand over his cheeks, sure that his face had turned red. Elsie looked so good, sitting there all relaxed with a wine in her hand, her dark eyes looking everywhere but at him. He wanted badly to turn around and look at her again, but he refrained, instead focusing on ordering his drink.

Damon thumped him on the back. 'What's with you? There's a beautiful lady there and you just ran a mile from her. If I didn't know better, I would say you were rude or that you didn't want to talk to her.'

He took his change from the bartender. Was it that obvious to others? 'We argued recently. She's bossy and thought she could tell me what to do with Ethan's future. One of those. You know. Think they know everything.'

'What about his future? Are you talking about when he leaves school to work?'

'He wants to go to uni. He and I can work it out. She pushed her nose into my business and I didn't appreciate it.'

By now both of them had their drinks in hand and headed for the beer garden which was on the opposite side of the building from where the teachers were sitting.

The area was crowded and they sat behind a bench that looked out onto the street. As the light started to dim, a few of the locals walked past, enjoying the balmy early evening. Kids on bikes raced each other up the street and a man walking a dog shook his fist at the kids and yelled out to 'Slow down!'

'Not much to do in these little towns for teenagers,' Matt said. 'I'm hoping Ethan gets a scholarship and goes to live in Townsville or maybe Rockhampton while he does his studies.'

'What did your beautiful date want him to do that made you argue?'

'She wanted him to look at different ways than usual to get accepted into his degree. Sort of a scholarship for disadvantaged kids. We don't take charity though so I dug my heels in.'

He watched as Damon gulped his beer down. They worked long hours on the fences and it had been a hot, busy week. Life at the moment just seemed about work, work, and more work. He couldn't complain though. The money coming in was plenty to get him and Ethan what they needed. Damon's next words caught him off guard. 'Are you interested in her or not?' He stared hard at Matt. 'Truth. Give it to me.'

Matt answered quickly, caught off guard at the questions. 'If you're talking about Elsie the answer is no. Not in the least interested in her. Why?'

'Do you reckon I'm too old for her?'

Matt nearly spat out his beer. 'Yes! Definitely too old. She's only twenty-five. You're fifteen years older.'

'That's not such a big age gap. Plenty of couples are years apart. Meryl and I have been separated for five years. Maybe I should ask her out?' Damon turned and looked through the louvres that separated the beer garden from the lounge bar. 'She's a looker. Smart and pretty. What do you reckon my chances are?'

For some reason Damon's words rankled Matt. Elsie was too young for him and Damon not only had Jeremy in year ten but he had a younger daughter as well. Both kids lived with him and only went to their mother's in the holidays. 'I don't think she'd want a relationship where there are kids involved.'

Damon tipped his glass up and guzzled the last of his beer. He burped loudly before answering. 'She's a teacher, mate. They love kids. Tell you what, someone like that would make my life a lot easier. I need a woman to help bring up that younger daughter of mine. She's going to be a handful.'

Matt felt a fire in his chest and the words flowed out of his mouth before he could even think about what he was saying. 'Well, I can tell you right now, Elsie's not the one for you. She's already spent most of her life looking after kids and family. She deserves the very best and for someone to spoil her and look after her. I think you should stay away and not even think along those lines.' He went to say more but Damon held his hands up.

'Whoa, steady on. I'm just dreaming.' He tipped his beer up and leaned over the table so that his face was nearer to Matt's. 'If I didn't know better it sounds to me like you got something for that girl.'

Rising to his feet, Matt swiftly finished the remnants of his beer. The mere notion of Damon vying for Elsie's attention and affection sparked a twinge of jealousy within him. 'I don't. I'm just saying she's not the right girl for you. My shout. Same again?'

27

Peter and Jane were due to arrive the weekend before the holidays. They were driving out together from Townsville and were going to stay for two nights. Jane would sleep in the bed with Elsie and she had borrowed a blow-up mattress from Penny for Peter to sleep on. As kids they had often slept in the same bed together and she grimaced, they had also often shared the same toothbrush. The three of them had always lived in survival mode and back when they were younger if Elsie kept them near her at night she could always ensure they were safe. Sometimes their mother had come home from the local RSL so drunk she could barely make it up the front stairs. They'd lie in bed together, listening to her stumble around on the verandah, trying to find her key to get in. If she was alone and none of her mates were with her with their supplies, she'd head to the kitchen, looking for more alcohol.

Elsie would whisper to Peter and Jane, who were only little kids back then, to pretend they were asleep if she came into their room. She rarely came looking for them though. If she did it was only to shake one of them and ask where they had hidden her spare cigarettes or if they had any money so she could go back out to the 7-Eleven store to buy some. Usually she was so drunk she'd crash on the lounge and fall asleep, her loud snores a signal that now they could relax and go to sleep themselves. Other nights she would be loud and aggressive. There had been a few occasions when Elsie had pushed a heavy dressing table up against the door so their mother couldn't get into where they were.

When her mother had been drinking, she usually directed her anger towards Elsie. Probably not only because Elsie was the eldest but she also had the smartest mouth. She would yell back at her mother and tell her to leave them all alone and go to sleep. By the time Peter got to high school, he also started to answer her back. His mouth was even quicker than Elsie's and he directed his insults straight like an arrow, letting her know she was a terrible mother and needed to get off the drugs and grog and act like an adult for once. Although Elsie tried to shut him up, knowing those types of comments only infuriated their mother more, he wouldn't stop and one night she had hit him so hard he had been out cold for a few minutes. Jane had started screaming at her that she'd killed him and the room had been full of swearing and yelling from everyone.

Lights had gone on in the houses on either side and also from the flats across the street. A man yelled out to, 'Shut the fuck up,' and a couple of dogs started barking loudly.'

Their mother had shut the windows and spat angry

words at them. 'They didn't deserve her. They were ruining her life. She had a terrible time and they didn't appreciate anything she did.'

They had heard it all before. Thank goodness for all those nights when their mother met a fella and didn't come home at all. It was easier for all of them. Elsie kept Peter and Jane in the same bedroom at night, right up until they had all moved out and went their separate ways. Now tonight, they would be all tucked up safely together again; the three of them snuggled up in her apartment without any negative influences.

It was the first time they had been under the same roof since Peter had moved out over three years ago and she was counting down the seconds until they arrived.

Elsie opened the door and swept the dust off the lounge room floor. A car had just pulled up and she recognised Mr Garranto getting out. Luckily she had already turned around and was walking back inside. She quickly shut the door behind her, standing still for a moment as she listened to the noises from outside. The door to the apartment next to her opened, and then shut again. He was paying his visit to Eliza next door. How disgusting, she thought.

Surveying the room, she hoped Peter and Jane would like where she lived. She had a few things planned for the weekend and the fact that they had a car was helpful. There were a few national parks and waterholes that Penny had told her how to get to and with the rain earlier in the year the scenery was amazing. Peter was into bush-walking so hopefully Jane would also be keen to do that. She rearranged a few pillows on the lounge and ran a cloth over the kitchen bench. Everything was basic and most things were second-hand or had been given to her, but it was her place, a haven to come home to every night and a place where she slept well and felt safe.

When someone knocked at the door she jumped up. Opening the door, she squealed with delight and then burst into tears as Peter and Jane stood in the doorway, looking at her with wide grins plastered across their faces. Peter pushed a large bunch of flowers in her arms and Jane flung her arms around her. For a long while they hugged and held each other, jumping up and down, the two girls squealing with delight. Peter laughed loudly and squeezed both of them in a group hug and Elsie found herself lifted off the ground. When they finally drew apart, they laughed even more and wiped tears from their eyes, still hanging onto each other's arms.

'Come in, come in,' Elsie said as she opened the door up further and pulled them inside. Out of the corner of her eye, she glimpsed Mr Garranto walking across the carpark to his car, a sullen look sent in their direction. She pushed his ugly face to the back of her mind and ignored him as he stopped and stood in the middle of the carpark and stared. Nothing was going to spoil this moment.

28

___

The first hour had been a jumble of conversations. Although they spoke on the phone regularly, being together in person was something else.

'I've got an internship with Davey Veterinary Clinic, right in the centre of Townsville,' Peter said. They're one of the biggest vet practices up this way and they have really looked after me. They have a string of clinics throughout the country and they're after someone who will be loyal to them. They pay seventy-five per cent of my rent, all my uni fees, plus bonuses on top of a generous pay. I never dreamed I'd earn this much money to begin with, before I even finish my studies.'

Bursting with pride, Elsie took a deep breath. 'You always aimed for this. You'll make a great vet. We're so proud of you.'

'It's all because of you,' Peter said. 'None of this would have happened without you.'

'Don't say that. We've all worked hard to get where we are.'

Jane added in. 'My internship is generous also. Maybe not as good as Peter's.' She threw an affectionate glance his way. 'Similar though. Good money and the best private hospital you could ask for. They're really looking after me and they roster my shifts around my study. Someone checks in with me regularly to ensure I'm not overloaded and that my studies are ticking along as they should be. The money's great.' She turned to Elsie. 'How are you going here?'

Elsie put her cup down on the table. 'Maybe not as good as you two but things are going okay. The kids are nice, most of the teachers are lovely and I've made a group of friends that are honest and dependable. I guess a couple of them sort of took me under their wing.'

Peter laughed. 'It's usually you doing that.'

'Yes, it was a bit strange at first. I'm not used to people helping me as much as these guys have. It's a nice feeling to know someone else is looking out for you. Especially in this place.'

'You mentioned the principal was an idiot,' Peter said.

'Garranto. Yes, regular pain in the bum. That was him in the carpark when you two arrived. He's having an affair with a teacher who lives next door. Eliza Tuls. It's common knowledge. He's a bully, but you know me, same as you two, no one pushes us Jackson kids around. I think he thought he could, but I'm not giving him an inch. Young teachers. He hates them. The school had several staff leave before I came. They just moved on. Told him to shove his job where it fitted and went in another direction. Not me though. I'm here to stay.'

Jane looked out through the kitchen window. 'I'm not being judgemental, but do you like living out here? There was nothing but dust and flies when we stopped an hour or so before we got to this place to have something to eat. I know it's greener around the town and the paddocks did look pretty with new shoots on all the trees and shrubs but we drove through the main street to get here. There isn't much happening and not a lot of shops.'

Elsie thought of her impressions of the small town when she first arrived and how different everything was from what she was used to. 'It isn't everyone's cup of tea. But look at where we come from. Everywhere is different and places have their pros and cons. I like it here.'

'How are you going without a car?' Peter asked.

'Struggling a bit. I don't do much on the weekends because of it, but that's okay. I'll get there.'

They talked for a bit longer and then she showed them where to put their bags and where they were going to sleep.

Peter wrapped his arm around her. 'Every time I think about growing up I remember that little bedroom where we all slept together. It took me a long time after I left home to sleep in a room by myself without you two girls.'

'You kept us safe, Elsie,' Jane sighed and put her overnight bag on the bed. 'God knows how the three of us survived. Do you ever talk to Mum?'

'Nope.' Elsie shook her head. 'All she does is complain or ask for money.'

Peter sighed. 'Sooner or later you have to get on with your own life. There are too many hurtful years there for me. I've moved on. Elsie's my Mum.' He squeezed her shoulders with his arm. It was strange that he was no longer the skinny kid she had inspected every morning before he went to school. Hopefully, he had grown out of his habit of wearing ill-matched socks and doing his buttons up wrong on his shirt. She licked her finger and held it in the air. 'Don't you dare,' he said, pulling back from her.

'You always had dirt on your face,' she replied, putting her hand back down.

'Those days of you wiping my face with your wet finger are gone.' He swivelled his head from side to side. 'Look at me now. Big, strong and super handsome.'

'And with an ego,' Elsie said, thinking that his description was spot on though. Both Peter and Jane had the same features as she did, although Peter was way taller than the two girls. Brown curly hair that she had once tried to keep in its place with some gel that someone at the charity shop had thrown in with their toiletry donations, had not even worked. She turned her gaze to Jane. The teachers at their school who had been there long enough to teach both Jane and Elsie, had said they were identical. Brown wavy hair, dark broody eyes and a slender build that never seemed to change over the years.

Jane threw a cushion at Peter. 'What an ego. I love your confidence. You've changed.'

'Never,' he replied. 'Always remember where you come from and what we've lived through. Never an ego. But I'll take the confidence compliment, thanks.'

'You know, it's a miracle that the three of us are still together and doing well. Thank God for you Elsie and those amazing teachers and support workers at the charity place. Do you ever question how we turned out all right, or how we ended up where we are? Thousands of others haven't. Were we just lucky or I don't know, what do you think?'

'I ponder the same question regularly,' Peter replied. 'Luckily we all loved school and learning, plus,' he threw a look Elsie's way, 'I think stubbornness, persistence and maybe just plain old pig-headed determination got us here.'

'I guess we did live in a street called, Resilience,' Elsie quipped. 'We definitely wouldn't have survived if it wasn't for the school and their staff. That's why I always wanted to teach. It's incredible what impact just one teacher can have on a child's life, never mind a whole team of them.'

As they walked back into the kitchen Elsie asked them what they wanted to do over the next couple of days. 'I thought we could go out to the National Park. There are some good walks out there. Maybe we could have dinner at the pub one night.'

'I checked ahead, Peter said. 'I've booked the three of us in for dinner at a restaurant on the hill. I think it was called *The Fortress*. It's my shout.'

'Come out to the car with us and help bring in the esky and other food we've brought with us,' Jane said. 'There's so much there, I think Peter thought he was feeding twenty people.'

There were a few cars parked in the carpark. Some new tenants had moved into the apartments further down the row and Elsie was no longer sure whose car belonged to who. They laughed and joked as they walked to Peter's new company car. Elsie looked at it with surprise. 'It's a Prado. They're worth a lot of money.'

'I told you I was getting paid well.'

Jane opened the car door. 'Close your eyes,' she told Elsie. 'We have something for you.'

'Hold your hand out and don't open your eyes,' Peter added as he grabbed her by the shoulders and steered her around to the other side of his car.

'What is it? Food? Wine? I'm excited.'

'Keep those eyes shut otherwise you won't get it. Open your hand out wide. Both of them,' ordered Jane.

She hadn't always been keen on surprises from these two, particularly Peter. Too often he had brought home lorikeets with broken wings or an old television he had found on the side of the road. The most troublesome gift or surprise had been three small kittens he had found in a hessian bag in the park. 'Mum won't know,' he said. 'She's never here anyway.' They had kept them hidden in the unused shed next door for a while and then Peter had re-located them to their bedroom once they were a bit bigger. It was hard to keep one kitten hidden, never mind three, and it hadn't taken long for their mother to discover them.

She had confronted them one morning before school. 'First,' she said as she stood leaning against the fridge, her long blonde hair, greasy and badly in need of a trim. 'Where's that jar you keep money in?' She directed her question at Elsie. 'I'm leaving in a couple of days. Big trip. Second, what the hell are those kittens doing in your bedroom?'

Elsie had been trying to find a clean uniform for Jane and shook her head at the question. She noticed a new tattoo on her mother's arm. Who knew where she found the money to pay for that? She glared at her mother. 'I don't have any money at the moment. I spent it on food this week.'

'You're working. Cleaning. Why don't you leave school and work full time?'

For some reason, that morning Elsie had enough. Her usual tactic was short answers or to ignore. But last night she had hardly slept. In between trying to study, rotating wet washing around the house to dry due to the torrential rain outside and being up with Peter half the night with some sort of vomiting bug, she wasn't in the mood for her mother's advice. She clenched her teeth, her words coming out angry and stilted. 'Because maybe, just maybe, I want more than to live in this shit-hole forever. Maybe I want a good job and not have to worry about where food or rent is going to come from.' She stood up from where she was crouched trying to help Jane with her shoelaces. The shoes were way too big for her and her socks were not dry. There was no choice this morning though. If her mother had been doing her job of looking after them, none of this would be a problem and she wouldn't be so tired that she could hardly hold her arms up to finish plaiting Jane's hair.

Walking towards her mother she felt the anger rising in her chest. She hated her. There was no emotional attachment to her at all. This wasn't about her, Elsie Jackson, this was about two small children who needed looking after. She vowed if she ever had children, she would be the best mother in the world. Now she stood in front of Peggie, as usual, her mother's eyes heavily made up with mascara and eyeliner. Her face showed the ravages of her addictions though and wrinkles ran from the corners of her mouth and eyes. Not happy lines like some of the old men who volunteered at the charity centre had. These were mean lines, drug lines, lines that could tell a thousand stories of woe and hardships. That was if her mother had any memory left. Yesterday she hadn't even been able to remember what grade Peter was in.

Elsie shoved her face up to her mother's. They weren't that different in height anymore and she looked Peggie straight in the eye. 'Maybe I want to be a better person than you. Maybe if I have kids I'll look after them. Maybe if I ring the authorities and let them know you're never here and we're looking after ourselves, maybe they'll stop your child payments that probably pay for your fucking ugly tattoos because they're not paying for our food or schooling.'

She took deep breaths, watching as her mother's face went as red as the ugly red earrings that dangled from her ears. One of her past boyfriends had given them to her and Elsie was surprised they hadn't been hocked like everything else that could be.

Peggie's hand came up to slap Elsie, but Elsie was quicker and she grabbed her mother's wrist and squeezed it. 'Don't you dare lay a hand on me, or the other two. No one will ever push me around or bully me, especially you.'

Jane's eyes were wide and Elsie grabbed her hand, picked up their school bags and walked towards the front door. Peter was standing in the doorway, his teeth clenched as he stood holding the door open for them to go through. 'Good on you, Elsie. Let's go,' he said as he took Jane's other hand in his.

WHEN THEY CAME HOME from school that afternoon, both the kittens and their mother were nowhere to be seen.

Peter had looked high and low for the kittens but there was no trace. His little face was covered in dirt and tears and the sight of him broke Elsie's heart. He had loved the kittens and looked after them every spare moment he had. Now they were gone.

Eventually he stopped looking for them and he buried the cracked saucer he had been using to feed them under the mango tree in the back yard. He made a cross out of sticks and placed it on top. He was only young but he already knew better than to ask what their mother had done with them. It was better not to know.

NOW ELSIE SQUEEZED her eyes tight, the memories of past presents and surprises pushed to the back of her mind. They had already given her flowers and wine. She wasn't allowed animals in the apartment. What had they bought her?

Something hard and metal was placed in her hands. 'Open your eyes,' Peter said.

She looked straight at both of them, their eyes fixed on her as she stared at their excited faces for a moment longer before looking at what was in her hands. They were keys. Car keys.

The other two stepped to the side, revealing a red car. Peter pulled the last of the car cover from it and she noticed a large ribbon decoration stuck to the windscreen. She was confused. Was it Jane's car? Why had they brought two cars with them?

Peter's voice was shaky. 'It's for you, sis. It's a brand new Rav 4, and you own it outright. Jane and I and paid for it and ....' He dug into his pockets, 'Here's the registration papers and the papers saying it's yours.'

'What?'

'It's yours,' the two of them said together.

She blinked several times, looking from one to the other. 'How? You can't do that. It's too much money.'

'It's not,' Jane said as she put her arm around Elsie, 'and we both owe you way more than that car. We want you to have it and not worry about having to save up for one. Do you like it?'

'Like it? Are you crazy? I can't believe it's mine. I can't let you do this. Have you gone into debt? You need to save for your own things.'

Peter's eyes shone with tears. 'We are both more than comfortable and no we didn't go into debt.'

Jane grabbed Elsie's hand and squeezed it. 'Peter and I talked about this not long after I left school. We've wanted to do it for ages. I got a bonus at Christmas time and well, Peter already has heaps of money.'

He laughed. 'I wouldn't say heaps but more money than we've ever had before.'

29

That night the three of them sat around the table and enjoyed fish and chips from the local take-away in town. It was, Peter declared, 'The best he'd ever had.'

'That's why they're always busy,' Elsie said, dividing out the crispy chips that were left. 'They do a roaring trade.' She picked up her chips and ate one. 'Remember that fish and chips shop where we all worked, at one stage or another.'

'Fisho's on Main,' Jane said, laughing at the memory. 'Greasy chips, soggy fish and a sliver of old lemon that had no juice left in it. Mr Peach. Peachy, or Mr Sleazy we used to call him.'

'At least we had some extra food to bring home. Some weeks that disgusting takeaway shop probably kept the three of us alive,' Peter added.

'Yeah, alright for you,' Elsie said. 'I spent my entire time trying to keep as far away from Peachy as possible. If you stayed next to his wife you were safer. He had stray hands.'

'I pulled a knife on him once,' Jane said. 'Do you remember? He patted my backside and then pushed up against me. Stupid idiot. I was cutting up the potatoes.'

'I remember,' Elsie said. 'I hadn't thought of that for a long time. You pushed the end into his stomach and threatened to gut him like the fish he sold. Good on you, Jane.'

'Well, he never tried it again. That job was good while we were at school. It gave us some income.'

Peter stuffed some more chips in his mouth. 'From talking to friends, it seemed like most of those jobs for kids were similar. They say the well-dressed guy at the servo was the worst. He preferred the boys.'

'Yuck.' Jane screwed her face up. 'Bloody lucky to get through those years alive.'

Elsie changed the direction of the conversation. 'Well, the people who own the fish and chip shop here in town are lovely. The kids love working there. I talk to them and I'm always checking in, you know asking subtle questions about how people treat them.'

'You seem to know a lot of people considering you've only been here a short while,' Jane said. 'I'm sure that boy in the shop charged us less than what he should have.'

'He did. He's one of my students but also the owner, George, told him to. I teach two of his girls also.'

'It's not a bad little community,' Peter said, as he picked up another chunk of fish. 'I reckon I could see myself eventually living in a place like this or maybe just a bit bigger. I plan on having my own business one day. Little towns need vets just like everywhere else.'

The three of them were silent for the first time since Peter and Jane had arrived. It was 'the best fish and chips' to be had and they made sure not to leave a crumb. Jane leaned back in her chair and patted her stomach. 'That's it. I'm full.'

'Has to be a decent meal for a Jackson to say they're full.' Peter wiped his hands and mouth on the paper towels Elsie had put out. 'I guess we learned to eat as much as we could when we could.'

'Plenty of times we had nothing,' Elsie said. 'If it wasn't for the handouts from the charities, we would have been even more hungry.'

'Bloody Mum,' Peter said. 'She didn't deserve to be a mother.'

'It's a vicious circle, Peter. You have to remember she didn't have it any better than we did and being a single mum can't have been easy. God knows what she went through as a kid.'

'I'd rather not know,' Jane said. 'It's better not to know.'

'Agreed', Peter said. 'Now, where are we going tomorrow and where's the map?'

30

The three of them lay awake for a long while that night, talking and reminiscing. They focused on the good times, the fun moments they had together. Peter lay on his air mattress just outside their bedroom door and the two girls lay on their stomachs facing the doorway, their heads resting on their hands as they chatted.

'Have you got a girlfriend, Peter?' Elsie asked. 'You seem to avoid that question when I ask you over the phone.'

He groaned and rolled onto his back, his eyes focused on the ceiling. 'I have met someone who I'm keen on. She is also a vet student. Comes from a small place like this actually. Bit further north though. Frankie. Her name is Frankie.'

'And?' Jane queried. 'Go on.'

'Well, there isn't much to tell at the moment. We go on dates every week but she's not giving anything much away about how she feels about me. Says she needs to concentrate on her studies. She comes from a working-class family and she doesn't seem to have much money to spare. Works at the chemist on weekends and some evenings. Doesn't leave much time for us.'

'What about you, Jane?' Elsie said, turning her head to look at her sister.

'Well, I was waiting to tell you once we were all together. I've met a really nice guy. His name is Sam and he's studying medicine also. We've been going out for a few months.'

Elsie rolled on her side and faced Jane. 'You had a couple of boyfriends at school. Is this one different?'

'He is. I'm in love with him. He's from India.'

'Indian?' Now she had Peter's full interest. 'Um, is this a rude question but is he Indian, you know with sort of brown skin or does he just live in India? You know, maybe English Indian.'

The two girls laughed. 'He's Indian and he's the most caring, gentle, kindest person I've ever met. His real name is, Samir, but everyone except his mother calls him, Sam.' Jane's eyes lit up when she talked about her new interest. He has gorgeous brown skin and dark eyes, sort of like ours. He's lived here in Australia nearly all his life. His father owns a taxation business. I've even met the family. Sam took me to Cairns where they live, to meet them.'

'And?' Elsie asked.

'I think they approved of me. There were a lot of family there. It's not just like we three are. There were endless aunties, uncles, and loads of kids who ran around, playing and eating. They all talked to me and wanted to know what I studied and what I thought of their food. I might add it was the best food I've ever tasted! Very different to anything I've ever experienced before. His mother gave me a lovely scarf and one of his sisters gave me these bangles.' She jiggled the brightly coloured bangles on her arm. 'They stand for friendship.'

Peter sat up on his mattress, looking in through the doorway. 'Sounds like you've been accepted.'

They were quiet for a moment and Elsie knew they were waiting for her to tell them about something or maybe someone.

'Come on Else,' Peter said. 'Surely, you've met someone out here. There seem to be more men in these small places than women. I would have thought someone would have been quick to snavel you. What happened after you went on that charity date?'

She looked at Peter. 'I didn't mind that fella. His name is Matt and I teach his younger brother. Matt is his guardian.'

'And?' Jane sat up also and gently nudged her sister on the shoulder.

'We argued. I wanted his brother, Ethan, to apply for a scholarship like the one you two won. A disadvantaged background scholarship. Ethan is highly intelligent. He'll top the year twelve cohort here at Matfield by a mile.'

'What does he want to do?' Peter asked.

'Speech Pathology at Townsville University. I had all the details for them to look over and we had a meeting about it. Matt and I argued because he didn't want Ethan to gain entry in that way. Pride. Stupid pride.'

Peter flopped back down on his mattress. 'The kid will probably get in anyway or just get him to apply for one of those other scholarships. Unis are keen for students these days. Bums on seats means money from the government for them.'

'You didn't put your Mother Therese hat on, did you?' Jane kicked Elsie's feet. 'That bossy, do as you're told teacher's voice?'

Elsie twisted her mouth and fluttered her eyes at Jane. 'Anyway, we haven't spoken since. It wasn't anything anyway. I'm going to sleep.' She turned her body around and pushed her head into the pillow. It had been a long day and they needed to be up early in the morning to walk before the heat set in. It was winter but temperatures were still up in the thirties.

'Nighty night,' Elsie said, smiling to herself when the other two replied with the same words.

She lay awake for a short while, a feeling of security and contentment enveloping her. What more could she ask for than for the three of them to be together in the same space? All tucked up, safe and happy. She thought about her new car as she drifted off to sleep. She must have the best brother and sister in the world.

31

———

The next day Peter decided that she should drive her new car. It would be good for her to get used to it and he was looking forward to being a passenger. 'Jane drove it out here. She followed me. I don't want to take the company car. It's not supposed to go off-road.'

'There isn't much dirt road and it's just been graded but,' she ran her hand over the shiny side of the car, 'it will get dusty.'

Jane looked around as the wind picked up some dry tumble grass and flung it across the footpath and onto the road. 'I think it will get dusty here anyway. It's meant to be used.'

The interior smelled new and she wiggled in the seat, adjusting everything so it was right for her. Oh my God, it has Bluetooth and a reversing camera! Look at this.' She played with the dials and switches, the upbeat tune of 'The Animal Song' filling the car. Jane squealed. 'Savage Garden. Do you remember how many times we watched that movie and listened to this song? Turn it up!'

Peter and Elsie jigged in their seats, swaying from side to side and singing along to the familiar lyrics. 'See, lots of good things came out of Resilience Street, Logan. We weren't the only ones who found success. What was that movie called? I remember this song playing at the end of the movie and you two rewinding the video and playing it over and over again.'

Elsie started the car. 'I think Savage Garden was a bit more successful than we are. Although I suppose success can be gauged in different ways.'

'The movie was called, *The Other Sister.*' Jane leaned over from the back seat and turned the music up louder as Elsie wound down her window. Elsie wanted the entire world to know that she had the best brother and sister in the world, a new car, and a radio that played great music from a singer who came from the same street as they did.

Eliza immediately came to stand outside her doorway, shaking her head and casting very cranky looks their way as Elsie practised reversing the car. She went back further than she needed to so that the back of the car was quite near to where Eliza stood, broom in hand.

'She looks like she could fly away on that,' Jane giggled as she looked back at her.

'That's my horrible neighbour, Eliza Tuls. 'Hey Eliza,' she said, sticking her head out of the window. 'Have a great day.'

Peter turned the music up louder and also wound his window down. He gave Eliza a wave and blew her a kiss, laughing loudly as they pulled out of the carpark and onto the road.

'She looked like she was about to pass out when you did that,' Jane said.

'I'll be up on more code of conducts by the return of school, Monday morning. Not that I care.'

'Live for the moment,' Peter said. 'You're only young once.'

JANE AND PETER were amazed at the landscape and she slowed down when a flock of emus ran alongside the car. Slowing to nearly a standstill she watched them also, intrigued by their size and the way they ran and then, yes, she knew it, the way they quickly changed direction and ran directly in front of her car. She stopped and they watched as the birds' long legs hammered across the road, their feet disappearing into the dust on the other side. Mottled feathers puffed out as they ran, holding their heads high, picking up speed and sprinting across an open area of land.

'I knew they would do that,' Elsie said as she started driving down the road again. 'I don't want any dents in my new car.' She had thanked Peter and Jane again and again last night. Finally, Peter told her she was not allowed to mention the gift again. 'Imagine if we listed everything you've given us. That's enough now.'

It felt like she had won the lotto and her initial concerns about how either of them had afforded the car had been put to rest. Peter and Jane were both in a good place. This also meant that she could use her savings for something else. What that might be she didn't know. But for the first time in her life she had some backup money in the bank. And that was a good feeling.

32

———

Their destination was a couple of hours from Matfield. Mrs Berry had drawn a map for Elsie with instructions on how to get there. 'It's a dirt road and it goes through private property,' she told Elsie. 'It's just been graded so you'll be alright even if you don't have a four-wheel drive. I was out there last week and the owners of the property don't mind if you drive through. Just shut any gates.'

Although the town and its close surrounds were green, once you got a bit further out the landscape became dusty and dry with only a few tufts of dried-up grass pushing through the red dirt. An occasional dry creek bed broke the flat landscape and Jane made her stop the car so she could take some photos of the vivid white gum trees that hung along the edges of the creek. 'Are you sure there's a waterhole out here?' she asked Elsie. 'There's no water to be seen.'

Peter pointed up into a large gum tree that hung

crookedly over the dry bed of what most likely was a waterway in the wet season. 'I love those galahs. Remember the tree at the back of the school? They used to sit in there in the afternoons and they'd nearly eat out of your hand if you had some bread.'

'They make me feel at peace,' Elsie said. 'There's something calming and beautiful about their colours and the way they're looking down at us.' They were all nestled in amongst the faded green leaves, shaded by the higher branches, looking like they were checking out the humans below. They watched as a baby bird squawked loudly, its cries only stopping when the mother bird fed it.

'An instinct,' Jane said. 'The mother looks after the little ones.' The message in her words wasn't lost on Peter or Elsie and they both gave Jane's shoulders a gentle squeeze.

'One day you'll have kids of your own, Jane. Maybe ones with olive skin and dark eyes. Then you can be the best mother in the world,' Peter said as he started walking back to the car. 'C'mon, let's get going. I'm going to need a swim to get all this dust off me.'

Soon the bushes around them thickened and they all peered ahead at a cluster of rocks and hills that rose on the horizon. 'That'll be where our waterhole is,' Elsie said. 'Mrs Berry said we would see the rocks long before we got there.'

As they got closer to the rocky structure, larger trees dotted the landscape, the white of the gums stark against the cloudless sky. They drove through a camping area with a few tents and a fire pit nestled in amongst the trees and when they came to the end of the road, they parked and got ready for the walk.

They had all made sure they had good walking boots on and Peter even had a fancy trekking stick. 'You can beat off the snakes with that,' Jane said, as she peered cautiously along either side of the track.

'I'm so glad we could come here,' Elsie said as she also nervously kept her eyes open for the brown and black snakes she had been told frequented the area.

'I can't believe you haven't already walked here,' Peter said. 'Surely there's a group you could join that goes bushwalking?'

'I haven't had time with all the school work I've had to do, and not having a car made everything a bit trickier. My aim in the holidays though is to find some activities. There's a pool in town but I've never been a good swimmer. I'll find something though.'

It had taken them a while to get started and Peter asked if they minded if he went ahead. Elsie was having a deep discussion with Jane about her boyfriend, Sam, and he wanted to stretch his muscles. 'I'll leave you two to talk romance. Just yell out if you encounter a snake. I'll come back and save you.'

He took the map from Elsie and grinned as he strode out in front of them, his stick poking the ground to the side as he traversed the rocky path. 'Good,' Jane said once he was out of earshot. 'He goes too fast for me. Now we can relax a little.'

At times there was no path visible, but they finally caught up to Peter who had stopped to wait for them and check the directions. Mrs Berry had been thorough though and as they squeezed between boulders and climbed higher up the rocky structure, they all felt a sense of adventure.

Peter stopped beside some trees, their roots clinging to gaps between the rocks. 'Bit different than climbing up the water tower back at home. I don't see any graffiti or used bongs lying around. Not even a cigarette butt in sight.' He held his hand over his eyes and looked out over the landscape below. Plains stretched out, their edges hazy as the heat threw mirages across the flat land. Here and there a tree held its head high, tufts of grass and other small shrubs pushing out of the red dirt. The sky was blue and cloudless, its colour distinct from the reds and faded greens below. 'Wow. Look at that view,' Peter said. 'That's well worth the walk.'

The three of them stood mesmerised and Elsie and Jane looked for so long that by the time they looked up, Peter had disappeared. Elsie took one last glimpse at the scene before following the path where Peter had disappeared. This part of the trail was well-marked and easy to follow and the two girls wound their way around rocks and bushes, all the while climbing higher and higher up into the rocky outcrop.

THEY STOPPED several times to take in the view and have a drink from their water bottles. 'It's an amazing country,' Elsie said, as she shielded her eyes against the sun. 'Look at those ranges to the west. Such flat dry land in between.'

'I love the air. It's dusty, but it's clean,' Jane inhaled deeply. 'It makes me feel alive out here. We're like specks in the desert. No one around for miles. I can't even see a car or for that matter, cattle or horses.'

'They're hoping for more rain soon,' Elsie started walking again. 'I did think we might run into others up here on the track. There seemed to be a few cars at the campground we passed.'

'Maybe you'll run into one of your students.' Jane also started walking. 'Okay, let's catch up to Peter. He can't be too far ahead.'

Soon they came to large boulders where the track wound through the narrow caverns between. The track started to get steeper and they could hear voices ahead. 'I think the waterhole can't be too far away,' Elsie said. 'I'm looking forward to a swim if there's any water in there.'

Jane looked around. 'But it doesn't look like it has rained here.'

'Apparently the waterhole doesn't dry up. The Indigenous people say it's a place of healing. They don't mind if people come here. They say it was always a meeting place and they're happy to share it as long as people respect it and don't leave any rubbish lying around.'

As they found their way around a huge boulder, Elsie heard the sound of Peter's laugh. He had obviously found other walkers to talk to.

Soon the circular waterhole was in front of them, its dark waters a cool contradiction to the surrounding landscape. Although the water was deep you could see right to the bottom and Elsie stared at the smooth boulders that formed the edge of the pool.

At first she was distracted by the colour of the water and the view of the plains beyond the edge of the hill. Suddenly she spotted Peter. He was seated down near the edge and had taken his boots off, his feet dangling in the cool water. In front of him were two men who were up to their waists in the rockpool. She blinked a couple of times but the scene did not change. The men in the water were Matt and Ethan. Peter waved and called out to the girls.

When Matt and Ethan looked towards Elsie and Jane, a surprised look crossed their faces. Ethan waved at Elsie and she hesitantly waved back.

'Ha,' Jane said. 'I knew you would run into kids from school. The other fella looks too old to be a student though.'

'The younger one is Ethan and the other one,' she turned around and rolled her eyes at Jane, 'the other one is as you labelled him, 'my hot date'. His name is Matt.'

Jane giggled. 'What are the chances?'

As the two girls approached, Matt ducked under the water and then bobbed up again, the water streaming over his body as he stood up. She tried to avert her eyes from his bare chest which was broad and toned. 'Cute,' Jane whispered behind her. 'Very cute.'

'Shut up. I can't believe they're here.'

She heard Peter say something as he looked from the men to his sisters. 'Oh, do you know my sister, Elsie?'

'She's my teacher,' Ethan said.

'Any good?'

Ethan laughed. 'She's the best.'

It was hard not to smile as they came closer to the pool. 'Hi,' Elsie said. 'I see you've met my brother, Peter. And this is my sister, Jane.'

Jane waved and flashed her best smile. 'And your names are?'

'Oh, sorry,' Elsie stumbled over her words. 'This is Ethan, and his brother Matt.'

Peter put his head on the side and Elsie could tell he was thinking. Silent words hammered into her mind. Please shut up, Peter, she thought as she glared hard at him, willing him not to open his mouth. Please don't talk. But it was too late. Peter looked from Elsie to Matt. 'Oh my God. You're the hot date, aren't you? Elsie won a date and it was you. Am I right, Elsie?'

Jane sat down beside Peter, and Elsie also sat near the edge of the pool. 'Yep. Matt was the date.'

'Come in for a swim, Miss,' Ethan said as he laid back and floated on his back. 'The water is beautiful.'

Matt stared at Elsie and she held his gaze, a strange fluttering in her stomach as a smile slowly spread across his face. 'I think I was the one who had the hot date. Not the other way around.'

'Oh, please,' she said. 'Flattery will get you nowhere. What are you two doing up here anyway? This is the first time I've been here.'

'We often come up here. Ethan and I walk all over this place. I did a lot of fencing for the lady who owns this property and she gave me directions on how to get to this pool and campground. They don't mind the locals using it, but they try and keep it quiet and unknown to tourists. You might not be able to see them but there are plenty of walking tracks. There are also some cave paintings further up the slope there. Sometimes we camp down the bottom, near the carpark.'

'I was just telling Elsie that she needs to join a walking club or do something on the weekends,' Peter piped in.

'I told her the same thing,' Matt said. 'She needs to get out more. All she does is work.'

Jane had taken off her t-shirt and shorts, her boots and socks in a neat row with Peter's. 'I'm going in. C'mon Elsie.'

PETER AND MATT started talking again. Peter must have told Matt what he was studying and how he worked for a vet clinic in Townsville. Their conversation went back and forth and Elsie was pleased that Matt was distracted and not looking as she slipped off her clothes and entered the water.

She joined Jane and Ethan who were floating in the middle of the waterhole. Elsie wore similar bikinis to Jane's, both yellow with the same flower design. It was uncanny how often they chose the same outfit, yet shopped in different locations. Not that Elsie had many clothes but the few she had bought over the years had usually coincided with something Jane had. At Peter's graduation and a couple of formal occasions when Jane was still at school, they had chosen the same outfits to wear, all bought at separate second-hand clothing shops. Now today they could pass as twins. Tiny bikinis, tanned skin and dark brown hair. Elsie was a little bit taller than Jane, but apart from that sometimes it was hard to tell the difference between them.

'You look like twins. Are you?' Ethan asked.

'No. We're seven years apart,' Elsie responded. 'Jane is the sister I told you about who's studying to be a doctor. She's at Townsville University.'

'I'm in first year,' Jane said.

'I'm just about to finish senior,' Ethan said. 'Only a couple of months to go. I'm hoping to get into Townsville University to study Speech Pathology.'

Elsie splashed water on her face. It was crystal clear and icy cold, the feel of it invigorating her body. She kept glancing back to Peter and Matt but they were in deep conversation. 'Ethan will have the highest marks in his grade, Jane. He's a top A student.'

'Good on you. You'll love uni,' Jane said.

'I can't wait.'

They floated on their backs, looking up at the cloudless sky. Elsie closed her eyes, the cool water like a dreamy pillow to lie on. When she opened her eyes, she watched a large eagle gliding above them. It looked downwards; its wings spread wide as it watched for small creatures in the rocks below. To her right was a cliff face, the steep sides soaring above where they swam. Among the blocks of solid rock were small ferns and other plants, their roots entwined in the crevices and hollows that marked the surface. A lone gum tree hung on to the side, its base rooted in a narrow ledge, tendrils hanging delicately over the sides. When she looked closer, she could see five galahs perched amongst the white limbs.

'Wow. Look at the colours of those birds,' she said, pointing the birds out to the others. Peter and Matt looked up as they all watched the birds who were staring down at them. 'There were a lot of them in the gum trees down the bottom of the hill.'

'Guess they must think it's a bit strange, people swimming in their waterhole,' Peter said.

Matt swam over towards Elsie, his strong arms

lifting out of the water. With a few strokes, he was standing right beside her, his white teeth flashing another one of those grins that made her stomach swirl. She could stay mad with him, or instead, she could enjoy the moment for what it was. How lucky was she to have her brother and sister with her at this special place and for them to meet two of the people she knew from Matfield.

Peter joined them and the five of them stood in the middle of the waterhole, all looking up as the galahs squawked loudly and then one by one flew out of the tree. 'The colours are incredible,' Jane said.

'A special moment,' Peter agreed.

The pink and white of the galahs was in stark contrast to the vivid blue sky and the red of the rockface. As the birds soared high and then plummeted into the valley below, their calls echoed across the vast plains and Elsie felt an overwhelming sense of happiness, as she watched their colours still visible against the dusty reds and browns of the plains below.

Soon they could no longer be heard or seen and as she looked back to the others she felt Matt's eyes on her. For a moment it was as if only he and she existed and their eyes held each other, her face softening and any tension she had at seeing him and Ethan easing from her body. She gave him a cheeky smile back and splashed water at him. 'For some reason you and I keep running into each other,' she said.

He flicked some water back at her. 'We do.'

'I have some exciting news,' she said. 'Jane and Peter bought me a car. A red Rav4. They bought it for me. It's mine.'

'Wow.' Ethan and Matt said at the same time and then both asked her a million questions.

'I know. I know. It's super exciting and I am very lucky.'

Peter wrapped his arm around her shoulders. 'No, we're lucky to have you, sis. Anyone would be lucky to have you in their life.'

33

Peter's last words were not lost on Matt. When he started talking to the bushwalker, Peter, who told him his sisters liked to walk slower than him and they would meet him at the rockpool, he would never have guessed he was talking to Elsie's brother. They had simply said hello to each other and then started talking. Conversations in this part of the country usually started with, 'Where are you from?' Matt knew Peter wasn't a local. He hadn't seen him before. When he asked where he lived, Peter had first said Logan and then Townsville. 'I went to Townsville to study a few years ago and now I have an internship. I'm lucky because I get to work and study at the same time.'

Matt had been instantly interested. This fella was friendly and easy to talk to. Also, he was in the line of work that Matt had always dreamed of. If only.

Of course, he hadn't thought to ask who his sisters were. He had assumed they were from out of town also. When Elsie's face and then her sister's appeared from around the corner of the boulder, he thought he was dreaming. Not only one Elsie, but two. The girls looked exactly the same, although once they were up a bit closer he could see the slight differences.

It had been hard to draw his eyes away from Elsie. She was beautiful. Her brown hair was tied up in a pony-tail, her dark eyes locking onto his. At first he wondered what her attitude towards him would be. They hadn't spoken since they argued, and she had avoided him if they happened to be in the same area. But today it was like she had let the barrier around her loosen a little. Maybe he had also. Perhaps it was this peaceful place. When she was with her brother and sister she was almost like a different person. The three of them were tight, he could tell straight away. Not only did they look alike and laugh the same, but they finished each other's sentences and also seemed to be continually looking out for one another.

He sensed Peter's protective stance towards Elsie. He might be the younger brother but it was clear that he adored her. When Peter wrestled with her and they tried to duck each other in the water, he'd been envious. What would it be like to be that familiar and close with her? How hard would it be to get her to let her guard down? He struggled to think of the right words to describe what he had found missing when they talked. Then it came to him. Trust. That's what it was. Every time he'd been with her, she'd been friendly and lovely, but there was an edge to her and he hadn't been able to put his finger on it until now. She didn't trust people. She hadn't trusted him. When they talked, she only let a little information go. Most she kept to herself. Lack of trust. That's what it was.

They all got out of the water at the same time. Ethan had a backpack full of food and drinks, and Matt spread what they had brought out on one of the towels. 'Join us,' he said glancing at Elsie. 'Get in quick though because Ethan eats like a horse.'

Jane added their food and the five of them sat around eating and drinking, listening to each other's stories. Ethan asked question after question. Peter and Jane were perfect fodder for his enquiries about university life and work. Matt listened also and Elsie relaxed even more. She had put her shorts and t-shirt back on and sat cross-legged next to Matt, who kept passing her food.

'You can eat a lot, Miss,' Ethan said.

Peter handed Ethan one of their custard tarts that he'd packed in a plastic container. 'Here, get one of these into you. I remember what it's like to be your age.'

'You remind me of Peter,' Elsie said as she looked towards Ethan. 'We could never fill him up or find enough food to satisfy him.'

Elsie thought back to the days when she had finished school, worked her part-time job and then visited the local charity centres to gather whatever food she could. Matt watched her. 'Penny for your thoughts,' he said.

She chewed on an apple, eating it down to the core with nothing to waste. 'We grew up in a tough household. There was never enough food.'

'Elsie used to make sure there was plenty for the three of us. We never starved but some of what we had to eat was pretty horrible sometimes,' Jane added.

Peter laughed. 'Do you remember those cabbages that someone gave us? We lived on them for a couple of weeks.'

'I learned how to make one hundred different dishes with cabbage.' Elsie laughed in between her words. 'I can't even remember where I got that produce from, but there were also two huge bags of zucchinis. Yuck, I still can't eat cabbage or zucchini to this day. Never again.'

'Would have kept you regular,' Ethan said. 'Where were your mum and dad?'

'There was no dad and our mother was not really a mother. We fended for ourselves,' Elsie said as she stretched her legs out in front of her.

'Elsie was our mum,' Peter squeezed her shoulders and playfully pushed her over. 'One bedroom, one cupboard and one toothbrush between us.'

Ethan screwed up his nose. 'That's the pits.'

'We survived. Only just, but we did,' Elsie looked at Matt and Ethan. 'We're all lucky we have brothers or sisters to look out for one another. You too Ethan. You just need that one person who will look out for you and get you through.'

As they stood up and packed away the lunch, Elsie took one last look at the rockpool and view. It was a day she would never forget. Peter and Jane together with her and then the bonus of meeting up with Matt and Ethan. The repercussions of her argument with Matt seemed to have been forgotten and she had relaxed and enjoyed the warm connection between everyone. She walked with Matt at the back of the group as they made their way down the hillside.

'What are you doing over the holidays?' he asked.

'I don't have much planned. I do have a car now though, so I might go exploring a bit around here. Not too far, but I'd like to have a look at some of the other places everyone talks about.'

'I have a few days off and I'm not working on the weekends. Ethan is going camping with one of the other families from your school. I'd like to take you walking somewhere, or show you some of the places I go to take photos. I've become interested in photography. That's if you'd like to.'

She hadn't realised at first that they'd stopped walking and stood facing each other on the narrow track. 'I'd love that. That's if you really want me to come with you.'

'I wouldn't have asked you otherwise. How about Wednesday next week? There are some waterholes out further and we could take some lunch. Do you still have my number?'

'Of course, I do.

'Anyway, I'll ring you and organise a time. I'll bring lunch and maybe you can bring a couple of drinks, soft drink or juice, like what we had today.'

'That would be lovely.'

'Are you going to keep walking?' He chuckled softly looking at the track ahead.

'Oh yes. Sorry. I stopped. Yes. Lovely. Wednesday.'

34

———

When they reached the carpark, they stood in a circle saying goodbye to each other. 'Don't forget, if you're ever in Townsville, look me up. Elsie will give you my number,' Peter said as the two men shook hands.

'And I'll be waiting to hear about your study plans,' Jane added, shaking hands with Ethan.

All eyes turned to Matt and Elsie when Matt said goodbye and then turned to Elsie. 'Wednesday. I'll message.'

Peter glanced from one to the other. 'Maybe we will see you two again. You know my beautiful sister Elsie may come across ....'

Elsie shoved him and shot him a stern glare. 'Be quiet please Peter. You don't need to say anything.'

He seemed determined to continue, but Elsie's gaze cut through him. Biting his lip, he shook his head. 'There's so much I want to tell, but I value my life. Good luck, Matt. That's all I can say.' Laughter erupted and Elsie playfully pummelled Peter's arm.

Speaking through gritted teeth she spoke quickly. 'I'm so glad you're leaving tomorrow.'

'Agh, you love me, Sis,' Peter teased, flinging his arm around her shoulder.

MATT WASN'T sure what had come over him. Up until a few hours ago he had still been angry with Elsie for trying to tell him what to do and how to organise Matt's life. Now his whole attitude had changed. From the moment her head had appeared around the corner of the boulder, he felt an undeniable attraction. Something about her that made him want to wrap his arms around her and draw her in close. Something that made him want to kiss her. To put his lips on her and press her body up against him. More than anything he wanted to gain her trust. To have that comfortable connection with her like she had with her brother and sister.

He shook his body as if trying to get rid of the feelings. When he had watched her get out of the water and stand beside the waterhole, the water streaming down her body, it had nearly been too much. There had been a couple of times when he felt like she was the only one there and that it was just the two of them in the middle of nowhere. What the hell was wrong with him? How could his feelings change so quickly?

Ethan had walked ahead and was waiting for him at the campsite. 'How lucky was that running into all of them? What a great day.'

'It was. It was. Lucky, and a great day,' Matt responded, his internal turmoil hidden beneath a veneer of casual conversation.

35

———

That night, Peter, Jane and Elsie had dinner together at *The Fortress*. Elsie looked over to the spot where she had sat with Matt, that very first time she had gone out with him. It seemed so long ago and back then she had been new to the town, unaccustomed to the way of life in an outback school and most of all, new to dating.

As they perused their menus, Peter demanded that they order whatever they wanted. 'My shout and we're going all out.' The restauranteur, Al, neared them, and Elsie's eyes lit up. Now with a bit more local knowledge under her belt, she knew that Al was Geno's father. Geno was a boy in her class and one of her favourites. 'We'll start with the oysters, thanks,' Peter said.

'Agh, the amazing kind-hearted teacher, Miss Jackson. My Geno hates everything else at that school except you. Never talks about anyone else there, well not in a good way anyway. But he says you are fair and you help him.

He's no genius the young Geno, but he's a good son. He works hard here for me.'

'He's a great kid. And he's doing above average in English. I have to push him a bit sometimes, but he does what he is supposed to.' Elsie turned to Peter and Jane. 'Geno has the best manners you'll ever find. He opens the door for me and offers to carry my books. You should be really proud of him, Al.'

They talked for a bit longer and Peter asked questions about where all the produce came from. Al loved nothing more than to talk about his restaurant and he was pleased to meet some of Elsie's family. 'You young people have also been brought up well. It is obvious. Your parents must be proud of you also.'

Peter made a funny chuckling noise and Al looked at him curiously.

'Elsie brought us up. She was the mum for us,' Peter said. 'Reared both of us and managed to finish school and go to university herself. I'm not sure how we got through as well as we did, but here we are, all because of this amazing person.'

Al poured them all a wine. 'Agh so there is more to Miss Jackson than what we see or should I say what meets the eye. Well, Miss Elsie Jackson, you should be congratulated.'

ELSIE SAT up straight as Al moved away to the table nearby to take other orders. She raised her glass which Al had filled more than usual, pouring from a bottle of wine that he said was on the house. 'Cheers,' she said, holding her glass high. She smiled when the three of their glasses clinked. 'Here's to the three of us and whatever comes next.'

THEY HAD all lain awake for hours after they got home. There was so much to talk about and they took turns relaying details of different events that had happened over the previous months. In the morning when it was time for Jane and Peter to leave, Elsie hugged them for a long time, not wanting to let go. It might be a while until they were all together again.

'Don't leave it too long. Drive to Townsville and we'll show you around. You've got a car now, so no excuses,' Peter called out the window as he pulled out of the carpark.

'Drive carefully,' she called out, blowing kisses back to Jane, who hung out the passenger's side window. She stood in the carpark until she could no longer hear Peter's car. It had been a fabulous weekend and not only had they talked about childhood memories but they had shared their hopes and dreams for the future. All of them had plenty to look forward to.

As she walked back inside, she didn't even need to look towards Eliza's window. Instead, she just flicked her middle finger in the air and pointed in that direction. Shortly after she heard a window shut. No doubt there would be questions to answer from Garranto at school on Monday. With only one more week until the holidays, she didn't care. In fact, she didn't care what he thought or did anyway. He was insignificant in her life.

36

It hadn't taken long on Monday morning for the first of Garranto's emails to hit her inbox. Did the man have nothing better to do than harass her? Obviously, he had too much spare time on his hands. She stood behind her desk at the front of the room. The students were silent for once, busy writing a news report. There had been some major fires about thirty kilometres south of Matfield and the dangers of summer and dry weather were a perfect topic for the unit of work they were doing next term.

She glanced down at the first email.

Once again you will need to report to my office at three o'clock sharp. Once again you will have to explain yourself and your actions and the company you had on the weekend. Teacher accommodation is not to be used for parties or for accommodating groups of friends. Also, noise is to be kept to a minimum at all times due to the respect that should be shown to those nearby. Have your explanations ready.

She had been oblivious to the fact that a student had

been standing in front of her while she was reading the email. Her reaction to the words on the screen was probably obvious on her face.

'Oh, sorry, Max. What can I help you with?'

'Get a bad email, Miss?'

She sighed. 'You might say that.'

'Garranto?'

'I can't divulge confidential emails.'

'He's a pig. We had a great teacher last year. She was first year out, but really, really good. I had her for maths and music. She wasn't a math teacher really, but she did okay. Everyone loved music lessons with her. She was so talented and loved teaching. He drove her away. She didn't tell us that but we knew. One of my mates, his mother teaches here and she said that Garranto was so mean to the music teacher she just left.'

Elsie bit her lip. Her students were like adults and she would have loved to let loose and tell them all she had to put up with. They weren't stupid. They knew what went on. Well, parts of it anyway. She tried to placate Max. 'I've worked in a variety of different places over the years, so I am used to those who are in charge. It's okay. Everything is good.'

'Don't go, Miss. You're one of the best teachers we've had. Teachers don't stay here. You should see how many we've had in the last few years. They come and then they go.'

'I can tell you one thing, Max. I would never complain about any of the students here. Ever. You are a great group of teenagers and I love working with you all. Now, what did you want?'

'Effie threw my book and my pencil case out the

window while you were reading your email. Can I go and get them, please.'

Elsie looked over to Effie who had her head down, writing, looking for all the world like the most conscientious student in the room. 'And why would she do that?'

'Does it matter?'

'Yes, if I am to give you permission to retrieve your belongings from the dust outside.'

Max turned red. 'I told her she was frickin hot and I wanted to take her to the rodeo next weekend.'

Elsie laughed out loud. 'So do her actions make you think that is a yes, or a no?'

'After Effie threw my stuff out, she must have thought about my question. Then she slipped me a note, that said, she would consider my offer. At the end of the note, she said she had decided, yes. You'd be pleased with her spelling, Miss, and she used some of those brilliant words you have on the board there to describe how she felt. Captivated. Fascinating. Agog.' He pointed to a list and Elsie closed her eyes.

This was what happened when you took your eyes off your students and read emails that came from the office during class time. She put on her cranky face. 'Okay. Hurry up. Go and get your pencil case and book, and...'

Max turned around, a cheeky grin on his face, his auburn hair hanging over his forehead looking like it needed a good cut. 'Yes, Miss?'

'Maybe try and ask Effie again. Perhaps use a better choice of words.'

'Yes, Miss.'

IT HAD BEEN A PARTICULARLY hot day and Elsie took her time once class had finished. She had been on bus duty until half past three, then she had grabbed a glass of water from the staffroom.

She looked at herself in the bathroom mirror before she left for the office. Her hair was tousled from the hat she had worn and she had a line of pen down the front part of her white shirt. At least that had happened in the last lesson so she hadn't been walking around with it on her shirt all day. She filled up her water bottle and walked slowly to the office. A few students passed her on the way and said goodbye. They were a friendly lot and after three terms at the school she was familiar with many of the students and the complicated processes that made up the school day. If it wasn't for the bullying nature of Garranto and his minions, life would be good.

Bron looked up from her desk when Elsie flung open the doors to the Admin building. The stalwart receptionist's eyes were wide and she shook her head, trying to silently deter Elsie from going any further. Elsie gave her a silly grin and held a cap high in the air, before plonking it on her head. The words, *Life is Good*, were embroidered on its tip and Elsie pointed to the saying before making her way down the hallway towards Garranto's office.

He had been waiting for her, his door wide open. Gwen sat in the corner, with pen in hand and a notebook on her lap. 'Come in, Miss Jackson. You are thirty minutes late,' he said.

'Gotcha,' Elsie said, quickly deciding to take on an even more relaxed attitude than usual. For some reason the emails and demands for meetings weren't making her angry, rather she was finding it more and more comical. 'Ta, Boss. Jees it's hot out there. I had bus duty.' She dragged a chair from near the door and put it straight in front of Garranto's desk. The chair scraped noisily along the wooden floor and she grimaced, exaggerating her response to the noise. Giving him a wave as she took a long drink out of her drink bottle, she plonked herself down, her legs stretched out casually in front of her as she leaned back in the chair. 'How are yous going? Long day for you fellas. What can I do for yus?'

She watched the colour rise in Garranto's face and Gwen sat up straighter. She could almost see the pious woman's nostrils flaring in and out as Mr Garranto stood up.

'I did not ask you to sit down,' he declared.

'Nah, all good. I'm used to looking after myself. What can I do for yus?' She took another swig from her bottle, holding it up high and glugging loudly. 'Jees, it's empty,' she said as she shook the bottle and held it up to the light. 'Empty as a pub with no patrons, or,' she giggled, 'a school with no kids.'

Both Garranto and Gwen were glaring at her and she noticed Garranto reading what was written on her hat. 'Right, okay, I'm listening. I'll fix the water problem later. Got plenty of time after school. Ain't really got that much to do.'

Mr Garranto was by now fuming and she delighted in watching him bluster and stutter when he spoke. She had really wound him up. This was fun. 'Miss Jackson. Can I remind you that you are in a formal setting. My office.'

She gave him a thumbs up. 'Gotcha.'

He put his hands on his desk and leaned over towards

her. 'Have you been drinking or are you high on something?'

She shook her bottle again and peered at it, an annoyed look on her face. 'High on something. Yeah, I'm high on something. Life.' Taking her hat off she held it out to Gwen and then Garranto. 'Life is Good,' she said, before placing the cap backwards on her head. She shifted it around until she was happy with the position of it.

'Gwen,' he spluttered. 'Can you please serve the code of conduct on Miss Jackson. Miss Jackson, you need to read over what you are being coded for. One — Teacher accommodation is for teachers and on occasion their families, only. It is not a space for friends to stay unless prior permission is acquired. Two —There is to be no partying or loud music or noises after six o'clock. Three —The teacher residing in the accommodation needs to get prior permission to have a partner visit or stay over. You are in violation of all of these rules. Please sign the bottom here and we will proceed with the subsequent actions.

She laughed loudly and took the papers from Gwen who stood up and walked over to hand them to her. 'Well, well, well. I'll be. I never did see anything like this before. Are these your own rules? Because they're very different to the ones Education Queensland has. They say it's okay to have people stay over as long as it's not in large numbers. That's the only rule here that I can see might be a problem in your list. And in your world,' she added.

'What do you have to say for yourself,' Garranto sat down and she watched his hands shake as they shuffled some papers in front of him. He really was an unfortunate looking person with broken veins running over his cheeks and oily hair that hung over to one side. The comb over, she thought. The good old comb-over.

She looked down at her shirt and rubbed the ink stain. 'Darn, she said. 'Pen. That's my good shirt. Sorry, did you ask me a question?'

No one spoke and she could feel the tension in the air. 'Oh, that's right. What have I got to say for myself? Not much. I do have a question. You said no noise after six o'clock. Is that am or pm?'

Garranto made a growling noise. 'That is pm, obviously.'

'Goodo, just checking. All good then?' She stood up and rearranged the papers Gwen had handed over. She pushed them up and down and stood them upright on the desk. Tapping them on the surface she played around until the edges were straight and neat. She then picked up a stapler that was in front of Garranto. 'Scuse me,' she quipped, once again throwing a smile his way. Stapling the papers a couple of times in the corner she then placed the stapler back on the desk. She looked at it and then moved it slightly to the side, then twisted it around a little.

'Right. Okay, I'll catch yus then.' She dumped the bundle of papers, now held firmly together with a staple in front of Garranto. As she turned to walk out, he called out to her.

'You need to take these documents with you. Read over them and sign.'

'No thanks. All good. None of that applies to me so we are tickety-boo.' As she strolled to the doorway, she shook her bottle again. 'Gonna get me some water.'

37

Nothing had ever felt so satisfying or empowering and she held both her hands up, giving a double thumbs up to Bron as she exited the office. She wanted to skip back to the staffroom, to laugh aloud. Idiots. She didn't care what they threw at her. She hadn't done anything wrong. If he was trying to push her out of the school then he would have to try a bit harder. Anyway, it was her choice. If it became too annoying, she would just leave. There were plenty of other schools around who would take her.

As if someone had read her mind, she felt her phone in her pocket ping with an incoming email. She pulled it out and read the words as she walked slowly back to the staffroom. From the first few lines, she could tell it was from one of the large private colleges in Townsville. They were looking for staff. She popped the phone back in her pocket. She'd read it later when she got home. Schools all over the state were trying to employ teachers and although she had no intention of leaving Matfield it would be interesting to see what this other school was offering.

By now most of the staff and students had left and she enjoyed the quiet of the usually noisy space. A couple of the cleaners called out to her and she waved back. Most people were so friendly. What a shame that just a few of the hierarchy spoiled what otherwise would have been the ideal teaching experience. No wonder other teachers had left the school.

BY THE TIME she got home she was hot and bothered and she turned the fans on high, hoping to get some breeze through the small apartment. The air-conditioning was broken and even though she had reported it several times no one had come to fix it. She would put up with it at the moment, but come October or November she would have to make a bit of noise so that someone would come and fix it. It would be impossible to sleep in the apartment during summer without air-con. Arming herself with a cold drink and a large piece of chocolate slice that Jane had baked, she flopped down on the lounge.

Even though it had been a trying day, the conversation in the principal's office had left her feeling invigorated and ready to take on the world. Now to read her email.

Dear Elsie Jackson,

We have been given your name by a colleague, Mrs Kirk, who I am acquainted with and met with recently. She noted that you had worked under her leadership and she had known you for several years. She also stated that you were interested in working in a regional area.

Elsie took a long sip of her cool drink and stretched out on the lounge. Her back was propped up by some luxurious cushions that Jane had brought as a house-warming gift. Over the years she had not collected that many household items and now every time she added to her belongings, whether it be new or second-hand, she felt like she had won the lotto. Mrs Kirk, who the letter mentioned, had been her principal at the school where she had undertaken some of her pracs. Elsie had also worked as a teacher aide there, as well as doing her cleaning job at night. Mrs Kirk was also the principal where she had gone to school and had always had a soft spot for Elsie and her siblings.

'I'd employ you over anyone,' Mrs Kirk had told her as she signed the paperwork to say Elsie had passed her prac at Kingsford High School. 'Students will be lucky to have you as their teacher.'

It had been a wonderful time learning the ropes under Mrs Kirk's guidance and Elsie felt like she had been well taken care of, the mentoring and support she had received more than anyone could ask for. Vastly different to what she was experiencing now, she thought.

She continued reading the email.

Mrs Kirk has told us of your experience and skills, and her recommendations could not come higher. We believe that you are contracted at a school this year, however we would like you to consider a placement with us for the following year. We are open to discussions about your pay rate as we are interested in paying higher than the award rate for your level, considering the recommendation that you would arrive with.

We also offer accommodation in a nearby suburb to the school, plus numerous remunerations for other requirements, including airfares back to Brisbane or anywhere of the same distance, twice a year, removal of furniture, settling in bonuses and a range of other payments that would go above what you are now receiving.

Please consider this offer carefully and we would love a reply to let us know what your thoughts are in regards to this offer. We would need to know by the end of term four if you are interested in a teaching position at our college for the following year.'

It was signed off by the principal. She read it again, her eyes scanning back and forth. An offer such as this one was something she hadn't seen coming. Her idea had been to settle in here at Matfield and stay for a solid length of time. It would be interesting to see how much extra the college was offering. 'Thank you, Mrs Kirk,' she muttered to herself.

38

By the time Thursday afternoon came, Elsie was well and truly ready for the holidays. She didn't even care if she just sat on her lounge and read books, ate chocolate and drank cups of tea for the entire two weeks. A well-earned break was needed. The students had become more and more restless with the holidays looming and it had been difficult to keep them on track, while deterrin them from not only annoying her, but also each other.

The air-conditioning had not been fixed and everyone was hot and cranky. There had been some arguments and even a fight in the classroom between some of the boys; it had taken all of her skills to keep everyone placated. Emails had been sent from the office stating that teachers were not to send students with behavioural problems to the office, or to contact the principal, or anyone else in the admin team unless it was a major medical emergency. They were busy!

'Think yourselves, lucky,' she had berated three of

the year ten boys as she sat them in different corners of her classroom. It was the first time she had raised her voice this year and she felt like she was on the edge of a precipice, about to completely lose her cool. 'This would usually merit a harsher consequence than just sitting in the corner of the room. Fighting is a major offence and I've had enough of the three of you. How dare you fight in my classroom. How dare you disrupt everyone and swear and carry on. How old are you? Three? I've had enough of all of you. Sit down and shut up!'

She couldn't believe she had said the 'shut up' word. Not once over the previous year had she lost her temper like she had this week, but the swearing, the fighting and the disrespectful behaviours were out of control. The kids knew that the office wasn't sending support or even remotely interested in the behaviour of the students this week. They were busy with other things.

One of the boys, Ken, looked up at her, his cheek red from where one of the others had punched him. He rubbed his hand over it. 'Don't look at me like that,' she said harshly. 'I have no sympathy for you, Ken. You pushed Robert so hard he slammed into Duncan. Duncan had no idea what was going on and his reaction was also impulsive. The three of you. I've had enough.' She crossed her arms as she looked between the three boys. The rest of the class was so quiet you could hear a pin drop. Good, she thought, they could all work in silence.

'What do you think, that you can just punch someone when you want to? The three of you will all have detentions with me next term. And don't think I'll forget, because I won't.' She had ranted some more and for the rest of the day the class worked in silence.

The following day, all three boys had waited behind and offered their apologies.

'Sorry, Miss Jackson,' Ken said. 'We were just hot and pissed off yesterday.' She glared at him and crossed her arms. He tried again. 'Sorry, I mean we were angry, 'cause it's real hot in here and none of us like being inside.'

Robert smiled and brought his hand from behind his back. 'We want you to have these. We're real sorry. Should'na punched each other in here. 'We appreciate that you pulled us apart. You sort of got right in the middle of us.'

She took the flowers and sniffed. They were great kids; deep down just nice boys who were a bit rough around the edges. 'Next time, stop fighting when I tell you to and better still don't start fighting. It won't solve anything.'

Duncan passed her a box of chocolates. 'You're pretty tough Miss.' He rubbed his arm. 'You were pretty brave when you dragged me off Robert and pulled us apart. We're all bigger than you.'

'Well it stopped you didn't it? Before you killed each other.'

They all stared down at their feet, before looking at her again. 'We're real sorry,' Ken said. 'We've never even heard you raise your voice before. It's a bit crazy how you broke us apart and stopped the fight.'

Duncan added, 'Yeah, other teachers, like Mrs Popple or even the sports teacher, won't come near any of us kids when we punch each other.'

'I shouldn't have either. I'm lucky that you boys had

the good sense to stop right away. I grew up in a rough school where everyone had to learn to look after themselves. I know that fighting isn't a solution for anything. You need to be quick with your words and clever to work your way out of tricky situations. Learn to control your temper. I know it's hot and we've all had enough this week.' She let a smile cross her face. 'Okay, I accept your apology and your gifts.' Her smile widened as Ken pulled a bottle of wine out from behind his back. 'Me mum bought this for you when I told her what happened. We've had this hidden all day in the middle room here. Lucky no one stole it from my bag.'

She inhaled sharply. 'Lucky no one did, or no one noticed and thought you had brought wine to school to drink.'

Ken pulled an innocent face. 'Awgh, Miss. As if we'd ever do that.'

They had all laughed and she accepted each of their hands for a handshake as they thanked her again. She shook her head as she watched them hitch their bags on their backs and walk out of the room, the three of them joking and jostling each other as they turned and waved to her.

39

On Saturday morning Elsie's phone woke her at ten thirty. The noise of it echoed throughout the apartment and she lay on her back staring at the ceiling. Could she be bothered getting out of bed and answering it? She had left it in the kitchen and she stretched her arms above her head, before snuggling back into her pillow.

She needed rest. Lots of it. The term had taken everything out of her. She had no more to give. Sleep. She closed her eyes and waited for the ringing to stop. It did, but then it started up again. Whoever was trying to reach her was persistent. Stumbling out of bed she pushed her hair from her face and made her way out of the bedroom. 'Hello,' she said, flopping back down on the lounge as she spoke.

'Elsie. It's Matt here.'

She instantly sat up. 'Oh. Hello. It's you.'

He chuckled. 'Yes, it's me. Did I wake you up? You sound half asleep.'

'Um, I won't lie. You did. I don't usually sleep in this late but I have to admit I'm exhausted.'

'Oh, well you might not welcome my suggestion. I wondered if you'd like to come with me to the lagoon out past Harold's Paddock. It's a beautiful spot and we could have lunch there and walk around. I often go there to take photos.'

She squeezed the phone in her hand. 'I'd love that. Yes, of course, I'd love to come.'

'Tomorrow? I can pick you up at about seven in the morning if that's not too early. If we go any later it will be too hot. I'll take my ute if that's okay. The road is dirt out that way.'

'Sure. I'd love that. What can I bring?'

'Just a bottle of juice or soft drink. I've got the rest covered. See you at seven then?'

'Thanks. Yes. I'll be ready.'

As she hung up she realised she was bouncing up and down on the lounge with delight. Matt. A date. Lunch. Walking. Apart from when Peter and Jane visited, it had been so long since she had been this excited. What would she wear? What shoes would be best? She jumped up and started getting her breakfast. There was so much to think about. What a great way to start the holidays.

THANK goodness for the bag of clothes that Jane had brought with her from Townsville. There were plenty of op shops near to where she lived and she had filled a bag of clothes for Elsie. 'I like all of these so I figured you would. One dollar each. They had a sale on.'

There hadn't been any time to look at them before today and now, as Elsie pulled them out she scrutinised each one. There was something for every occasion and she counted how many items of clothing were in the bag. Thirty-two. Thirty-two dollars for that amount of clothes. Blue jeans that looked like they had never been worn, floral blouses with the new price tags still on them and .... she pulled out what she knew straight away was going to be her favourite. A floral fitted dress with a v-neckline and a drawn-in waist. She pulled it over her head and swirled in front of the mirror. She loved it.

Drawing her hands over the fabric she looked at it closely. Tiny floral patterns that filled the fabric gave it a summery look and she stood up straight and turned around. The hemline was exactly where she liked it. Just above her knee. This would be the perfect dress to wear to the pub or maybe she might go to a restaurant again one night. Who knew what the holidays might bring?

40

The next morning Elsie was awake at five. She showered and had breakfast before putting on what she had decided to wear the day before. She looked wistfully at the floral dress but that would not be suitable for today's outing. Pulling on a khaki pair of shorts, she zipped them up and turned to gaze at herself in the mirror. A loose-fitting cotton shirt sat nicely on her body, the length of it just sitting below her waist. It was a crème colour and she hoped that the dust wouldn't show up on it too much. She wore a black singlet top under it. If they were going to be doing some walking she might get hot and at least she could take the blouse off.

A well-worn straw hat would protect her from the sun and a pair of hiking boots that were in the bag from Jane fitted perfectly. She looked prepared. Like she was ready to go exploring. As she checked how she looked again, a flicker of excitement surged through her body. She looked good. Even if she might say that herself. It wasn't often that she complimented herself but today she was going to allow it.

Matt arrived just before seven. He knocked on the door and she jumped, the anticipation of going out with him, making her a bit nervous. She grabbed her bag with the drinks in it and opened the door.

At first, he didn't speak and they just stared at each other. Finally, he spoke. 'Wow. You look good. I'm used to seeing you in your work clothes.'

She followed him out and closed the door behind her. 'No work clothes for two weeks. Just play clothes.'

Matt was also dressed to go walking and she checked out his sturdy boots and thick cotton shorts. His legs and arms were well-toned and she admired how tanned he was, the blue t-shirt he had on, contrasting against the colour of his skin. 'Are you up for some walking today?' he asked as he opened the ute door for her.

'Definitely. I need some exercise.' She settled into the seat, pleasantly surprised that the ute had been cleaned. Wriggling her nose, she thought she could still smell some of the cleaning product. The dashboard shone and there wasn't a single piece of paper or any drink bottles at her feet. Surely he hadn't cleaned the ute just for her. Was he trying to impress her? Shaking her head as if to rid herself of what she told herself were stupid ideas, she looked at him as he sat behind the wheel.

His eyes were bright in the early morning light and the way he looked at her made her feel like a teenager on a first date. 'Ready?' he asked.

'Yes,' she replied.

THEY TALKED non-stop on the way to the lagoon. Matt rattled off the history of the area and the different families he had worked for. 'Always work for fencing mobs out here. I'll never be out of a job.'

'What did you want to do when you were at school?' she asked. 'Did you think you'd be working out here in the dust?'

'No way. I didn't even know where the outback was. We grew up in Inala, on the western side of Brisbane.'

'Oh, I know where Inala is. It's probably a bit the same as where I come from in Logan.'

He nodded in agreement. 'All I ever wanted to do was what your brother Peter is doing. I wanted to be a vet. To be with animals and mend them.' He sighed and looked sideways at her. 'You know what it's like. Sometimes dreams aren't that easy to reach.'

She relaxed back in her seat. 'It can be tough. It's hard enough to get through the maze of teenage life when everything is going okay. Sometimes though, the odds can be insurmountable and choices are taken out of your hands.'

'Yeah. I had no option but to leave school, and then home.' He glanced at her as if he wanted to say something but wasn't sure.

'What else?' she asked.

'One of my older brothers ended up in jail. The other brother went to live with him when he got out and now they both live in Western Australia. I haven't seen them for years. Ethan doesn't even really remember them. Our parents had addictions and that's why I have guardianship over Ethan. He'll only need me until he finishes school, but if I'd left him at home with them it would have been too hard for him. No support. He didn't have an Elsie at home to push him through and make sure he was looked after.'

She accepted the subtle compliment. 'Must have been hard for you, to leave and let him be there by himself.'

'I was only sixteen when I left home. Never finished school. My old man had a thing for me. A hatred for some reason that he didn't have for the others. Who knows. Maybe he wasn't even my father. But one thing I did know, if I stayed at home he was going to kill me.' Matt ran his hand over his chin. 'He liked to punch.'

'Oh,' Elsie said, her heart sinking at the thought of what Matt must have endured.

'He never hit Ethan, just me. They didn't look after him though. They signed the paperwork with no questions. Glad to give me the responsibility, they said.'

''FUPs we call them,' Elsie muttered.

'What does that stand for?'

She changed the first word. 'Effed up parents.'

He made a hmph noise. 'I get it. I haven't heard that expression but that pretty much describes it. Anyway, we're doing okay and Ethan has had a good year. Even better than I imagined. Thanks to you also.'

'Oh, I've not done anything. That kid does it all himself.'

'You know the last thing they said to me, our parents that is?'

'What?'

'They said, he'll be just like you and never amount to anything. Happy for you both to piss off.'

Silence filled the car and Elsie could sense the hurt that Matt still so clearly carried. 'FUP. No other words to describe it,' she mumbled. It was easy for her to understand the situation and she sympathised with Matt and for Ethan. Thank goodness they had come to Matfield and not thrown away Ethan's last year of schooling. For a split second, the thought of the scholarship crossed her mind. She pushed the idea away. The others were right. It wasn't any of her business. She'd given them the information and it was up to them to decide.

Matt stopped talking and she wondered if he was waiting for her to share some of her childhood with him. There were plenty of stories to tell. A lifetime of them. But that wasn't something she was ready for. There was too much hurt and angst. It was better to keep the past closed.

41

As they pulled into the carpark of the lagoon area, Elsie sat up and peered through the windscreen. The sun was starting to rise in the eastern sky and flocks of galahs filled the sky above. Their noises echoed across the vast plains and she jumped out of the car and stood with Matt, both looking up at the sky that was blocked with flocks of birds. She felt a splat on her nose and nearly went cross-eyed trying to look at what it was. Matt laughed and reached into the car. He pulled out a tissue which he wiped firmly across her nose.

'Bird shit. Galah shit to be precise,' he said between snorts of laughter.

'Fifty million miles of nothing and one bird shits on me. What are your chances?' She also laughed and grabbed the tissue off him to make sure her face was clean. Tilting her head up to his, she asked. 'Gone?'

His thumb touched her cheek and she felt like an electric shock ran through her body. Had he felt the same thing? Was that why he was now staring at her and not moving?

'Um, yes. Now it is.' He drew his hand away. 'They say it's good luck if a bird craps on you.'

She was lost for words and continued to look into his eyes which hadn't moved from hers. 'Should we go for a walk,' she asked quietly.

He shook his head as if to clear some thoughts. 'Sure. Yes. Let's get going.'

MATT'S FINGERS were still tingling from where they had touched Elsie's skin. He had not wanted to draw his hand away, but it would have been strange just to rest it there. If touching her slightly like that felt so good, what would .... He admonished himself and pulled a backpack from the ute. Walk. That's what they needed to do. Walk.

The birds that had blocked the sky a few moments ago were now a dark shape in the distance. As he pulled his camera out of the car and slung it over his shoulder he had a sudden impulse to take a photo of Elsie. He didn't usually like people in his photos, but, well, today, today was different.

'Elsie,' he called out to her and waved her back to where he was. She had started to walk towards the gum trees that bordered the carpark and he saw her looking up into the branches of the tallest tree.

'There's a nest up there. In the hollow. I can see chicks. Baby galahs.'

'Stay there. Hang on.'

He jogged over to where she was and without her

knowing started clicking photos of her as she looked up into the tree, her hand shading the glare from the rising sun. When he crouched down to get a different perspective, she finally turned to him. 'Look into the camera, Elsie.'

'How embarrassing,' she said. 'You don't need to take photos of me.'

He stood up and looked at the photos he had taken. 'You're beautiful. You should see yourself. The look on your face. It's like, a look of wonder. Your reaction to what you're seeing. Like you've never seen something like it before.'

'Maybe you're wasted as a fencer. You should write poetry or stories.'

'I always see the depth in what I'm taking photos of. When you look through the lens it's a different perspective and, like just now, it's almost like I can, well it sounds stupid.'

'Go on.'

'It's like I can see your emotions, feel what you're feeling and look into your soul.'

'Wow.'

'It doesn't happen that often and usually it's with Ethan or one of the older men I work with. Usually, I know someone well before that happens. You know, that I can see their emotions.'

ELSIE WAS CONFUSED. This was a different side to Matt and she almost felt like she was listening to one of the speakers at some of the literature courses she had been to. He spoke eloquently, precise and bared his emotions. She gulped. That was more than she did. As he flung his camera back over his shoulder and led the way to the lagoon she thought about his words. He had said she was beautiful. No one except her brother had ever told her that.

When they reached the destination, she was speechless. In front of them, glassy green water filled the lagoon, the surface dotted with hundreds of large lily pads. White crane-like birds waded in the shallows and a flock of budgerigars exploded into the air, departing the tree where they had been hiding.

'What do you think?' Matt stood close to her and she swore she could feel an electrical pulse between the hairs on their arms. She pulled her arm away and rubbed it, conscious that he was staring at her and waiting for a response.

'It's amazing. I've never been anywhere like this. An oasis in the middle of the dry plains. Can we walk right around it?'

'At the moment you can. When we get more rain, you won't be able to as the river will flow and the swampland behind it will be filled also. Today though we should be able to go all the way round. Ready?'

She smiled at him and for a moment she wondered what it would be like to be kissed by those lips. His eyes bored into hers and she looked away, flustered by the feelings that were raging in her body.

'You okay?' he asked. 'You seem a little out of sorts.'

'No. I'm fine. Just overwhelmed at the natural beauty of these places out here.'

'Way different from where we grew up,' he replied as

he started to follow a track that led around the lagoon. 'No bitumen, traffic lights, sirens or drivers yelling at each other. I don't think I'll ever be able to go back to the city to live.'

She walked faster to keep up with him, the path wide enough for them to walk side-by-side. 'I feel the same. I've only been out here for a short while but I can't see me leaving. I love the little towns, although...'

She stopped talking. She hadn't meant to tell him so much and she hadn't shared the offer of the job in Townsville with anyone. A move like that hadn't entered her head before the email arrived.

'Go on,' he prompted. 'What did you want to say.'

She stopped when he did, watching as he pointed his camera towards a large bird that had landed on the other side of the lagoon. 'Jabiru,' he whispered.

'I had a strange email arrive last week.'

'Strange?' he said, his eyes not moving away from where he was looking through the camera. 'What do you mean?'

'I got an offer from a large private college in Townsville. They've dangled a carrot; higher pay, great conditions, transport and housing as well as a range of other things that I don't get at Matfield. The principal is a friend of my old principal where I went to school. I also worked for her as a teacher aide when I was studying.'

Matt stopped in his tracks and put the camera away. 'That's crazy. You're great at your job. I suppose it's not surprising that you will get offers. What are you going to do? The kids at Matfield will be devastated to lose you.'

She laughed. 'Oh, I'm not going to accept it. I've become attached to the kids at school and this one in

Townsville is a private college. Way out of my league.'
When she told him the name of the college he nodded.

'I know the place. Heaps of country kids go there. It's
well set up for boarders.'

'I want to help kids, particularly kids who have challenges to overcome. I don't think I'd get that at a place
like that.'

'Sure you would. Kids everywhere have problems.
Just because you might come from money or maybe a
large property out west, doesn't mean you don't have
something you need help with.'

'Can you imagine me in amongst all those posh
teachers? I'm from Logan. It's a whole different world to
what that college would be like.'

'What happened to stepping outside your comfort
zone? Challenging yourself. A school like Matfield will
always be after teachers but offers like that one don't
come along every day. You'd be mad not to at least look
into it.'

She continued to walk. Up until now she has just
dismissed the idea. It was ridiculous really. She was only
a new teacher and just learning the ropes. On the other
hand, Gantarro was a pain in the neck and next year she
knew he wouldn't have to give her spares or any of the
other considerations that had been promised for her
beginning year.

'How much more money are they offering?' Matt
asked.

'A substantial amount. Thousands more a year.'

They walked in silence, her thoughts now swirling as
she thought that perhaps she should look at the offer
more closely. If she knocked it back it wouldn't ever come

up again. Maybe Matt was right. She could always come back to Matfield or somewhere similar if the other didn't work out.

By the time they reached the other side of the lagoon the sun was high in the sky. Luckily there was a grove of trees that offered shade and a grassy area to sit. 'Just watch for snakes,' Matt offered as he sat down on the picnic blanket next to her.'

The food he had brought was delicious and before long the topic of the job offer was forgotten and she relaxed in his conversation, his stories of trying to keep food up to Ethan and making him keep his room tidy causing her to laugh so much that tears rolled down her face. 'Teenage boys,' she giggled. 'That kid has every teacher at school, excuse the pun, eating out of his hand. Charm with a capital C.'

'He confessed to me that everyone was feeding him, plus the ladies in the library keep a special stash of fruit cake for him when he goes to study class on a Thursday afternoon. They even pack him some extra to take home. I can't believe that everyone thought I didn't have enough money to feed him.

'He's too smart for his own good.' She took a break from eating. Matt had packed a yummy lunch and she wondered if it was rude to eat another lamington. As if he read her mind, he picked one up and passed it to her. 'Have another one. They're good for you.'

They had laughed and talked for another hour or so before packing up and walking back around the lagoon. There were another couple of cars in the carpark, but considering it was school holidays the area was quiet. The lack of people was another aspect that Elsie liked.

Living in Matfield she didn't need to contend with crowds or busy shops. She was sorry when the walk finished and they approached Matt's ute. As he opened the door for her to get in she looked up at him and smiled. 'Thank you. Thank you for a lovely day.'

He paused, holding the door open. 'My pleasure. I've also enjoyed it.'

THEY WENT out another three times that week. Matt would ring her and suggest they go somewhere. A couple of times the trips were in the afternoon, after he finished work. One afternoon they'd driven out to a rocky outcrop that was in the middle of nowhere. Matt had brought a bottle of wine and a beautiful platter of food. 'Wow,' she said. 'You're going all out. You'll have to let me bring the next lunch or dinner.'

He passed her a cracker that had a slice of some sort of cheese on it that she had never seen before. It didn't look like the regular Homebrand one she kept in her fridge and she closed her eyes when she tasted it. 'What is that? I love it.'

'Double Brie Ash Cheese. I bought it at the deli. I can't have these types of food in my fridge when Ethan is home. He would eat that entire block in one go. Two bites and it would be gone.'

Together they watched the sun set over the western plains. Flashes of pink, orange and red spread out above the horizon and it seemed like the entire sky was on fire. The earth glowed with a red tinge and beyond the colours of the sunset a deep blue filled the vast expanse above. Soon tiny stars flickered in the distance and she sat mesmerised as the sun sank below the low ridge of mountains on the horizon. Flocks of galahs flew above them. 'They're going down to the river, to nest in those trees we saw them in last week.'

'You love those birds, don't you?' Matt sat close, next to her and his arm rubbed against hers. Over the past week she had waited for his phone calls and then spent the entire time until he picked her up, thinking about what to wear and where they would go. She knew that her feelings for him had changed and it scared her to think of what might come next. What if he didn't feel the same? What if he was just being a good friend and showing her the places around town? What if when school started back everything just went back to the way it was and her days consisted of work, work and more work?

Over the last week, her life had changed and she liked how she now spent her time. As she watched the last of the birds disappear into the distance, she felt the urge to snuggle up against him. But she didn't. It had been so long since she had been out with anyone that she was a bit lost as to how to act or what to do. If he had picked up on her uneasiness, he didn't show it. He seemed at ease and relaxed, and she wondered what he was thinking.

She jumped a little when he spoke, her ponderings and silent questions pushed aside. 'Would you like to go for dinner at *The Fortress*, Saturday night? I thought seeing it was school holidays we should go out and celebrate. I'd love to shout you if that's okay. Sort of a thank you for teaching Ethan this year.'

'That would be lovely,' she replied, holding the hand

that he offered to help her up. The sun had disappeared and the cool of the early evening filtered around them. 'But I'd rather pay half if that's okay.'

He grinned at her and for a moment she thought he was going to kiss her. But he didn't and she turned away so that he couldn't see the look in her eyes.

THE FLORAL DRESS that Jane had given her was the perfect outfit for Saturday night. She breathed in and stood side on to the mirror, pleased with how she looked. Her hair was shiny and held back on one side with a hair clip. The dress clung to her slim body and she pressed her hands over it, smoothing the fabric so that it sat just right. A pair of strappy sandals showed off her brightly coloured toenails and she pushed her hands out in front. She had even painted her fingernails.

When she had rung Jane for some makeup advice the two of them had talked and giggled like they were kids. 'Has he kissed you yet?' Jane asked. 'It seems like he might be building up to it.'

'No, he hasn't. There have been a few times when I thought that he might but he's been the perfect gentle-man. I wish he would kiss me though.'

'Oh my God. I never thought I'd hear you say that.'

'I think I like him. You know, more than just a friend.'

'I'd say you've completely fallen for him. I've met him. It wouldn't be hard to fall in love with him.'

'I wouldn't go that far but I definitely want to see him all the time. I wait for his calls. Is that pathetic?'

Jane laughed. 'No, not at all. Now send me a photo of

what you're going to wear and I'll check everything is okay.'

NOW THAT JANE was at uni and living away from home she had become more of a confidante and Elsie was starting to rely on her for advice about clothes, makeup and men. The tables had turned and it was nice to have someone to turn to. Heaven knows, at the moment she needed all the advice she could get.

42

―――

Matt picked her up right on the dot of six o'clock. He rapped loudly on the door and then swung it open when she called out to come in. She tried not to stare with her mouth open but for goodness' sake, he looked handsome. Really handsome. His hair was combed back and sat neatly, showing off his handsome face. He had shaved and she resisted the impulse to reach up and stroke his cheek. His skin looked smooth and her gaze wandered to his bare arms, tanned and muscled from the work he did.

Well-fitting jeans were matched with a blue chambray shirt and she noted the shiny riding boots that he wore. 'Got new boots from the store in town,' he said. 'Now I don't want to get any dust on them.'

'You look great. Really great,' she said, stumbling over her words as she tried not to stare.

Matt was still watching her and she giggled nervously as his eyes looked her up and down. He reached up and pushed a stray piece of hair behind her ear, tucking it in until it stayed in place. Their eyes hadn't left each other and she held her breath as he took her hand in his. 'You are beautiful. I've told you before but, in that dress, well, the way you wear it. I'm lost for words. Beautiful.'

'Thank you, Matt,' she said, loving the feeling of her hand in his. 'Should we go?'

'Yes, oh yes. Of course. I forgot why I was here. *The Fortress*. Let's get going.'

He had let go of her hand and for a long while after she could still feel the warmth that had radiated from his fingers as they entwined through hers. If that was what his fingers felt like on her hands what would ...' She stopped herself in mid-thought. Dinner. Drinks. Food. That was the plan. Nothing more.

Al and Anita made a huge fuss, welcoming them as if they were long-lost family. Elsie was worried that she never got to see the bottom of her wine glass. 'Al is keeping me topped up tonight,' she exclaimed, before winding her spaghetti around her fork and placing it in her mouth. 'I don't think I ever went to a restaurant before I moved here, and now in one year, I have been here three times already. Life is good.'

'What? How did you not go to a restaurant? There are heaps in Brisbane, in every suburb. Surely you went sometimes.'

'No. There wasn't time or money.' She didn't continue talking, instead, she put more pasta in her mouth and listened as Matt talked about the different places he had eaten out. Ethan was obviously a large influence and it sounded like when they came into town, he worked hard to coerce Matt to take him to different eateries.

'I'd like to take you out again if you want to. Maybe we

can visit some of the other small towns nearby. Try some of their restaurants.'

'I'd like that.'

'You know Elsie, I've told you a lot about my life, now and before we came here, but you don't reveal too much about yours.'

She pushed her empty bowl to one side and dabbed at her mouth with the serviette. She was so full that she felt like she would burst. 'There's not much to tell.'

He leaned back in his chair and pushed his empty bowl to the side. 'I'm sure there is.'

'No. nothing exciting.'

Luckily at that moment, Al appeared with the dessert menu. 'Agh you are bella tonight,' he said, his sultry voice like honey as he complimented her. She blushed and Matt put his hand on her arm. 'She is Bella, Al. I told Elsie that when I picked her up. Beautiful.'

She could feel her face getting redder. Compliments were not something she was used to, or for that matter men revealing their feelings. This was a new experience and she grappled with her emotions as Matt's fingers seemed to burn through her skin. Why was his touch having such an effect on her?

43

By the time they finished dessert and the last of the wine, Elsie felt like she was tipsy. Matt must have noticed because he steadied her as they stood up. Al fussed over them and passed Matt a complementary bottle of wine as they prepared to leave. 'Maybe have a couple of drinks when you get home.' Al waved his hand upwards. 'It is a full moon and love is in the air.'

Elsie pretended not to hear him, her focus on trying to walk straight enough to concentrate on. When they reached her apartment, she wasn't ready to say goodnight to Matt. 'I'd love it if you'd come in. I wouldn't mind another glass of wine.'

He raised his eyebrows. 'I thought you would have had enough of listening to me by now.'

When she didn't reply he grabbed the bottle of wine and got out of the ute. She laughed loudly when she saw the curtains in the apartment next door open a little, a sliver of light shining through from Eliza's front room.

'This will give her something to report on,' Elsie said as she unlocked her front door.

Matt followed her in and they sat at the kitchen table, a large glass of wine in their hand. Soon they were laughing and talking together as Matt relayed some of the funny stories from his days of fencing in remote areas. He'd met a lot of interesting characters along the way and he had a wonderful way of describing them and their antics. It was as if she could picture them in her head when he talked and she became involved in his stories, wishing that one day she might travel to the different places he talked about.

'I worked on some of the biggest cattle properties there are up in the Northern Territory. Some of them over a hundred thousand hectares in size. Last job before I came here, I was mustering wild buffalo. They sold them to the domestic market but also some of them were exported overseas. Plenty of rain where I was, next to Kakadu National Park.'

'I'd love to see water buffalo in the wild.'

'You want to see their horns. Over a couple of metres across on some of them. It was tough work but I loved it. Have you been to many places in Queensland?'

She thought how few places she had been. For years she had borrowed beautiful hard-covered books from the library, pouring over the photos of Australia's top places to visit. 'Matfield is the only other place I've been, apart from Brisbane and the Gold Coast. I would love to see different places, especially the remote places. Where's your favourite spot?'

He thought for a while. 'I have so many. You can't beat the beaches up around Cairns and Port Douglas but then there's the amazing national parks, like Kakadu. I worked a fair bit around Mataranka and even went with some of the local boys onto Elsey Station for some work. I reckon it's my pick. It's a bit like here is at the moment. They'd had a good season of rain so it was looking its best.'

The sound of Matt's voice was mesmerising and she was intrigued by where he had been. 'Why did you like that place so much.'

'You have to see it one day, Elsie.' He grinned. 'Same name as you. It's like you're on another planet, a million miles from anywhere. I loved the remoteness and the billabongs that are filled with bird life during the wet. That area has everything; flood plains, black soils and incredible ridge country. The history of the place is really interesting also. You probably haven't heard of it but it's where the movie, *We of the Never Never*, was filmed.'

She smiled. Now he was talking about something she knew about. 'Matt, I'm an English teacher. Before there was a movie there was a book. I've read that book quite a few times over the years. I can't believe you've actually been to the place.' The wine was cool and refreshing to drink and she took some more sips before continuing. 'That's somewhere I'd like to go. Elsey Station. The home of Jeannie, the little Missus, and Bett Bett. I think I could nearly recite the book off by heart.'

When she had lived on Resilience Street, books had been her saviour. As long as she had a torch that worked and a book from the library, she could get through the tough times. The words between the pages let her mind go to places that were as far away as possible from where she lay in her bed, listening to the neighbours' dogs barking, occasionally someone screaming at someone else and the sound of sirens in the streets nearby. 'When I was a kid, I read lots of books that were set in remote areas of Australia. Maybe that's why I ended up here.' She mused over that thought. It was the first time she had made the connection between what she had read about and where she had come to teach. 'Reading was an 'out' for me. It blocked out a lot of other things.'

'Like what?'

Her stomach tightened and she took a sharp intake of breath. No one else needed to know about her past. It was too depressing. Matt squeezed the last drop of wine into her glass and she could tell he was waiting for her to tell him more. Change the subject, she thought. Standing up, she remembered that she had some beers in the fridge. 'You don't have any wine left in your glass either,' she said. 'Do you want a beer? There is a heap left over from when Peter was here.'

He'd welcomed that idea, and once she finished her glass of wine she followed up with a couple of beers also. They lost track of time and how much they had drunk. She kept him talking about the different places he'd been and the interesting people he had worked with and met. At one stage she wondered if she was slurring a bit. Not that she cared. She hadn't laughed so much or enjoyed someone's company like this, well, ever, she thought.

Elsie wasn't sure exactly how the next part of the night started. She had stood up to get another beer from the fridge when Matt grabbed her hand as she walked past him. His fingers were warm and they sent electric shocks through her body. She stopped and looked down at him where he sat staring up at her. Neither spoke and she wasn't sure why she did it but she bent down and pushed her lips onto his. When he stood up and pulled her in towards him, she responded and their bodies pressed together. Sensations rippled through her body and she stopped thinking about anything else.

His kisses were warm and soft on her mouth and she kissed him back, only stopping when they both needed to breathe. When his blue eyes looked straight into hers, her legs went weak and she clung to him pressing her lips back onto his. His hands caressed her face before he wrapped his arms around her, his hands moving up and down her back. She held him tightly, and slid her hands inside his shirt, relishing the feel of his smooth skin.

It was as if they couldn't get enough of each other and their bodies tangled together, his hands stroking her hair, her back, as his arms drew around drawing her in closer.

When they pulled apart, they looked at each other for a while until Elsie grabbed his hand and led him into her bedroom. Matt sat on the bed and pulled his shirt off and she held her breath as she gazed at his body which was firm and well-toned. She ran her hands over his chest and he pulled her in towards him. Shivers ran through her body as his hands moved up along her leg and caressed her thighs. The sensations rippling along her skin were irresistible and she pushed him back on the bed, their bodies entwining as their lips pressed together.

When he muttered that he didn't have a condom with him, she jumped up and foraged in her top drawer. 'I have all these sample toiletry packages that I was given. Yes,' she said, triumphantly holding a condom in the air. 'I thought I'd seen one in here.'

Everything moved quickly after that. Her dress, bra and undies were soon removed as were the rest of his clothes. When he looked at her and touched her body, she felt her entire world explode and she responded wildly, her body starved too long of attention and love.

MATT'S BODY responded with a fervour as if every touch were a first. Elsie was nothing short of amazing — her allure, a potent combination of sensuality and a yearning for love. Each glance at her stirred an intense desire within him, a longing to intimately explore every inch of her being. In that moment he had tried to slow down time, wanting to savour every second. Yet the pull between them proved too strong and their bodies were drawn together, refusing to be restrained. Neither held back and time blurred in a moment of urgency and shared longings as the sounds of their passion echoed through the room. Time seemed to lose its grip until all that remained was the intoxicating embrace of two souls drawn together.

AFTERWARDS, as they lay side by side, he found himself caught in the aftermath of what had just happened. His chest rose up and down and the effects of the alcohol left his head spinning. He had never experienced love-making like this before. Gazing down at Elsie as she lay naked beside him, he stroked her head that rested on his shoulder; her shallow breathing a sign that she was asleep. The intensity of what had just happened lingered in the air and he knew she had let herself completely go, free of inhibitions or trying to hold back her feelings. As he lay there his thoughts became elusive, blurred by the haze of the excessive alcohol. Both of them had indulged a bit too much. His mind was too foggy to process anything and he closed his eyes, surrendering to sleep. The last sensation he could recall before drifting off was the gentle touch of her hand, a fleeting reminder of the intimacy they had just shared.

44

When Elsie woke in the morning all trace of Matt had gone. She rolled on her side, scanning the room as she put her hand on her head. It was thumping and she ran her tongue around her mouth. Dry. Tacky; a stale wine taste. She pulled the sheet over her nakedness and closed her eyes. Her body tingled as she thought about Matt and the way he had made love to her. Even with a thumping headache and what she could tell was shaping up to be one hell of a hangover, she couldn't help but smile. She stretched and breathed in deeply. Was that what the best sex in the world felt like? Had she just had the ultimate experience with someone who she now couldn't refute she had strong feelings for?

She sat up. But why had he left? It was a Sunday. Surely he didn't have to work today? He hadn't said anything last night about fencing jobs today. She dragged herself to the shower, revelling in the cool water that ran over her body. Lathering herself, she tried to ignore the ache in her body as she recalled last night. Standing for a long time in the shower she thought about Matt, visualising his strong arms, his muscly body and ... her body quivered, those blue eyes that seemed to be able to look straight into her soul.

Several times that morning, in between cups of tea that she hoped would make her feel a bit better, and lying on the couch after taking more Panadol, she had checked her phone. She thought that he would ring or message even if he was working. She held a wet washer to her face and closed her eyes.

KNOCKING on the door broke her sleep and she moaned, rolling on her side on the uncomfortable couch. Goodness knows how long she had been asleep for. A smile crossed her face. Matt. It had to be him knocking. Maybe he had brought her flowers or better still, food. Would he kiss her again? Was he back to make love to her again? A shiver of pleasure ran through her and she pushed her hair back from her face, trying to make herself look respectable. Shaking her body to relieve the stiffness in her limbs from lying on the couch, she walked to the door and then opened it.

A smile was fixed on her face as she looked straight up into Matt's eyes. But the look on his face did not reflect her romantic dreams or sensual feelings. His hair was messy, his eyes bloodshot and he wore old shorts and a t-shirt; not work gear, so he mustn't have been at work.

His voice was low and husky and she wondered if

there was something wrong. 'Can I come in?' he said as he looked at the ground.

She gave him a flirty grin as she opened the door and let him in. 'Sure. Anytime.'

He immediately sat down on the couch, his hands running through his hair in an agitated state. She sat down beside him and placed her hand on his arm. It didn't matter what was wrong, she was going to make sure he knew her feelings towards him. She was sick of not being upfront. Last night had changed everything for her and she wanted to be with him every second of the day. To talk to him, share her thoughts and dreams, to have him hold her and most of al,l to make love with him.

Those thoughts started to fade however when he looked at her again. His gaze held hers and her heart thumped hard. For a split second, she had doubts. What if he didn't feel the same way? What if last night had been a one-off for him? What if the experience evoked different emotions for him than it had for her?

His words came out stilted. 'I'm so sorry, Elsie. So sorry about what happened last night.'

She stiffened. 'Sorry? Really?'

'Yes. Both of us were drunk. Too much to drink. I should never have come back here. I should have gone home after the restaurant. What happened should never have happened. It was a huge mistake.'

Anger bubbled and she bit her lip before her words tumbled out. 'A mistake. Apologies. Shouldn't have happened.' She blinked as her mind tried to wrap around what he was saying. 'Okay, I see. Is that what you've come to tell me?' His words were not the words she would have used to describe last night. He was on a completely different page than she was.

She stood up and he looked up at her, shaking his head. 'What a disastrous end to a good night. I'm so sorry. I should never have done what I did. It was the alcohol.'

She nearly spat her next words out. 'The alcohol. Right. If that's what you've come to tell me then I guess you can go.' She walked to the door and held it open. She tried not to look at him as he stayed sitting on the couch, his hands wrapped around his head as he looked towards the floor again. 'I said you can go,' she repeated, her chest moving up and down as she tried to quell the anger rising in her body.

He stood up slowly and she turned away, her eyes downcast as he walked past her and out the door. She didn't look up until she could hear the sound of his ute driving out of the carpark.

As she stood at the kitchen sink sipping a cold glass of water, she tried to stop the tears from coming. It felt like someone had kicked her in the gut. As if the excitement of how she had felt when she woke up this morning had been stolen. It felt like...she took a long sip of water. It felt like someone had broken her heart.

45

As Matt drove away he also felt like he had been kicked in the guts. Guilt and shame plagued him and he gripped the steering wheel harder, the look on Elsie's face when she asked him to leave imprinted in his memory. Last night he had thrown caution to the wind and taken advantage of the one girl who, for the first time in a very long while, he had felt he was forming a connection to. She was lonely, vulnerable and last night she also had been very drunk. If only he had stopped drinking at the restaurant and not continued when they went back to her apartment. If only he had gone straight home. He could have just dropped her home and done the polite thing. Maybe just a kiss on the cheek to let her know he had enjoyed her company.

Instead, he had taken her home and allowed his desires to take over. He had thought of nothing else except...he gulped...except his sexual need for her. The problem was she deserved more than a fleeting encounter; a wild romp that was the consequence of too much alcohol. Guilt surged within him, a powerful punch as he grappled with his actions. He had betrayed her trust. The one quality she had trouble believing in. Her belief in not trusting anyone was now justified. No wonder, over the months they had known each other, she never gave him more information than what she needed to. She held back on sharing the personal and unhappy stories; she had never trusted him. And now she would trust him less. Thank goodness Ethan was still away. At least he didn't have to face him straight away.

Jees, Ethan. He inhaled sharply. Another layer of betrayal unfolded in his mind. He had just slept with his brother's teacher. He slammed his hands against the steering wheel, a wave of nausea engulfing him.

46

Elsie spent the rest of the holidays immersing herself in schoolwork so that she would be ready for the last term of the year. She hadn't replied to the email from the private college in Townsville. Before her night out with Matt she had decided not to accept their generous offer. Now however, she was tempted. Maybe she needed another change, to step away from the small country town and the never-ending harassment of Garranto. It would also mean she wouldn't run the risk of running into Matt.

When the new term started, she didn't have the same enthusiasm or drive she had started the year with. Was it because she had been pushed away from the one person she thought she had formed a connection with or was she, as Penny had warned, burnt out?

The steady flow of emails, the daily meetings and unrealistic expectations for forms to be filled in and submitted along with data collection and student reporting were relentless; and that was before she had even thought about assessment, marking, correspondence to parents and students, or assisting students with their work. It was piling up and as the second week of term four came about, she felt like she was drowning.

Penny and the others helped as much as they could, but they were also snowed under. Sometimes she took solace from the fact that although many of them were experienced teachers, they were having trouble keeping up with Garranto's demands too. How the hell was she supposed to cope when even they were struggling? At least he had stopped harassing her about the code of conduct and the word was that his wife was giving him such a hard time that he had lost focus on his administration jobs. Good, she thought. At least that's one less thing for me to contend with.

Ethan had returned to school with plenty of stories about his camping trips over the holidays. He hadn't said anything about Matt to her and she doubted he knew they had even gone out on a date. That suited her fine. The last thing she needed was for one of her students to find out about 'the mistake'.

Matt's words still rankled with her and she tried hard to push all thoughts of him from her mind. The loss of his company and conversation left her feeling down; she wished she could see him and talk about what had happened. Did he realise that even though it had been a wild night, she had been in full control of her actions and hadn't participated in anything she wouldn't do again with him? Berating herself, she tried to push the thoughts of him away. Why had she trusted that he would continue after that night? She had fallen for his charms, for his looks, and most of all just that amazing connection that she had thought they shared. How could she have been so wrong?

47

As the days of spring dwindled and the heat of summer set in, Matt threw himself into his work. Long days in the heat and dust were taking it out of him and he came home at night tired and cranky. Ethan wondered what was wrong with him. 'What's up big brother? You're out of sorts. Is it something I've done?'

Matt lay on his bed staring at the ceiling, his hands behind his head. He didn't look at Ethan when he spoke. 'No mate, nothing's wrong. Just hot and tired. Long days at work. What's happening with your scholarship offers?' He could tell that Ethan wasn't convinced, but at least he had changed the subject and no more questions came his way.

'I find out tomorrow. Miss Jackson said the offers will be emailed out. I'm a bit nervous. There are quite a few in year twelve who have gone for them.'

'You have the marks. You should get one.'

'I hope so.'

Ethan had retreated to his room and left Matt alone with the weight of his thoughts. Since the night at Elsie's, a deep sense of melancholy had settled over him. Nothing seemed to bring joy, and as much as he tried to join in with the conversations around the fire at night with the other workers, his heart just wasn't in it. The cloud of depression lingered and for a while he considered going to see her again. To apologise all over again and perhaps find a way to ease his guilt over what he had done. But the look of scorn on her face when she had seen him to the door, was etched into his memory, a reminder that trust had been lost. During the night, images of her face came to him in his dreams and he woke in a cold sweat, devastated that he couldn't reach out and stroke her arm or hold her tightly. He punched the pillow and stared at the wall. Like the trust he had failed to earn, sleep eluded him until the early hours of the morning, leaving him grappling with the consequences of his actions.

48

Sleep at night did not come easily to Elsie either and the couple of hours that she was managing to grab before the sun came up left her feeling run-down and exhausted. As the temperature rose into the high thirties, she once again emailed the department to request the air-conditioning in her apartment be fixed. She had given up asking Garranto and now went above his head. She was past caring what he thought and as the days passed she was more and more leaning towards the idea of leaving Matfield and moving to Townsville to teach. She would be near to Peter and Jane if she did that. Some of the other teachers were moving on also, and although she felt sorry for the students with so many changes, she knew that it wasn't her fault. It was a broken system and what she had observed over the past year made it easy to see why teachers either left the profession or moved to other schools that perhaps offered better support.

She counted down the weeks. Only two more to go.

She could make it. Just keep going she told herself as she pulled out of the carpark and onto the road. Thank goodness she had her red car. It would not have been practical to walk back and forth to work in this heat, and she gave silent thanks to her siblings for being so generous. As she drove down the road a few students waved to her. The girls' skirts were hitched up as high as they could go and their collared white blouses were tight on their teenage bodies. One of them tried to hide a cigarette behind her back and Elsie grimaced, but pushed it to the back of her mind. The group reminded her of her own school days. Short skirts, tiny blouses and walking with the boys to school. The solace of school. The one safe place in amongst the turmoil and chaos of their family life.

As she passed the group, she waved and continued down the road. She peered through the windscreen of the car after noticing a billowing mushroom cloud of smoke rising to the south of the town. There had been plenty of warnings about fires. The area further out had not had the rain the town had enjoyed and, with no rain forecast, everything was tinder dry. She looked again. The fire was large, and in the distance she could hear sirens as fire trucks raced towards the smoke. There was a new estate out that way and Elsie had ridden there on her bicycle before she got her car. Probably about thirty houses she thought. Brick houses on smaller blocks, all with similar fencing and carports. She had noticed their neat yards and similar style of buildings. 'It's where the rich people live,' Penny had told her. 'Garranto has a huge house out there. Imagine living next door to him.' She wondered how serious the fire was. Unused to rural fire seasons, she was unsure about the distances that fires travelled, or if that fire would endanger the town or school.

Pulling into the carpark at school she noticed some of the other staff getting into their cars and driving away. Elizabeth drove into the space next to her and gave her a wave. The two of them stood together, both peering at the cloud of smoke that seemed to be getting larger very quickly. 'We should be okay here,' Elizabeth said. 'The wind is going in the other direction. I'm not sure if that is the housing estate or the bush behind it. Those teachers and cleaners leaving are in the SES and rural fire service. They'll be sent out there to help.'

Elsie shielded her eyes from the sun and looked fearfully at the smoke. 'I've never seen a bushfire. There seems to be a lot of dust swirling around also.'

'Messy,' Elizabeth said. 'Dangerous, and hopefully it won't change direction. Let's go in. For sure there will be a meeting to let us know what's going on.'

For the first time, Elsie actually wanted to be at a meeting. She needed to know what they did in an emergency and what the news was on the fire.

STRANGELY IT WASN'T Garranto who spoke at the meeting. He was nowhere to be found and there were some whispers about where he was. One of the deputies took the meeting and Elsie listened carefully to the plans that would need to be put in place if the wind was to change and the fire unable to be contained. Everyone else seemed to know exactly what to do. They'd all been through this before.

As she walked back to the staffroom with Penny and Elizabeth, she listened to them talk about how the fire would be contained, and what the chances were of it jumping the river and crossing over into the property behind. Elizabeth turned to Elsie who was trying to get a glimpse of the smoke in between the school buildings. 'You do know how it started, don't you?' Elizabeth asked, her eyebrows high on her forehead and the most pious look on her face.

Penny added in. 'Elizabeth got all the goss from Bron up in the office.' Elizabeth stopped walking and they huddled in a group. She kept her voice low and looked around to make sure no students were listening. 'Not that it matters. The word will quickly get out. Bron from the office told me that Garranto's wife, Penelope, threw all his clothes, books and other belongings out into the middle of their yard. She piled them all up and lit a match. Set them on fire.'

Elsie took a sharp intake of breath, looking from Penny to Elizabeth. 'What?'

Elizabeth was now taking great delight in relaying the story and adding extra drama and emphasis to her words. 'Shoes, trophies, paintings that he'd done, clothes and,' she laughed and gave them a wicked smile, 'the piece de resistance, his beloved golf clubs. She raised her hands in the air. 'Poof! Gone! All of it.'

'You're joking,' Penny said, her eyes wide, her eyes blinking quickly.

'Gone. Everything. Up in smoke.'

The three of them stood wide-eyed, looking at each other. Elizabeth lowered her voice again and took on the tone of a stern teacher. 'The trouble was...' she paused for emphasis, 'the fire got away. Penelope got in her car and went into town to do some shopping. She thought she had put it out. She told the police when she left there was only a pile of ash left and a few metal pieces resembling the remnants of a golf club.'

'But it had got away?' Elsie questioned.

'Yes. It skimmed across their lawn, burnt the timber fence next door and then it took off. They have a heap of scrub at the back of their place and once it spread to there, nothing could stop it.'

'Where's Garranto?' Penny asked.

'Apparently, he's down at the police station also. The word is at this stage no property has been lost, although everyone is worried that the fire mightn't be contained. Even the policemen know about Garranto's antics and I can tell you I bet they're on his wife's side.'

'Will she get fined or go to jail?' Elsie asked.

'There's a fine, but Bessy said all the women Penelope plays bridge with have already started a collection to pay for her fine. They said anything left over will be donated to the local firefighters and SES. Bessy tells me there are already thousands of dollars donated. Penelope is a well-respected woman in this town. She's on a lot of committees and has helped a lot of people over the years, not to mention all the crap she's had to put up with from that dreadful man.'

49

The students were restless in class and Elsie eventually gave up trying to make them do any work. Assessment had been completed for the year and half the class was away attending work experience. Everyone was hot and bothered as well as worried about the fire. The smell of smoke wafted throughout the room, and as she passed handfuls of word searches around to fill in some time, she wondered if the firemen had been successful in putting the fire out.

When someone from the office came to collect Ethan from her class, she didn't think much of it. He had found out the week before that he had been awarded a scholarship for the course he wanted. When he had told her the exciting news, she had broken the rules and let him hug her. 'Thank you, Miss. I wouldn't have got through this year and done so well in English if it wasn't for you.'

'I couldn't be prouder of you, Ethan,' she said. 'You did it your way and you still received a scholarship. It will make so much difference for you.'

'It's thirty thousand dollars over four years, plus accommodation and meals. I still can't believe it.'

'You deserve it,' she told him. She wanted to know what his brother thought of his success in not only landing the scholarship but also receiving early notice of his successful entry. But she refrained from asking. Although Ethan hadn't mentioned anything about Matt, she had an idea that he sensed something wasn't right between the two of them.

Now she watched as he got up and followed the admin lady to the office. Perhaps he would receive some more information about the course, or further details about the university accommodation where he would be staying. She wandered around the room, stopping next to a student who put his hand up and waved the word search in front of her. 'Miss, look here in this word search. The C word is here. Look,' he pointed, 'right there. C U...'

'Stop,' she yelled out, causing the student to jump and stop speaking. Peering with dread at where he pointed, she gasped, her hand over her mouth. 'Trust you to find that one, Jaiden. I note that you have not found another word in the entire puzzle that you were supposed to, just that one.'

For a moment she contemplated collecting them all up and throwing them in the bin. She had downloaded the word search from the English Department folder so didn't really consider herself to be at fault. By now the rest of the class were talking noisily and helping each other find the word that Jaiden had been so clever to find.

As much as she tried she couldn't seem to stay out of trouble. Only last week she had received a lecture from Gantarro about a documentary she had shown without watching first. Surely, she wasn't expected to go through every word search, word by word. Although Gantarro had been leaving her alone lately, he had recently taken great delight in using her as an example at a staff meeting. He had gone on and on about the dangers of showing documentaries or films without fully watching them first. The intended shame he had tried to bring about for her had not worked, and instead when he name-shamed her and revealed the error she had made, his accusations backfired and the majority of teachers had laughed and talked over him when he was trying to continue his tirade.

Many of them had made an effort and found her after the meeting. 'Done similar myself heaps of time,' one of the history teachers told her.

'That's nothing,' a stern senior science teacher whispered. I accidentally put up a clip of Fifty Shades of Grey, instead of Grey Matter Science World. I'd walked out for a moment when the ads were playing before the clip, to get something from the staffroom. While I was absent the kids thoroughly enjoyed a very explicit sex scene. When I came back in, the class was in an uproar and I ripped the electrical socket and some other plugs out of the wall to stop the picture from showing up on the whiteboard. Of course, it was the last plug I pulled that stopped the film rolling. Your 'Travels through Rome' are nothing to worry about.'

The documentary Elsie had shown had been about a middle-aged English actor who was re-tracing the travels he had made in his twenties. The well-spoken English man had travelled around Europe in a tiny two-door car and was re-creating the journey, describing with great detail the buildings, culture and people as he went. The class had been enthralled, as had she, until right near the end he started explaining how many times he had enjoyed sex with a variety of different girls in the back seat of that tiny car. He twisted his body to show how cramped it had been and how they had to accommodate the squishy conditions. It had taken a while for her to respond, her mind stalling in shock as if she hadn't properly heard what he was saying.

When she hit every key on her computer to try and delete the images, the class roared with laughter and she felt her face burn as she pulled the plug out of the wall, unfortunately making the whiteboard screen freeze in a particular part where the actor was thrusting his body forward to demonstrate the difficulties he had encountered in the back of his tiny Fiat.

Elsie thought she had learned her lesson after that and she scrutinised every piece of work or film that was recommended for her use, even if it meant sitting up until midnight watching one documentary after the other. At least it would ensure there was nothing inappropriate for students to watch. Last week she had shown a travel documentary about Italy and the Renaissance. The class had been working on a writing piece that should reflect the architecture and style of the Renaissance period and she thought it a good idea to show a clip that depicted the very subject they were writing about. She had watched nearly all of the show at home the night before, but had fallen asleep before it finished. It had been suitable though. Nothing inappropriate was shown and no explicit language used. Just a run-of-the-mill travel journey through many of the amazing buildings and artworks she hoped would inspire some extraordinary writing. At the end of the film the narrator suggested that viewers go onto Google Earth and take the 3D, walk-through tour, of the famous Duomo in Florence.

Jaiden had been the first to get onto Google Earth and she was pleased that for once he seemed focused and interested in what they were learning about. She was even more impressed when he asked if he could project Google Earth onto the large whiteboard, and show the other students how to navigate their way through the different chapels, steps, and narrow walkways that led to the top of the church and ultimately the magnificent view of Florence.

Overcome by his enthusiasm, she agreed and watched as he plugged his laptop into the whiteboard system and started taking the students through the tour. Most of them watched his tour instead of bothering to look for it themselves. Typical she thought, whatever is easiest is what they want. The least amount of work the better was their standard motto.

Jaiden, much like today when he had promptly found the C word in amongst a million other letters, had a keen eye for detail and she was about to find out why he was so enthusiastic to share the scene. As he zoomed in on some of the graffiti that visitors had drawn on the walls at the top of the Duomo, she experienced a sinking feeling in her stomach. Swear words flashed across the screen and Jaiden zoomed in closer. The class gasped loudly and those who had not been watching Jaiden's tour all looked up. He had the full attention of the entire class.

'And here,' he said pointing to the screen, 'We have the fine art of Mr Michelangelo himself. Although you might notice it has been done with a Sharpie pen so maybe it's not that old.' He zoomed in to reveal a very detailed and explicit drawing, of firstly, the male reproductive system and then secondly, an even more detailed drawing of the female parts. The drawings were surrounded by other inappropriate drawings of couples in different sexual positions, the crude but well-done sketches larger than life on her classroom whiteboard.

'It's the Kama Sutra,' one girl called out. Another stood up and walked closer to the whiteboard to get a better look. The class erupted, the noise of everyone calling out and yelling what they considered to be funny remarks filling the classroom.

The drawings were well-crafted, very detailed caricatures, with some parts of the appendages enlarged to add emphasis to their importance. Behind the drawings were the rails surrounding the dome and then further beyond, a vast view of the city of Florence. The Renaissance style buildings stretched out in every direction, the red tiled roofs colourful and uniquely Italian. But no one was interested in that part of the picture. Their eyes were drawn elsewhere.

She strode across the room to Jaiden and his laptop, as the class erupted into louder laughter.

He grinned at her. 'It's graffiti Miss. Look there's some other drawings here that are even better. Men with men.'

Raising her voice she slammed his laptop down. 'Stop!' Unfortunately, the picture remained frozen on the screen and she pushed every button on the whiteboard, trying to turn the stupid thing off. When she finally pulled the plug out from the wall, thankfully the picture faded and then disappeared. The trouble was it was embedded in her and the entire class's memory.

Through gritted teeth she thanked Jaiden for sharing his findings and directed him to sit down. It had taken her ages to get the class to quieten down and to move on to the next task. Now, today again Jaiden had shown his tenacity in finding the extraordinary in the ordinary. In a classroom, it seemed, nothing was ever simple.

50

Ethan had burst into the room in a panicked state. Her heart leapt in her throat as she looked at his face. He was distraught and he strode across the room to her. Everyone quietened and she waited for him to speak. His words were choked. 'Matt's in hospital. He was helping with the fire and a tree fell on him. He's in a bad way. They say his leg is busted but mostly they're worried about head injuries.'

She led him into the middle room between the two classrooms. It was a small room and she pushed him down into a seat while she opened the dividing wall to gain Penny's attention. Penny came towards them, her face anxious when she looked at Ethan.

'Can you mind my class. They've got a word search to do. Matt's been hurt. Something to do with the fire. There's only half an hour left so I'm going to take Ethan and drive to the hospital, or wherever Matt is.'

Ethan looked up at them both. 'I spoke to the fella Matt works with. He said he thought they were flying him down to a Brisbane hospital. They were worried about a head injury.'

'That doesn't sound good,' Penny said. 'The trouble is you won't get a plane out of here for Brisbane. You'd have to drive to one of the larger towns and wait until there is a flight down that way. It might be quicker just to drive there.'

Ethan looked up at her and she knew straight away what they needed to do. She turned to Penny. 'I'm going to take Ethan now and try and find out some more information. Probably the best thing to do is grab some clothes and drive to Brisbane. Ethan needs to be with his brother.' She didn't add she also wanted to make sure that Matt was okay. She hoped with all her heart that he would be.

Penny nodded. 'I can take care of everything here. You've got the weekend and if you have to, take a couple of days off next week. Just drive carefully.'

'I will.'

They both stood up and she directed Ethan to grab his bag and follow her. Penny went in to talk to Elsie's class and she and Matt slipped out through Penny's classroom door. The last thing she wanted was to explain what was happening to the class. She just wanted to find out further details of the accident and see what they could do as soon as possible.

As they walked to the car, she rang the office. Thankfully she got Bron. 'I'm signing Ethan out and I'm leaving also. We'll head down to the police station first and find out what we can. Thanks, Bron,' she said, 'I will. Don't worry, I'll look after him and make sure we do everything we can.'

Jeff, the policeman, gave them some more informa-tion about what had happened. 'I was down there myself, at the fire that is. They'd nearly got it under control. Matt'd been fencing out there and was giving some of the Rural Fire blokes a hand moving livestock that were trapped in one of the corners of the bushland. A tree that had been burnt fell on him.' He stopped talking so much when he saw the distressed look on Ethan's face. Speaking slower, he lessened the details. 'I'm not sure what Matt's injuries are but they were concerned about his head being knocked by the tree, so they flew him straight down to Brisbane.'

'Was he conscious?' Elsie asked, her throat dry and dread building in her stomach.

Jeff's reply was short. 'No.'

ELSIE DROVE Ethan to where he and Matt lived. None of the other workers were there and she figured they must still be out where the fire was. Dark smoke drifted across the plains to the south and her mind whirled with the thought of what Matt's injuries might be. She waited on the doorstep while Ethan grabbed some clothes and food from the fridge. He closed the door behind him. 'The other fellas will keep an eye on everything. Thanks for being so helpful, Miss Jackson. I don't know how I'd get to Brisbane otherwise. The train doesn't run until Wednesday next week and there's no other way I could get down there.' His voice wobbled a bit. 'I need to be with him. He and I are all each other have. Do you think he'll be alright?'

She threw his bag in the back of the car. 'They don't seem to be able to tell us anything. When we get to my place, we'll ring the hospital and see what we can find out. That way we can also let them know you're coming.'

Thankfully Elsie got onto someone at the hospital who was very helpful. The woman's voice was calm and reassuring and she could tell she was someone who had dealt with these types of calamities before. 'Yes, the rescue flight has landed. Only a short time ago though,' she said. She did not have an up-to-date report on how the patient was but she could assure Elsie that if they were to drive to Brisbane, the patient, Matt Maloney, would be there. 'Do you have somewhere to stay?' she asked. Elsie and Matt looked at each other as they sat at the table in Elsie's apartment. She had put the phone on speaker so Matt could also hear the conversation. 'I suggest you try the Light Motel at Annerley. It's cheap plus it's clean and close to the hospital.'

'Thank you, Elsie replied. 'I guess we'll be there tomorrow if we start driving soon.'

'I'll be back on shift by the time you arrive. My name is Marion. Just look out for me and I'll try and help you however I can.' She told them where to go and who to ask for. 'They've just brought your Matt in, but that's all I can tell you at the moment. We will see you both tomorrow.'

Elsie grabbed a bag and threw some clothes into it. She gathered her toiletries and tried to think of anything else she might need. The drive to Brisbane would take just over ten hours. If they left now, they would at least have another four hours of light. That would let them reach the main highway and be off the backroads before it got dark. She didn't relish the idea of driving in the dark with so many kangaroos around. Not everywhere had experienced rain and the paddocks further south were dry. The wildlife would be looking for any hint of green grass on the sides of the roads.

'You alright?' she asked Ethan.

'Yep. Have you got everything you need?' he questioned her back.

'Yes. Let's get going.' As she got into her car and made sure Ethan was settled in and had everything he needed, her thoughts turned to Matt. Surely he would be okay. The fact that he had been taken to Brisbane worried her. That sounded serious. Stress filled her and she tried to remain calm. Matt was all Ethan had and the thought of anything happening to him was unbearable.

51

It had taken them ten hours to reach the outskirts of Brisbane. It was four o'clock in the morning and she glanced over at Ethan who had dozed off a few hours ago. The length of the drive didn't concern her although she was pleased when they turned onto the Bruce Highway and the distance between the small towns became less. As they passed more and more buildings and houses on the sides of the highway, the chances of hitting kangaroos or other wildlife diminished. Now they drove on well-lit highways that criss-crossed the outlying areas of Brisbane.

Light started to peep over the eastern horizon and she relaxed a little, grateful that they had reached their desti-nation without any problems. They had stopped a couple of times at service stations for petrol and some food, and it was amazing to see Ethan step into the role of adult instead of the student who she was more familiar with.

She asked him to ring ahead and book two rooms for them at the motel that the nurse had recommended. It did appear to be close to the hospital. 'We could get one room and I'll sleep on the couch or the floor,' Ethan said. 'This is going to cost a bit.'

'Don't worry about the cost. I have some spare money saved and I'm probably already in enough trouble for driving you here. We have to have two rooms.' She found it refreshing that he obviously didn't even think of the complexities of sharing a room. He thought of her as a teacher and to her he was a student and Matt's brother. She had no doubt that 'shit would hit the fan' when Gantarro found out that she had left school and taken Ethan with her.

The policeman had thought it a good idea for her to drive Ethan to Brisbane. He hadn't found anything odd about it, nor had Bron or Penny. The most important thing was to get Ethan to his brother. Matt would need someone there with him. At the thought of him lying alone in a hospital bed, her heart ached. Why hadn't she talked to him before now? Even if he didn't feel the same way about her as she did about him, they could have still been friends. They got on well and had shared stories and laughter. Blinking at the brightness of the street lights she thought how they had shared way more than that. If only there had been a better ending than what there had been.

52

———————

Ethan woke up as they neared the suburb where they would be staying. Elsie knew her way around Brisbane well and she had no trouble locating the rooms they would be staying in at Annerley. They were as the website described—practical, comfortable and close to public transport. As she threw her bag on the bed, she looked around the sparsely furnished room. The room was clean and it would do for now. She was paying for two rooms so they had wanted the cheapest they could find near to the hospital where Matt had been flown to.

Ethan was in the room next door and she told him they would meet back out at her car in half an hour. 'We need to have a shower, freshen up and we'll grab a coffee and maybe some breakfast before we go in. Is that okay?' From the look on his face, now that they had arrived, she could see he was in a state of anxiety. 'It will be okay, Ethan. We're here now and we'll get to Matt as soon as we can. They may not even let us in to see him if he's in the emergency ward. Go and have a shower. We've been sitting in that car for over ten hours.'

He had done as he was told, and when she met him back at her car, they both looked a lot better than what they had done half an hour earlier.

Ethan had changed into jeans and a neat collared shirt. He also had joggers on that looked new and he had neatened his hair. He looked much like Matt. Just a younger version. 'Thanks, Miss. I would have gone straight to the hospital. But you're right. It's better to clean up and feel refreshed.'

She had also changed and wore a floral skirt that came to just above her knee and a knitted top that fitted nicely. Thank goodness for Jane and her bag of clothes, she thought for the thousandth time. 'We might be at the hospital for a long time.' Nerves fluttered in her stomach when she thought of what they might find out. 'C'mon. Let's go.'

Ethan looked at her as she settled into the driver's seat. 'You know, Miss. I appreciate this. I'll pay you back for everything you've spent. There's no way I could have got here so fast without you. Thank you.'

'No worries, Ethan. You need to be here.'

BOTH WERE SUBDUED when they walked through the foyer of the hospital and the seriousness of the situation hit them with full force. The smell of a hospital, the sterile surroundings, and the staff who rushed around with folders or clipboards in their hands all relayed a sense of urgency and gravity. There were also other patients in wheelchairs and families and friends sitting anxiously, waiting for who knew what?

She put her hand on Ethan's shoulder. 'It's okay. Hospitals are a bit overwhelming. Just remember he's in the best place he can be.'

Ethan's voice was a whisper. 'Thanks, Miss.'

Elsie walked up to the front desk and was soon directed to another desk, then a room where they were told to take a seat and someone would see them soon. They sat in silence and she tried to stop fidgeting. It was nerve-wracking waiting and she was worried about Ethan whose face had drained of colour. They both jumped when the door opened and a doctor greeted them before sitting down across from them.

'I'm Doctor Best,' he offered his hand to them both. They shook it and Elsie introduced herself and then Ethan. 'Ethan is Matt's younger brother,' she said, the doctor nodding his head as he listened.

He explained to them what had happened. A large tree that had already been burnt in a previous fire had given way with the new flames and wind that had whipped up. 'Apparently your Matt was bringing some supplies to the firies when the entire tree came down on him. Luckily for him there were medical people out there and he received help straight away. It appeared though, that he had head injuries as well as a broken leg.' Ethan sat up straight and breathed in sharply. The doctor continued, 'We've got him settled now and we've already run a lot of tests.'

He paused and Elsie didn't breathe. Her body stiffened and she prepared herself for what was coming next. The doctor let out a long breath. His eyes were red and he looked like he hadn't slept in a long while. 'Matt appears at this stage to not have major head injuries. We feel that he has been severely concussed but there is nothing else there to suggest anything more sinister. The medics did the right thing flying him down here because this could have easily gone in another direction.'

Ethan's hand gripped Elsie's arm and for the first time since he had received the news a faint smile crossed his lips. 'So, he's going to be okay?' he asked.

'He still has other injuries. The leg is going to take a long while to heal and we will need to operate once everything else is okay. But yes, you could say he has escaped the worst.' The doctor stood up and Elsie and Ethan followed suit.

'Thank you so much,' Elsie said. 'This is the best news we could have hoped for.'

'You're welcome,' the doctor replied.

'When can we see him?' Ethan asked.

Doctor Best ran his hand through his hair and thought hard. 'I'd say by tomorrow you might be able to go in for a quick visit. Actually, if he comes out of this okay this morning, maybe I could let you sneak in to say hello this afternoon. How does that sound?'

Ethan gripped the doctor's hand, his eyes full of tears. 'Great. Thank you.'

Doctor Best covered Ethan's hand with his and squeezed it. 'Good. When he wakes, I'll tell him his brother and sister are here to see him.'

Elsie went to contradict him, but he had already started to leave the room. No doubt he had a line of patients and families to talk to. They stood looking at each other. 'Okay, now we have a sister,' Ethan said, a smile on his face.

'I was going to say something, but he left,' Elsie said.

'It doesn't matter. Nothing does. Nothing except Matt is going to be okay.'

53

Matt had woken to white walls and stark surroundings. He looked straight down to his arm where a tube pumped something into his veins. He closed his eyes and felt the thumping in his head. His eyes shot open and he tried to look down at his legs. Something had happened. Fire. Trucks. Smoke. Men in orange uniforms. Burnt out paddocks and bushes. A tree. He drifted back to sleep.

When he woke again later, he looked up to see a nurse moving tubes around that were attached to some sort of machine. Now and again the machine beeped and she pressed buttons, shaking her head and pushing more to stop the beeping. She readjusted some other tubes and turned around to look at him. 'Oh my. Look at you my love,' she said. 'Mr Blue Eyes. It's nice to see them finally open.' She was middle aged and her words comforted him, even though he had no idea where he was.

'Where am I?'

'PA Hospital, Brisbane. A tree fell on you and they

flew you down here so we could put you back together again.' She moved his sheets around and adjusted something down near his feet.

'My leg. Is it still there? I can't feel it.'

'That's good. Yes, it's still there but it's broken and you're pumped full of painkillers.'

'Oh,' he tried to move his legs, but neither would budge.

'It was your head we were worried about. The doctor will fill you in, but everything seems to be going okay.'

He ran his tongue around his mouth which was drier than the worst hangover he had ever had. 'Can I have some water, please?' he asked.

'My name is Janice and I'll be looking after you 'til change of shift this afternoon. We'll have to wait until the doctor comes, and then we can ask about water and what the program is going to be for your recovery. How does that sound?'

Matt instantly liked Sister Janice. She was matter-of-fact; from the way she moved around and did things he could tell she knew her stuff. He sank back into the pillow. He was in good hands.

HE MUST HAVE DRIFTED off to sleep because the next time he opened his eyes a doctor was looking down at him. The doctor's face broke into a smile when Matt opened his eyes and he tried to smile back. His lips felt dry though and he wasn't sure if he moved any muscles in his face. Janice leaned over him from the other side of the bed and put some ointment on his lips.

'You've had a narrow escape, young man,' the doctor said. 'Severe concussion and a broken leg. All the tests are good and by tomorrow or the day after we'll move you up into the ward.'

Matt's mind had started to clear a bit and he asked the doctor a string of questions. Doctor Best filled him in on everything that had happened, right from when the firies had rescued him from under the burning tree, to the flight to Brisbane and then the last twenty-four hours. He had been lucky. He managed to hold one of his bandaged hands up and he looked at it like it didn't belong to him.

'You're on painkillers,' Janice said. 'Things might appear a bit different at the moment.'

'Is that why I feel so sleepy?' he asked. 'What's wrong with my hands.'

'You have a few minor burns on your hands. That's why we have the bandages on them. Nothing serious though. You were lucky the men got to you quickly.'

They'd talked for a bit longer until he could no longer keep his eyes open. The last thing he remembered the doctor saying was, 'I've given permission for your brother and sister to visit you this afternoon.'

As he drifted off, he thought how the doctor must have mixed him up with someone else. One, he didn't have a sister and two, Ethan was in Matfield, no doubt without Matt there to supervise, eating everything in the fridge and cupboard.

54

J anice had come back in just as he woke up. She bustled around and his eyes followed her. He was in awe of her and the other two nurses who came in and out during the day. So professional and caring even though he could tell from their chatter they were tired and had worked long shifts. 'You're awake, young Matt. And might I say looking much better than this morning.'

He moved a little in the bed, stiffening quickly as he felt a shooting pain in his leg. Broken leg. That's right. He'd need a bit of time to get his head around that one. Janice must have noticed him wince.

'You need to stay still. Doctor Best is coming in to see you this evening to let you know what's going to happen next in your recovery. No use thinking too far ahead until you see him.'

'Thanks, Janice.' He threw a smile her way and was rewarded with one back.

She wiped a cool washer over his face and it felt like

the best sensation in the world. His thoughts were still a little jumbled, but the series of events, and what he had wrong with him, were starting to settle into his mind a little more each time he woke up.

'I'm going to leave you for a short while. Cuppa time for me. You have visitors.'

'Really?'

'Who?'

'Your brother and sister. They're only allowed to stay for a short visit. But it will do you good. Just say when you've had enough, though. You need your rest. Here, press this.' She handed him a buzzer. 'One of the other nurses will come in and I'll let them know that it's a sign you need your visitors to go.' With that she bustled out of the room, leaving the door open for the two people who entered.

At first, he only saw Ethan. His younger brother wore an anxious look and was dressed in clothes he would normally wear out to somewhere special. Ethan approached his bed and when Matt put his arm up, his younger brother gently gripped his bandaged hand with both of his. Matt felt a tear slide down his cheek as the enormity of what had happened hit him. He might have died under that tree and then who would have looked out for Ethan? 'Good to see you, brother,' Matt said, using his other bandaged hand to wipe his tears away.

Ethan looked a bit shocked and Matt could see his eyes moving around the room taking in all the tubes and machines that surrounded the bed. 'It's okay Mate,' he said. 'I'm going to be okay. Doc says most of this stuff'll get taken off tonight. It's just my leg they have to work on. Luckily my hard head is okay.'

Ethan was struggling to keep his tears back and Matt waved their lightly gripped hands from side to side when his brother's words eventually came. 'I thought you were going to die. I didn't know what I'd do without you.'

'It's okay, Ethan. Everything is going to be okay. Not sure how I'm going to function with a broken leg, but considering what it could've been, I feel very lucky.'

Matt drew his eyes away from Ethan's when he noticed someone else standing behind him. His heart leapt in his chest and this time his tears flowed, his bandage brushing continually across his face as he tried to wipe them away. Through the blur of tears, he saw a tissue that Ethan was offering. He took it and composed himself. 'Elsie. What are you doing here?'

She didn't speak and he could tell she wanted to but the words wouldn't come. Her eyes never left him. He reached out and she took his bandaged hand gently in hers as his smile tried to dispel the worried expression on her face. 'You've brought Ethan here, haven't you? I wondered how he got here so fast. Only you would get him here that quickly.'

She still didn't speak and it appeared to him that she was trying to stay composed. He looked from Elsie to Ethan, a surge of warmth and love filling him. No matter what was broken or burnt, he knew he was going to be okay. He reached out and took her hand from where it hung by her side. Gently pressing her hand to his cheek he closed his eyes. 'Are you the sister?'

55

Elsie had found no words when she stood next to the hospital bed and looked down at Matt's scratched and bruised face, the bandages on his hand and the cast on his leg. Goodness only knew what the rest of his body had suffered. The reaction she had to the drip going into his arm and the noise of the machines monitoring him, had caught her off guard. It had been a long time since she had visited someone in hospital or been in one herself. Her thoughts raced back to a time when she had needed to have her tonsils removed. She had only been ten and she couldn't recall who had dropped her off. No one had stayed with her though and she had been alone in a bed, in a room full of other kids who all had a parent, siblings or other friends and family as visitors. When it was visiting hours, she would pretend she was asleep. Lying still in her bed she could hear the other conversations going on between the kids and those who had come to visit.

What would it feel like to have someone care about

you so much that they had taken weeks off work to sleep next to your bed at night? How many hours could a father or mother sit beside a bed and even sleep on it during the day? What was it like to be spoilt with new toys or yummy things to eat? The memories came back to her like it was yesterday. She hadn't thought of that time for years and she sniffed the air. It was the smell. The same smell that all hospitals had.

She had some type of infection after the tonsil operation and stayed in hospital for a week. The nurses had fussed over her and spoilt her with books and a pack of cards that had remained her favourite possession for a long while afterwards. Her mother had not been there to reassure her though, and she remembered being in pain and frightened about what was happening to her. When it had come time to leave, her mother was four hours late picking her up. It seemed just like yesterday that she had sat in the room next to where all the nurses were, waiting to be collected.

Back then she had been grateful to see her mother. Goodness knows why. She had received no comfort, sympathy or attention. There had only been lectures about how much trouble she was and how much money her mother had to waste on a taxi to get to the train station to come and pick her up. She had sat next to her on the train ride home and then walked in the hot sun to get back to their house, feeling like she was the biggest nuisance in the world.

Now, when she tried to talk to Matt no words would come out. Her heart palpitated with anxiety when she looked into his eyes All she could think about was the tubes and machines, a childhood experience; memories that had laid dormant for years. But then he smiled, and her memories slipped away and she smiled back. She had missed him so much. His face, his laughter, and most of all his companionship. Now she was here right next to him. Her heart plunged though. Just because she had brought Ethan to the hospital, nothing had changed. Matt had said what he thought. He had made a mistake.

She stepped back and let Ethan talk, but when Matt reached out, she moved beside the bed, took his hand, and looked properly at him. It was strange to see him laid up and she wanted to push the hair back from his forehead and wipe his tears.

His comment about being his sister had broken her reverie. 'That was not my fault,' she said, her voice quiet. 'The doctor assumed that and we didn't have time to correct him.'

'It's a good thing.' He looked towards a sign on the wall. 'Family only, allowed in this section.'

Their smiles held and she found it hard to drag her eyes away from him. Ethan thankfully broke the moment. 'Elsie and I are staying at Annerley. We have a room each and it's not far from here. Elsie helped me pack up what I needed and she drove straight here.'

'The school knows. I signed him out at the office. We drove straight through,' she added. 'I took it easy though. I was a bit worried about kangaroos, but we had no problems.'

'Thank you. You have no idea how good it is to see both your faces. No idea.'

'The nurse said they're going to operate on your leg tomorrow and that you might get out in a few days,' Ethan said.

'Yeah, the doc did mention that. He's worried about who's going to look after me when I get back home. Patrick left me a message and said that work will pay me compo and that I'm not to worry about money or income. They'll cover what's needed.' He sighed. 'I guess that's a good thing but I'm not sure how I'm going to cope with not going to work, or being cooped up in that small donga.'

Elsie could see that Matt was starting to get tired. The exertion of seeing them and then talking so much about what had happened was starting to take its toll. 'I think Ethan and I should go. You look tired.'

'I don't want you to go, but,' he closed his eyes and then opened them again. 'I am starting to doze off. Painkillers. Got to get off them. The doctor will give me more info tomorrow after the operation.'

She'd wanted to give him a kiss on the cheek before she left but she didn't. At least they seemed to be friends again. If that was what he wanted she'd have to settle for just friendship. At the moment all she cared about was that he was going to be okay.

56

The visit the following day had also been short. The operation had been performed in the morning and had gone well, but Matt was still groggy and they only stayed long enough to say hello, let him know they were around and would see him the following day.

It had been upsetting to see him in the state he was in and once again Elsie's thoughts were dragged back to her lonely memories of being in hospital. Ethan had gone for a walk in the city but she had declined to join him. She was tired. Tired from the drive, tired from worrying about Matt and also just worn out from the end of the school year. The minute her head hit the lumpy pillow in the motel bed she was asleep.

She woke to her phone ringing. An unknown number. Sitting up, she answered it. 'Elsie Jackson speaking,' she said.

'I hope I haven't got you at a bad time. It's Lea Smith

here. I'm the deputy at the primary school. Mrs Berry gave me your number.'

'Hi. It's not a bad time. Is everything alright?'

'Yes, it's fine. Your principal, Mr Garranto, has had to take leave and they've brought me in to do his job until the end of the term, which,' she chuckled, 'thankfully for all of us, is just around the corner.'

Elsie was intrigued as to why Lea was ringing her. She listened as the deputy continued. 'I've been filled in about what happened to Ethan Maloney's brother and how you drove Ethan down to Brisbane. Penny tells me you're a family friend of theirs.'

'Yes, that's right,' she replied, in her mind a drum roll playing in her head as she waited for the tirade that no doubt would follow.

'I just want to check if you need the entire week off. It's not a problem if you do. I can see you haven't taken a day off all year and there isn't much happening here at school with it being so near to the end of the year. I have an extra teacher here who is more than happy to take your classes. Before I put anything into place, I just wanted to check with you first that those arrangements would suit you.'

'Um, yes. Thank you. That's an unexpected offer but I might take you up on it. Matt is doing fine. The head injury is not as bad as they thought it would be, and he's just had his leg operated on today. All things considered, he's been lucky; Ethan is a lot calmer now that's he's with his brother. If I was able to have the week off, there's a possibility that I might be able to drive Matt back home when he's allowed out.'

'Excellent! Lea said. 'That sounds like a plan. Don't

worry about anything at this end, it'll all be taken care of, and if you happen to need some extra time off just ring me back. You have my number now. The main thing is that you look after your friends and yourself. The teachers I know, and the high school students I've worked with when they come here for work experience, have always spoken very highly of you. Everyone is worried for Ethan's brother and it'll be good to let them know that he's doing well and is being taken care of. Righto. I'd better go. I have some other phone calls to make to ensure the next two weeks run smoothly. Adios and I look forward to talking to you when you get back. Don't forget, just ring if you need more time.'

Elsie still held the phone to her ear, even for a long time after Lea had hung up. She was in a state of shock. Had she just had that conversation or had she dreamt it? How long was this deputy going to be staying and how long was Garranto going to be gone for? Intriguing. No doubt Penny would fill her in when she talked to her next. She lay back down on the bed and stretched out. An entire week off. In Brisbane. And she would still get paid.

THE WEEK PASSED QUICKLY and although it seemed like there would be a lot of spare hours, the visits to the hospital, getting there and back, took up most of their time. Every time they visited, Matt had improved and now that the bruising had gone from his face and arms, and the hand bandages were off, he looked a bit more like the Matt of old. She sensed none of the antagonism or unfriendliness that he had shown when they had argued, and she once again relaxed in his company, falling into the ease of conversation had by good friends. Once he was able to think clearly, he made sure that he had given Ethan money that would not only pay for their accommodation but also any food or other items they needed. At first she had refused, but he had been adamant and threatened to get out of the bed and walk her to the canteen downstairs if she refused. 'You've lost weight, Elsie. Are you eating okay? I know you live by a strict budget, you told me that once. If you don't take this money and spend it on food, I will make a scene.'

She had given in and that afternoon she and Ethan walked down to the Brisbane River to sat in one of the restaurants, just like it was the sort of thing that they did every day. Ethan ate so much she thought he would burst and she had to agree it was the best steak she had ever tasted. She had gone even further and ordered dessert and then coffee. If Matt was going to insist on paying and leave her no options, then she should make the most of it.

So far she hadn't been alone with him. Ethan was always there. She wondered if he would act differently once his brother wasn't around. Would he make sure she knew they were only friends and that the 'mistake' was never going to happen again? Or would he thank her for bringing Ethan down to Brisbane, and treat her like she was just Ethan's teacher and nothing more?

The questions bounced around in her mind as she opened the door to his hospital room and went to walk in. Ethan was behind her and they both stopped in shock at the sight of Matt standing on crutches next to his bed. 'The family has arrived,' Janice said. 'You're a lucky man to have these two to look after you.'

'They've been here every day,' he said, sitting back down on the bed. 'I couldn't ask for anything more.'

Janice positioned his leg and started running off a list of instructions for Ethan and Elsie about how to look after him once they got him back home. 'Main thing is,' she patted Matt firmly on the back. 'He's going to have to do as he's told. Do you hear me, young Matt?' She manoeuvred herself around so that her face was in front of him. 'Do as you're told and don't do anything stupid. It's going to be a long recovery and you don't want to mess around with that leg.'

'Yes Ma'am,' he quipped, saluting her as she straightened up.

'He'll need all the help he can get,' she turned towards Elsie and Ethan. 'But you two look capable and I'm hoping that your sister here is as bossy as most are?'

Elsie folded her arms. 'He will do as he's told. I'm also a teacher, so I'm extra bossy. Don't worry, he won't get away with anything. Ethan and I will make sure he rests and does his exercises when he's supposed to. I'll keep a daily report for you.'

Matt frowned. 'I'm not used to anyone telling me what to do.'

'Well get used to it,' Janice said as she repositioned his pillow. She passed and raised her eyebrows, before pretending to cough. 'Your ha hum, sister here will make you rest. You have a couple more days here and then these two are going to drive you home.'

57

———————

Elsie had been on the phone with Peter and Jane throughout the week. When they asked if there was anything between her and Matt she reassured them that there wasn't, and that she was in Brisbane as a support for Ethan and now to help Matt get back home.

Jane had plenty to talk about with her new romance going stronger than ever. She had loved being part of Sam's family when they drove up to Cairns to visit them. 'His family argue sometimes but then they make up and just get on with it,' she told Elsie. 'It's so different to anything I've ever experienced before. I love it. They're all so caring and make sure they include me in everything.' She paused and then added. 'Sam has told me he loves me. Did you hear me, Elsie? He said he loves me.'

Elsie laughed on the other end of the line. 'I heard you. Be careful. You're both only young and you don't want to go rushing into anything.'

'We've talked about the future. We both have years of

study in front of us, so we'll see how we go in the next few years. At the moment I'm just loving going out with him and spending time with him and his family. It makes me realise how much we missed out on growing up.'

'We did. But now you have everything ahead of you. Don't look back.'

'I don't. We all need to move on and hopefully one day we'll all have our own kids.'

Peter had also been up for a chat. 'Actually, I thought about Matt last week. The company I work for are looking for a new employee. They want someone who's in their twenties or thirties and is interested in pursuing study in the field of Veterinary Science. They're having trouble finding people. Everyone heads out to the mines. It's quicker to reach the big pay and I don't think many people are prepared to put in all the years of study or pay the uni fees. They're talking about something like I have. An internship, where you work and learn on the job and then they pay for the study. It's probably not a good time to broach the idea to Matt, but from what he told me that day at the rock pool, this type of job was all he ever used to dream about.'

Elsie thought long and hard before replying. 'He's a bit stubborn about staying in the fencing business. His problem is he doesn't think he's capable of doing Vet Science now that he's been out of school for so long. He didn't finish year twelve.'

'They're not worried about that, and that's why they're chasing a mature age person. As long as he passes some of their tests, they can get him entry to university through different avenues. It's a lot of years of study as you know, but it would be well worth it if that's what he wants.'

'I'm not sure he'd be open to those ideas at the moment. He really doubts his academic ability, which is probably nonsense going on what he has told me, his marks when he left school were above and beyond anyone else in his year level.' She thought for a bit. 'Just look at Ethan. He's probably much the same as he is. He's really in the realm of the gifted and talented. Not just smart, there's a difference and when you see the work Ethan does, it's way beyond what other kids hand in.'

'So do you think Matt'd be interested?'

'Why don't you email the forms or whatever is needed to me? I'll talk to Ethan about it and see what he thinks. Perhaps if we approach this together, Ethan and I, we might be able to convince him. We have a lot of hours to waste on that drive home. Send the info through and thanks, Peter, it's good of you to think of him.'

58

___

The night before they were due to drive back to Matfield, Elsie read over the job proposal and selection criteria. The company Peter worked for were after someone exactly like Matt. They wanted someone with a bit of life experience and who had done different jobs. They needed to be in their mid-twenties to thirties, keen to study, loyal and hardworking. They preferred someone who had completed their senior years of study but they were willing to take an application from someone who hadn't. They could apply as long as they were prepared to put in the hard yards, both working in the veterinarian business and then undertaking study. The point that might not sit well however, was that the applicant had to be prepared to work and live in Townsville. Basic accommodation would be provided that would suit a couple and also a pet if needed.

She read over the last bit time and time again. Even if Matt was interested in the job, she didn't think he would be prepared to move to Townsville. Then again, Ethan would be living there next year and going to university and ... she tapped her pen on the table, the doctor had said that it would be six months before Matt would be able to return to work as a fencer. The break had been tricky to fix and if he had an office job or one that didn't require physical activity, he would have been able to resume work earlier, but fencing—the doctor had shaken his head and looked sternly at Matt. 'None of that strenuous hard work for at least six months.'

59

Even with the visits back and forth from the hospital Elsie had managed to fit in some extra sleep and long walks that had taken her in different directions through the inner Brisbane suburbs. They weren't areas that she had been that familiar with when she lived in Logan. Coming from the outer southern suburbs, the only time she had passed through these places was when she caught the train to her cleaning job in the city.

When she wandered through the parks that spread out along the reaches of the river, she mused about how her life had changed from the one she had when she lived in Resilience Street. The sprawling fig trees above her threw a shady canopy to walk under and she dawdled, content to watch the rowers on the river and the occasional riverboats that raced along, filled with passengers on their way to the city. It was a far different world from where she had grown up and vastly different to

Matfield. Where would she eventually end up, she wondered? Would she one day want to return to Brisbane or another city, or was she destined to live her life in small rural towns, teaching country kids?

She stopped and watched a young family as they made their way along the concrete footpath that followed the course of the river. The young dad pushed a pram that had a baby in the top part and a toddler sitting in a seat at the front. He was dressed in tidy shorts and shirt, and while one hand pushed the pram the other held fast to his wife's hand. She had long hair that was tied back in a ponytail and she looked back and forth over the river, pointing different things out to him. Elsie couldn't hear their conversation, but from the look on their faces she could tell they were both talking and happy about being together. A child that was maybe about six rode a push-bike just in front of them, every so often stopping and turning around to make sure he wasn't getting too far in front of them.

They looked like the perfect family and she watched them, envious of their togetherness. It was a big city and, although there were a lot of people around, now that she wasn't with Matt and Ethan, she felt like a speck on the grass, as if she didn't belong to anyone or that no-one belonged to her. A heavy feeling filled her and she watched the family until they rounded the corner and were no longer visible. At least at Matfield she had some good friends at the school, people who cared about her. And then there was Matt. She started walking, her pace getting faster and faster as she tried to push the thoughts of him from her mind.

THAT AFTERNOON she made her way to Southbank and caught up with her train friends, Maurie and Matilda. Neither had changed a bit and they still had the same funny stories about the people they came across as they completed their jobs. Once she had asked them what seemed like a million questions about what they had been up to, they then started firing questions at her. She had rung them a couple of times over the last year but they had only been short conversations. Now they wanted to know everything.

'What are the kids like?' Matilda asked. 'I bet country kids are more polite and better behaved than these ratbags in the city. They don't even get up to give me a seat on the train. No manners.'

'You'd be surprised, Matilda.' She thought about the kids she had taught this year. 'Kids are the same wherever you go. They have their share of different problems and don't worry, some of them can be just as rude as the ones you find in the city. Overall though, I have loved teaching them. They're great kids and I feel like I've found my feet and confidence this last term. The teachers have also been helpful.' She left out of the titbits around Garranto and his crew. It was too long to go into, besides who would believe some of the antics that occurred at the school.

Maurie hugged her tightly when it was time to say goodbye. 'We think of you often and wonder how you're going. All those years you struggled with the jobs and study. Mighty proud of you, Elsie. You've really found your spot.'

Matilda was emotional and Elsie found it hard to say goodbye. It might be a long while until she saw them again. 'Now all you need is a good man,' Matilda said. 'A decent, kind, hard-working fella who will look after you.'

She laughed. 'I don't need anyone to look after me. You know me. I've always managed to look after myself.'

As she sat on the bus heading back towards Annerley, she thought about how she was so used to being alone. Was it always going to be that way? She sighed as she looked at the peak-hour crowds rushing along the footpaths, the roads choked with traffic. At least she was living and working somewhere different, and when she went back maybe she'd spruce up her apartment a bit. She'd have to find something to fill in her time. Just her, she thought. It was always just her.

By the time Elsie returned to Matfield she felt rested. A week in Brisbane away from school and her classes had done her the world of good. The trip back had been longer because they needed to stop every so often so that Matt could get out and move around. They had stacked pillows around him on the back seat and his broken leg was stretched out with more pillows propping it up. Elsie could see that the trip was tiring him, so she made sure to stop in the afternoon so that they could all have a break from the car. 'Stop at that motel there,' Matt called out from the back.

'That looks expensive,' she replied. 'I think there's an older one up further here.'

'Pull over now, or I'll jump out,' he laughed and leaned forward, tapping her on her arm.

Matt sent Ethan in to book two rooms. 'Here take my card. Don't worry about the cost. I'm paying. We all need to be comfortable for the rest of the drive tomorrow.'

Matt and Ethan shared a room while Elsie stayed in another. She had argued with Matt about paying for her room but she had not got her way.

'There is no way you're paying. You've done enough for us. Maybe sometime you should do as you're told.' He had probably meant it as a joke but his remarks had annoyed her. Who was he to tell her what to do and why should she listen to him? To him, she was just a 'mistake', an accidental interlude that he had done everything to forget about.

***

The next day they started early. With Ethan in the front seat next to her, she concentrated on talking to him about his plans after leaving school. The conversation flowed and Matt often joined in. A couple of times when she looked back at him, he had drifted off to sleep. His eyes were closed and a peaceful look rested on his face. As the doctor had said, it was going to be a long recovery to get the full use of his leg back to normal.

Ethan was due to sit his driver's test shortly, so they had discussed how getting his licence soon might help, as Matt wouldn't be able to drive for quite a while. She offered any help she could give. I'll be on school holidays and I have nothing else to do. I'll do the groceries for you and pick up anything else you need.

Now, as they pulled into the dusty driveway where Matt and Ethan lived, she thought about how difficult it was going to be for Matt. The donga was small with not much room to move around. Summer was in full swing and outside was hot and dusty where the men spent their spare time, sitting around the fire and sharing their stories.

It was a Saturday and Matt's workmates were there to greet him. Patrick had laid out a path made out of rubber matting, which might be easier to navigate with crutches rather than the undulating dusty ground. Rusty had a basket filled with fruit waiting on the table outside Matt's donga, as well as some groceries. An awning someone had rigged up was attached to the donga, throwing some shade from the unrelenting sun. A collection of chairs and a table were placed under it. The group of men welcomed them home and Elsie found herself chatting to them like she had always known them. They were friendly as she had met some of them at the pub over the past year. However this was the first time she'd had a proper conversation with any of them.

Now they made sure she sat down at the table with them. Pedro put out plates and cutlery and Patrick arrived with platters of salad and cold meats. They had prepared a huge spread and Ethan's eyes lit up like lights on a Christmas tree. Food. And lots of it.

Patrick reassured Elsie that they would look after Ethan and Matt when they were here. It might just be a bit tricky when they were out working, although Ethan would be around to help out.

'I'll be here Wednesday afternoon to pick him up,' she

told them, 'to pick him up and take him for his visit to the doctor in town.'

'Oye. Don't talk about me like I'm not here,' Matt said, a wide grin on his face. He leaned back in his chair and she could tell he was happy to be home, amongst his friends and familiar surroundings.

Ethan added, 'The nurse at the hospital told him he has to do as Miss Jackson tells him. She was a bit scary. I think he needs to do as he's told.'

They all laughed and Elsie thought now was a good time to leave. She didn't want to outstay her welcome. When she stood up, she could feel Matt's eyes follow her as she walked around the table and said goodbye to everyone. She waved to him and he waved back, giving her a huge smile. He looked tired but happy. 'Thank you,' he said. 'Thank you for everything. You looked after both of us and I don't know what we would've done without you.'

She dismissed his gratitude. 'I'll see you Wednesday afternoon at four. Ring me if you need anything and in the meantime do everything as you were told to.'

WHEN SHE DROVE AWAY from Matt it felt strange. He had been a constant in her life for the past week and now she almost felt as if she was deserting him. But he had Ethan and the other men there to help him. He would be fine. Now she needed to re-organise her life and get everything ready for the last week of school. One more to go and then the school year would be ended. Six weeks of holidays loomed ahead of her.

When she pulled into her apartment block, she sat in the car for a while before getting out, staring out through the front windscreen. Six weeks. What was she going to do? Most of the other teachers were going away. Some of them were travelling overseas or going on cruises. Maybe she should start saving to go somewhere. She'd have to go by herself, but that was okay. She was used to going solo. That's what she'd do. Save for a trip. She needed something to aim for, otherwise life didn't seem to have any purpose.

Waiting for Eliza to come out and spy on her, she was surprised when there was no movement of curtains or Eliza's door didn't swing open. The apartment looked empty and the small table and chairs plus the ugly cactus pot plant that were usually out the front had disappeared. Eliza's car was not in the carpark and even the broom that always leaned against her front wall was missing. Had she moved out? Wouldn't that be nice, she thought.

Walking inside her apartment she stopped and looked around. Everything was just as she had left it and it seemed strange that it was just over a week since she and Ethan had left. It seemed a lot longer. The road at the front was quiet and she realised that she had been surrounded by noise for the last week; cars, traffic, the sounds of the hospital, and then over the last couple of days, the chatter between Ethan and Matt as well as the noisy banter of the men who worked with Matt.

Picking up a drooping plant that was badly in need of water she went to the kitchen sink to water it. The water soon filled the pot and she stood there for a long while, looking out the window at nothing much in particular. A galah landed on the fence nearby and when she moved to see it better, it cocked its head to the side as if it was looking at her. Another one soon joined it and then some more, until there was a line of them on the fence. They seemed to be staring at her. She scowled back at them as she spoke aloud, 'Yep. Just me. Just me and you guys.'

It was refreshing to immerse herself in the work routine, especially with only a few days remaining. The students had gradually tapered off as some of them began their holiday break early. Ethan was there on Monday and Tuesday. The school bus had stopped running so Patrick drove him in and picked him up in the afternoon. 'I can drop you home Wednesday if you like,' Elsie offered Ethan. 'I'm picking Matt up for his doctor's visit so we can go there together after school.'

'That would be great. It'll save Jeremy a trip.'

MATT WAS WAITING outside the dongas and waved as she drove in and parked next to where he stood. The other men must still be at work, she thought, because there didn't seem to be anyone around.

Matt looked so much better than he had last week. The colour had come back to his face and she was pleased to see him standing without too much trouble when she walked towards him. Ethan disappeared into the donga, calling out as he went inside. 'Gotta eat. Be back out soon.'

Matt pulled out a chair next to him. 'Come and sit. You must be tired after work. I should have got one of the fellas to take me in.'

He had a jug full of cold water waiting, the ice floating on the top as he poured her a drink. He pulled a tea towel away from a plate, exposing an array of biscuits and cake. 'Rusty's wife's been sending out food for us. You should see the fridge. It's full. Ethan's in his element.'

She relaxed back in the chair and sipped her drink. Beyond where they sat the paddocks stretched out, a dusty haze settling on the horizon. She could see the outline of the mountains where they had walked to the rock pools and she thought about that day and what a great time they had all had together.

'Are you thinking about the rock pool?' he asked, as if he could read her mind.

'I am. It was a lovely day. I often think about it.'

Matt asked about Peter and Jane and she answered his questions, adding that they had been asking after him and wished him all the best for his recovery.

She wondered if she should talk to him about the internship that Peter had sent the paperwork through for, but thought better of it. He'd only give all the negatives about why it wouldn't be any good for him. Plus, he had plenty of other things to think about at the moment, mainly about recovery and rehabilitation exercises.

When she walked with him to the car she was surprised at how much better he was moving, even within the space of a few days. 'I'm going to have to go back to work earlier,' he told her as he got into the passenger's side of the car. 'I'll go stir crazy sitting around here for a month, never mind six. I can't do it.'

She started the car. 'You don't have a choice. You're going to have to be patient. It was a major break.'

'Patient. That's something I'm not good at.'

'Well. That's the way it is.'

'You're not very sympathetic.'

She glanced over at him. He also looked at her, waiting to see what her response was. 'No, I'm not sympathetic towards anyone who doesn't want to help themselves, and in this case that means you need to do what is required to get the leg working properly again. The nurses made it very clear you were to do as you're told and this would be not a quick fix.'

He looked away and stared out the side window. It was almost like he wanted to say something but thought better of it. They drove the rest of the way in silence and he didn't speak until they pulled up outside the doctors. 'Can we go to the café or even have an early meal at *The Fortress* before you drop me home? I need to get out. It's only been a few days but I'm telling you, I'm going to go nuts stuck out there with no work. There're only so many crosswords you can do and I'm over watching movies already.'

She opened the car door for him. 'It's up to you. If that's what you'd like to do. I'm not exactly dressed for the restaurant but I don't have anything else to do. Did you want to go for a drink at the pub?'

He answered quickly. 'No. No alcohol.'

'Right.'

61

———

By the time Matt came out from his doctor's visit it was six o'clock. Thank goodness there was a slight breeze to ease the heat of the day. 'How about we go to the new café on the main street,' she offered. 'Apparently, they make great hamburgers.'

'That'd be perfect. I'll admit I'm a bit tired but I have enough energy for that and I don't want to go straight home.'

The new café did have delicious food and she was pleased she had suggested it instead of the restaurant. *The Fortress* threw up too many memories of their last night there and she didn't want to have alcohol either when she was with him. It had caused enough trouble last time.

A large milkshake each and a huge hamburger that Ethan would have loved filled them both. They laughed when they shared stories that had happened when he was in hospital. and she felt like they had gained the rapport back that they once had.

When she dropped him home, he kissed her on the cheek and held her hand. 'You've done so much for us Elsie. Sometimes I don't think I deserve it. You're amazing.'

'Pleased to be able to help,' she said as she made a hasty retreat to her car. 'Catcha. Give me a ring when you need to come in for a break from being out there or need something. Like I said I'm here all the time.'

62

When her phone rang at one o'clock in the morning, she knew it was probably bad news. She hadn't heard from Matt for a week or more but now he was on the phone and he sounded like he was out of breath. Ethan was away in Townsville. He'd caught the train in and was staying at the university, attending a pre-course in preparation for his studies the following year.

The heat of summer was at its peak and this afternoon she had wanted to ring him and check he was okay. She was worried about him being in such a confined space. But her pride had held her back and she reminded herself that he would ring if he needed anything.

Now she sat up in bed. 'What's wrong? Are you okay?'

'I'm okay. Don't panic but can you come and get me? I'm not that bad to call the ambulance, but I think I need you to take me to the after-hours clinic. I've got a lot of pain in my leg. I think it's where the stitches were.'

'I'm already getting changed. Hang on, I'll grab my keys. I'm out the door. Be there soon.'

He nearly yelled down the phone at her. 'Don't hurry. Don't you dare drive fast. I'm okay. I'm just worried that I might get worse. Sorry to ring you but the other fellas aren't here. Most of them have knocked off for the Christmas break.'

She kept talking to him as she started the car up and backed out of the carpark. 'Why didn't you tell me there wasn't anyone there? You need to tell me stuff like that. I knew Ethan was away, but I thought Rusty and Pedro were out there. I'm hanging up. See you soon.'

He was waiting outside for her and she watched as he wiped a hand towel across his forehead which was covered in beads of sweat. His face was red and she quickly helped him to the car.

'I brought a bag with some clothes in it.' He grimaced. 'Hopefully, I don't need these but just in case they decide I need to go to hospital. Rusty got a call from his wife late last night and he had to leave in a hurry. I've been fine by myself until now.'

Fortunately, a doctor was on duty. In the waiting room, the clock on the wall seemed to tick away at a sluggish pace as she anxiously waited for him. Time felt stretched, and her nerves were on edge, her concern growing as time passed. What if his condition worsened? She would have to get him to one of the hospitals on the coast. Where she had brought him to was only a medical clinic; the town no longer had a hospital or specialists who could help with major problems. The doctor appeared in the doorway and beckoned her to follow him into the room where he had taken Matt. Matt lay on a bed, a drip attached to his arm.

'We're just going to pump some antibiotics into him. There's a bit of infection there and I want to nip it in the bud before it turns into something worse,' he said as he pulled out a chair for Elsie to sit down. The doctor continued and she struggled to understand what he was saying as he talked fast and had a strong accent. She asked some more questions and then felt relieved. He seemed to be sure of the treatment he was giving Matt and assured them that the antibiotics would kick in over the next few hours, and Matt could then follow up with a dose of tablets.

'He is lucky he has you to look after him,' the doctor said as he leaned back on the wall, watching the fluid drain into Matt's arms. The doctor's name was Guvit and while they waited Elsie talked to him about where he had studied and worked. Matt also listened and it helped pass the time to hear the man's story. He hadn't always been a doctor. He had started his working life as a floor tiler, before moving on to detailed mosaic work that he said was still on the floors of some of the fanciest mansions in Mumbai. 'I always knew though that tiling was not my lot in life.' He patted his knees. 'These would soon wear out, plus I wanted to help people, sick people.'

Against all odds he had gone back to school and then onto further study. 'I studied day and night, night and day, until my grades were so high that one of your universities here accepted me to study medicine. It cost every cent I had saved over ten years, but it has all been worth it.' He walked over and disconnected the drip, offering Matt his hand as he helped him up to a sitting position.

In India, there are so many people that you have to study hard and be the best to even stand out a little. If you can get to the top and show promise of succeeding, there may be opportunities that will come your way. Now I am doing exactly as I always wanted.'

Elsie was intrigued by his story. I wish some of the kids I teach could hear your words. I'm not sure many of them appreciate what they have at school, or value education like those who have had to work and study hard to get to where they want to be.'

The doctor turned to Matt. 'Your wife sounds like she must be a great teacher. We need to remember that behind every doctor, lawyer, chemist, carpenter or tiler there is a teacher who has educated them to be who they want to be.'

Matt shook the doctor's hand. 'Thank you. I will see you tomorrow as you asked and yes, she is the best teacher anyone could ask for.'

63

Elsie drove straight from the surgery back to her apartment. 'In the words of the great nurse, Janice, you will do as you're told and tonight you can sleep at my place.' She held up her hand as he went to speak. 'No, stop. I don't want to hear anything you have to say. I will sleep on the camp mattress in the lounge and you will have my bed. No,' her hand went up again. 'Be quiet. My bathroom has a lot more room than yours at the donga and it will be easier for you to shower and move around. Tomorrow we can see how you feel and work it out from there.'

She could tell he was feeling unwell and needed to lie down because there were no more complaints from him and he let her hold his arm and help him inside and into her bedroom. There must have been a worried look on her face because after he flopped back on the bed and passed her his crutches, he looked up at her, his voice shaky. 'Don't worry. I'll be okay. I just need to sleep.'

She left the bathroom light on so that he could see

where to go if he needed to get up during the night. Both of them must have fallen asleep because when she woke up it was after midday. She cranked the fans up, annoyed that once again the air conditioning was not working properly. Although she had asked several times for it to be fixed, no one had even come to look at it. When she peeked in to see how Matt was going, she was surprised to see he was still fast asleep. He must have been up during the night because all he had on was his shorts. His chest was bare and she struggled to take her eyes away, watching him as he lay on his back with one arm tucked up behind his head.

At least he looked like he was sleeping comfortably and his face was no longer red or sweaty. Thankfully he hadn't argued about sleeping at her place, because it made sense rather than having her going back and forth to the camp. The apartment had a lot more room for him to move around and was also close to the medical centre if she needed to rush him back there.

64

———

Matt slept solidly to begin with when they had come home from the doctor's. After a few hours though he had needed to get up to go to the toilet. Elsie had left the light on so he could see where he was going. He passed where she slept on the lounge and he couldn't help but look at her as she lay on her side, her bare legs stretched out, the tiny shorts she wore revealing her toned skin and slender body. She wore only a strappy singlet and the shape of her shoulders and arms was clear in the dim light. He stopped in his tracks and closed his eyes for a moment. Why had he been so stupid that one night? She meant everything to him. When he lay in the hospital for the week after the accident, he could think of nothing else except her. His life meant nothing without her and even though he had made such an unforgivable mistake, maybe they could work past that problem and try again. Maybe there was a slim chance the past could be mended.

He wasn't sure how to start that process though, and

now he had a broken leg as well as no transport to add to his problems. The last thing he wanted to do was to burden her with all of that. She had always looked after others her entire life. He didn't want her weighed down by him. He moved away quietly from where she slept, careful his crutches didn't scrape on the floor and wake her. The antibiotics the doctor had pumped into him must have kicked in, because he was starting to feel a lot better.

MOST OF THE following day he slept. Elsie's room was a lot larger than his back at the donga and the airflow and space allowed him to have the best sleep since coming home from Brisbane. There was also room to walk around when he wasn't resting and over the next few days he could feel his leg improving, not only because it was recovering from the infection, but also because the muscles were strengthening from moving around more.

'I don't know why you didn't let me know the men had left you there by yourself,' she said.

'They didn't realise that Ethan was going to Townville and Patrick was supposed to be there for the next month. He got a phone call a couple of days ago and had to rush back to Gladstone because his mum's crook. He only left me there because Rusty was still there and I assured him I'd ring you in the morning.'

'But you didn't ring me. How the hell did you think you were going to look after yourself?'

'I can drive. I had a go the other day. I've got to start doing stuff for myself.'

'Not on my watch. You need to take the medication the doctor gave you. Here,' she held a glass of water and two tablets out to him. 'Take these now.' Elsie also made sure he did his exercises. She was a hard taskmaster and he didn't dare argue when she gave instructions. After three days he suggested that he might have outstayed his welcome and perhaps he should go back home. Not that he particularly wanted to, but he didn't want to cramp her style. She was on school holidays and might want her own space back. But she didn't seem to mind him being there and now that she had her camp mattress set up she was more than happy for him to stay as long as he wanted.

The other men had checked on him. Rusty invited him to come and stay at his place but he assured them that Elsie had everything under control. She could hear the conversation and added in so that Rusty could hear. 'Matt is staying here until I say otherwise. Don't worry Rusty, I've got him sorted.'

Together they had gone out and collected what food was in his fridge and made sure that everything was in order and locked up. The camp had shut up for the Christmas break. 'No fencing for anyone until the new year,' he told her.

Once he started to move around better, he talked her into taking him shopping in town so he could get some Christmas presents. 'What day is it on?' she asked. 'I don't usually bother too much with Christmas.'

'It's really for kids,' he said. 'But seeing we're here together and Ethan won't be back for another few weeks, I thought we should have a Christmas tree and some festive food and decorations.'

'Really,' she seemed bemused. 'I've never had a tree before.'

It was his turn to be shocked. 'Even my family had a tree. It was usually a scrappy one we found at the dump the year before, or one someone went and cut down from in the pine forest out the back of where we lived. But we did have a tree.'

'Nope. Never had one.'

'Okay. Well this year you will. C'mon, get your car keys and drive me. We're going into town.'

Although most of the trees had already been sold there was one decent one left and Matt also bought some decorations to put on it. She left him for a while to go and pick up some groceries at the store. 'I'll meet you back at the car in half an hour,' she said, amused as she watched him trying to work out what to buy.

'Do we want two trees?' he asked. 'I just found another one.'

'Matt. No. Just one.'

She smiled to herself as she walked to get the groceries. Although they were confined to the apartment, they had been having fun. She taught him how to play Canasta and he showed her how to play Gin Rummy. He'd cooked breakfast for her and she showed him how to make her famous gravy which she poured over the thick tasty steaks he'd bought at the local butcher's. Sometimes they watched a movie on her small television that she had to hit on the top to get a clear picture. Other times he lay on the couch and she sat on the lounge chair and they read. He had discovered her bookcase and although he hadn't read since he had been at school, in the space of a couple of weeks he had ploughed his way through most of her favourites.

He had the same taste in literature as she did. Adventure, murder mysteries and historical fiction. He had even read some of the soppy romance novels Jane had brought with her the last time she visited.

When Ethan rang to see how they were going, Matt talked at length about the books he was reading and how he had been filling his time. The accommodation the university had organised was suiting Ethan fine and he had lined up a job at a local bakery, to start in the new year. He had done a few of the lead-in courses but now it was holiday time and he was enjoying finding his way around the city of Townsville. 'Where I'm staying has great views across the water and I've been up the top of the hill that's near the city. You can see for miles. Boxing Day I've been invited by one of the other students who I've been studying with, to join her and her family while they sail over to Magnetic Island. We'll be away overnight and all I have to bring are my clothes and swimmers.'

There was a wistfulness in Matt's voice when he talked to Ethan, and Elsie understood. His little brother was growing up and didn't seem to need Matt so much anymore. When Matt hung up he sat quietly, rubbing his hands together and staring into space. She passed him a cup of tea. 'Here have this and stop sulking. He was going to grow up sooner or later and not need you so much. It's a fact of life.'

He frowned. 'How did you know what I was thinking.'

'Because I felt the same when Peter left, and then Jane. You're like me. We've been a mother and a father all in one.'

'He just seems so grown up and independent. He's always had to be independent anyway, but over this last year I felt like he needed me. Now he doesn't need me at all.'

'It's how it should be. We've done what we've had to, to get them on their feet. Now it's up to them.'

That night Matt cooked her the best meal ever. It was a curry and he had bought prawns from the fishos in town as well as some delicious fish. 'Better than going to a restaurant,' she told him, 'plus, there is so much here to eat without Ethan to share it with.'

They'd laughed and joked and she had enjoyed a couple of beers with dinner. It wasn't lost on her that Matt hadn't drunk any alcohol since his accident. Perhaps he hadn't drunk any since the night with her. Who knew. And after a few beers, who cared?

Before they went to sleep he fussed over the Christmas tree. It was decorated with an odd assortment of decorations. Some were from the second-hand shop and others had been the last ones left at the shop in town. The tree did look lovely and she smiled as he put the Christmas lights on, the colourful blinking bulbs lighting up the reindeer and assortment of Santas that hug from the branches of the tree. 'You're excited about this, aren't you? You remind me of a little kid,' she teased.

'Look at it. Bloody beautiful. The best Christmas tree in Matfield. And wait 'til you see the breakfast that I have planned for us in the morning. This is going to be a Christmas to remember, Miss Jackson.'

SHE SLEPT SOUNDLY, the beers making her sink into a deep sleep. Contentment also filled her and she pondered about why that was. Was it because her friendship with Matt had returned to what it once was, or did she love having him here with her? Whatever it was, she was happy.

ALTHOUGH HE TURNED the Christmas lights off and went to bed at the same time as Elsie, Matt had not fallen asleep for a long while. He read and then lay awake, his mind going over the last month since the accident. Why was it, even with a broken leg, no physical work allowed for months, living in someone else's house while they had to sleep on the couch and relying on Elsie for everything he needed, did he feel so happy? Tonight, he had felt like he was a kid again, and happiness had filled him as he laughed and joked with Elsie about his placement of the decorations. He had even loved it when she had moved some of them to where she thought they looked better or more balanced. Now as he crept to his doorway and made sure she was sleeping, he felt excited at what the morning would bring.

Her breathing was shallow and steady and he knew she was asleep. Hidden in a bag under the bed was a present. He had bought it when she had left him for a while in town to get some groceries. The lady in the shop had wrapped it for him and helped him take it out to the car and hide it in the boot before Elsie came back. It had taken a lot of effort to keep the present concealed from her. After all, her apartment was only small and she tidied each day, picking up anything left on the floor. His secret had remained hidden though and now as he placed it carefully under the tree he couldn't wait for the morning to see her reaction.

When he returned to bed he lay awake for a long while, the conversations and moments they had spent together swirling through his thoughts. Thank goodness their friendship had retained its earlier closeness. Even though she was still guarded and didn't reveal much of her past, or talk about anything that encroached on her privacy, he felt like the connection that had been there before that night had been restored. A connection that had been made in this very bed where he was now sleeping. Flashes of the night came back to him and he nearly groaned out loud. Did she mean more than a friend to him? Was there any chance of anything more?

65

Elsie's excited squeal woke him in the morning. Sometimes, when he first opened his eyes, he forgot for a second that his leg was broken and still in plaster. But as soon as he went to move, he was reminded. It took him a bit longer to get out of bed than before the accident, but this morning he moved quickly. Swinging himself around so he could put his legs over the edge of the bed, he pulled on his t-shirt and picked up his crutches. No doubt he looked a sight with his old shorts on and tousled hair still unbrushed. He couldn't wait though and he looked through his doorway to see Elsie sitting cross-legged in front of the Christmas tree.

'Santa came,' he said. 'You must have been good.'

She jumped up, still in her pyjamas. Taking a sharp intake of breath, he tried not to stare at her shapely legs and slender body, the way the matching shorts and pyjama top hung loosely on her body sending a pleasant shiver through him. 'I haven't got you anything,' she said. 'That's not fair.'

He manoeuvred himself into one of the lounge chairs and rested his crutches next to him. 'Are you going to open it?'

She jumped up and down. 'It's big. Why didn't you tell me so I could have got you a present also.'

'You've done heaps for me over the last month. It's a thank you, and a Merry Christmas from me.'

She leaned under the tree and pulled the present out from underneath. It was large and for a moment she was hidden behind it. When she sat down on the lounge and placed it on her lap she looked like a kid opening the first present of the day. Carefully she undid the string and then the bow that the shop lady had so fastidiously wrapped around it. Her dark hair hung down and he was mesmerised by the way it rested on her shoulders. For a moment he wanted to reach over and run his fingers through it.

'Oh my goodness.' She squealed loudly again as some of the paper ripped, revealing a little of what was inside. 'It's a painting. The sticker on the back here says it's from the Matfield Art Gallery. I saw some of these paintings displayed in the shop we were in. You are very sneaky. I can't believe I didn't spot this. Where did you hide it?

'Firstly, in the boot of your car. Then when I got it back here, I put it under your bed. I just had to hope you didn't decide to clean under the bed.'

When she pulled the paper away and looked fully at the picture her eyes were wide. He wished he had his camera with him to take a photo of the look of delight on her face. He leaned forward, excited at seeing how happy she was. 'Do you like it? I thought you needed something on your wall.'

She turned it around and propped it up on the back of the lounge as she jumped up and stood back to look at it. 'Like it, I love it! It's stunning.' A pair of galahs took centre place in the painting. They were perched on a log, the bright pink and grey of their feathers vivid against the backdrop of an outback sunset. The grass in the dusty paddocks behind them glowed red, and above that the space above the horizon boasted flashing colours of orange and vivid blues. It was such a familiar scene, and they had watched similar sunsets together when they had gone exploring.

'It's beautiful. Thank you. I'll treasure it. Always.' She touched it again and then started looking around the room to see where she could hang it.

'I liked that it had a pair of galahs on it. You always watch those birds in the trees. The artist is local but she also exhibits in some of the bigger galleries in the cities.'

'It's exquisite and I love it. I'll have it forever.'

Matt had got out of the chair and wobbled a little on his feet as he went to stand next to her. He leaned on his crutches as he stared at the painting. 'I knew you'd love it.'

'I do.'

'I have another small present for you.' He passed her a small present that was wrapped in Christmas paper.

'No way. This is not allowed. I didn't get you anything.'

'This is just something small.'

As she pulled the paper away, he watched her expression as she saw what he had given her. For a while she didn't talk, her eyes resting on the gift. Running her hand over the small frame she looked up at him. 'It's beautiful. It's me.'

The lady at the shop where he bought the painting had helped him to organise the photo and frame that Elsie now held. It was the photo Matt had taken of her at the lagoon as she watched the galahs. The angle he had taken it from showed the delight on her face and when he saw it in the frame, he knew he had captured the moment perfectly. The look on her face now was just as exquisite and he felt like someone had hit him in the chest. He couldn't keep going like this.

He turned to her and rested his hand gently on her shoulder. 'We need to talk, Elsie. I don't want to mess things up between us again, but I can't keep pretending that nothing happened between us.'

As she faced him, a flicker of anger ignited in her eyes. It didn't take much to fire her up. He needed to be careful this time to get his words right and say precisely what he meant. Her questions came out before he could speak. 'Why do you have to spoil such a perfect morning? You've already made it clear how you see me and what you think of our *mistake*.'

Striving for an even tone he asked again, 'Please let me explain. I was so confused after what happened and I don't think I chose the right words or explanation for how I felt.'

Her gaze met his, her cheeks flushed. "You think I viewed it as just a fling? I woke up the next day certain about my feelings for you. It's a shame you didn't feel the same and you made that crystal clear."

He talked quickly, before she could stop him. 'I was so ashamed that I'd taken advantage of you. I'd broken your trust that had taken me a long time to win.' He adjusted the crutch under his arm and she could see he was trying to balance on his one good leg. Usually, she'd tell him he needed to sit down but this time she didn't.

'You're such a good person and I proved that night that I wasn't. You deserve better.'

She locked eyes with him, her tone cutting, her cheeks flushed. 'I never thought of it as just a fling. That night I wanted you as much as you wanted me. The difference was that the next day I had no doubts about how I felt about you. It was just a shame that you didn't reciprocate those feelings.'

He countered with more excuses. 'It wasn't that I didn't care about you, the problem was I cared too much and I had it in my head that you'd only slept with me because you were drunk. If you'd been sober you wouldn't have.'

'That's bullshit. It wouldn't have made any difference. I may have been drunk but I knew exactly what I was doing. We're both adults.'

'Wasn't your initial reaction towards what had happened, misgiving? Weren't you angry about what had happened? Didn't you feel like you'd never be able to trust me? You must have doubted me.'

'No. I didn't feel like you had broken my trust at all. Not once did I think that. Did I ever say that?'

'No. But you were angry the next morning. You can't deny that. I could see it in your eyes and you told me to leave.'

'You told me it had all been a mistake. How was I supposed to react?'

'I meant it was a mistake because we had been drunk

and I felt you wouldn't have been with me otherwise.' His mind whirled with confusion. 'Tell me what you think about what happened between us. Don't hold back. Tell me what you really thought the next morning. You put the barriers up sometimes and I find it difficult to tell what you're thinking.'

'You want to know what I thought?' She blinked and he could see tears in her eyes. 'I thought that night had been the best night of my life. I thought that I'd finally found someone I could maybe have a relationship with. Someone who I could talk to and laugh with and, maybe after a while, let my guard down. I felt like I'd finally given my body to someone with no regrets. It didn't matter that I'd been drinking, I was very clear about what I was doing.'

She stopped and wiped her hand across her eyes. 'And then you said it was a mistake and we should never have done it.'

'I was protecting you. I felt like I'd taken advantage and what made it worse was that you were Ethan's teacher.'

'I didn't care about any of that.'

He ran a hand through his hair and she put her hand out to steady him as he teetered a bit on the one leg he was standing on. 'I've stuffed this up completely. I've made everything complicated between us, by giving you space and time to think. I wanted you to have time to move on, but ever since that night I've been doing nothing but thinking of you and feeling guilty that you were angry with me because of what happened.'

Her voice was barely audible. 'I loved what we had together that night. I was angry because you ran away.'

She had turned away from him and he knew she didn't want him to see her upset. Now he had distressed her even more. When he put his hand on her shoulder she didn't move. 'Please Elsie, turn around. I don't want to hurt you even more.'

Tears streamed down her face. 'What do you want me to do?'

'I want you to tell me how you feel.'

'No. I did tell you that night and now I don't want to feel like an idiot again and ...'

He pulled her towards him. He needed to ensure that she realised how much he cared about her. This might be his last chance. 'Maybe then I can tell you how I feel. Maybe we can start again. Before that night I'd always thought that you considered me a friend, Ethan's brother and someone to hang out with. We got on great, we liked similar things and I could talk to you. You listened to me.' He could see he wasn't getting anywhere, a stony look set on her face. 'I'm just going to lay it on the line and if I make a fool of myself, well, then so be it. I'm in love with you. I want to be with you all the time and never be apart. I want to hold you so close that you'll never be able to leave me, and most of all I want you to trust me and know that I'm in this for the long haul. I'm not after a one-night stand or a short relationship. I'm looking for something serious.'

She didn't reply and he hobbled forward and pulled her towards him. 'I love you. If you don't feel anything for me, well I'll leave you be, but I'm very clear about how I feel and if I'm honest about it I felt something for you even before that night. I just didn't think you had the same feelings.'

As Elsie stood in his embrace, the weight of unspoken words hung between them. He could feel her hesitation, her vulnerability and he knew this was the moment to bare their souls.

Gently he stroked her face. 'Elsie, I've never wanted anything more in my life. Please, give me another chance and only walk away if you don't feel the same.'

In that moment, the burden of silent emotions lifted and his heart filled as she pressed her lips to his. Her kisses were soft and passionate and he held her firmly with one arm. She wrapped her arms around him to steady him as he teetered on his good leg.

He waited as he looked into her eyes. Her words were clear and sure, and she took a deep breath, like an inhalation of relief. 'I was so upset that you left that morning. That's why I felt my trust was broken, not because of what happened the night before.' She took another deep breath. 'I'm not great at letting my barriers down. It's a survival technique that has got me through life so far. But if this is going to go anywhere, I'm going to, well,' she looked down and then back into his eyes, 'I'm going to be honest. I love you too, Matt. I knew that night I loved you and when I woke the next morning I was so completely and utterly sure of my feelings for you. That realisation was the happiest moment in my life. I just didn't approach you because I was so hurt that you didn't care. And also, you weren't that great at telling me how you actually felt. Maybe if we had talked about it that morning we could have sorted it out.'

'The trouble was I did care. I cared too much about you and I'll never do anything to hurt you ever. That's a lesson for me to talk to you and be honest about what's worrying me and you need to do the same with me.' They hugged and it felt like a million firecrackers went off as she pushed against him and he felt any angst or tension leave her body. As they slowly released each other she laughed and laid her head on his chest. 'I think you should sit down. You're a bit wobbly.'

66

It had been a Christmas Day like no other, and when Peter and Jane rang to wish her Merry Christmas, she put her phone on speaker so that Matt could be included in the conversation.

'So,' Jane said, her voice excited. 'Why is Matt there with you on Christmas Day?'

Matt had beamed and grabbed Elsie's hand as he answered. 'Because today is our first day of being a couple. Can I say it, Elsie?' She nodded and he laughed out loud. 'We love each other. Simple as that.'

Jane breathed an audible sigh of relief. 'At last. Thank goodness because I thought there was a spark there when we saw you talking on the bushwalk that day. I guess most relationships have tricky parts sometimes. I'm so pleased you have both come to your senses.'

Peter had also been delighted when Matt told him that Elsie and he had talked and laid their feelings on the line. 'You should see my painting, Pete,' Elsie said. 'You'd love it. A pair of galahs and a sunset done by a local artist.'

'Don't spoil her, mate,' Peter advised, 'she'll get used to it.'

Matt leaned over and wrapped his arm around Elsie's shoulder. 'I look forward to spoiling her. She's one special person.'

'Do you want me to fill you in on what you need to be careful of? Don't ever talk to her when she's trying to do a crossword, don't touch her toothbrush or move her hairbrush. Your life won't be worth living, and ....'

Elsie grabbed the phone from Matt. 'Thank you, Peter. Matt doesn't need to know any more. Time for us to go.'

They had all laughed and when Peter hung up she came and sat on Matt's lap. Wrapping her arms around his neck she leaned in and kissed him. His arms encircled her and a warm feeling enveloped them. 'Merry Christmas.' he muttered as he rubbed his nose in her hair. 'May it be the first of many.'

67

That night Elsie decided that some things needed to change. She swung her head around the doorway, watching as Matt clambered into bed. 'Just to note,' she said, as she walked towards him and turned off the bedroom light. 'I'm coming to sleep with you in my bed.'

'Do you want me to go on the camp mattress?' he asked, pushing the sheet back and preparing to get up.

Turning a bedside lamp on, she dimmed it until she was happy with the subdued light in the room. She stood at the side of the bed and put on her most nonchalant voice. 'No. We're going to sleep together.'

He lay still on his side, propping his head up with his hand. 'Oh.'

She pulled the sheet back and crawled in beside him. He still hadn't moved and she giggled. 'You look worried.'

He managed to laugh. 'I am. I have a broken leg. I can't move very much.'

She lay down next to him, her head on the pillow as

she looked into his eyes. They were blue. Mr Blue Eyes she thought. Reaching up, she stroked his cheek and his hand touched her arm. He stroked it gently and she moved in closer to him. 'I hope your hands still work,' she said.

He threw his head back and laughed. 'I see you're not going to hold back on what you want anymore. Lay those feelings bare.'

'No. This is the real me. So watch out. You might be sorry you ever encouraged me to let down my barriers.' When she sat up and slowly took off her shirt, he closed his eyes for a moment. Reaching out he touched her softly before drawing her body down onto his. The touch of his hands on her skin sent pulsating tremors through her body and she ached for him.

When she whispered in his ear he rolled on his side and his hands moved over her as they found a comfortable position together. He moaned softly as her hands stroked his body and she reassured him again that a broken leg was not a worry. She was from Resilience Street and there were ways and means of adjusting to life and anything it threw at you to get the result you wanted. 'No mistake this time,' she giggled.

68

They had hardly left the apartment for the past two weeks and this morning Matt was cooking her another scrumptious breakfast. It was as if their love-making had worked as a therapy for his leg and most days he was hardly using his crutches at all. His muscles had lost their stiffness and he told her that it was the best he had felt since the accident.

She stood at the kitchen sink, washing up some of their dishes from dinner the night before. 'It must be your innovative love-making,' he said as he stood behind her, kissing up and down her neck.

Closing her eyes she revelled in the sensations that rippled over her skin. When she turned around she flung her arms around him and straight away felt the need in his body. Whirling back around she continued with the dishes. 'Matt. Really. I can feel what you want. No more this morning. Are you going for the record? I'll never get to eat breakfast.'

He stood next to her. 'Wait until I get this plaster off. Then we'll never get out of bed.'

She waited until they were sitting down eating to talk to him about an email she had received last night.

'I want to talk to you about something and I don't want you to get cranky or defensive about it. It doesn't matter what you think or if you don't want to do anything about it, but whatever, you have to promise me that you won't get angry with me.'

He held his little finger up and hooked it around hers. 'Pinky promise. What have you done?'

'I may have been a bit naughty.'

He leaned back in his chair and threw a very charismatic sexy look her way. 'You are naughty. You don't need to remind me of that.'

Blushing, she pushed her food around her plate. 'Not in that way. I've done something, sort of behind your back.'

Now she had his full attention and he leaned forward, resting his elbows on the table. 'Okay. What have you done?'

She tried to word what she was about to say very carefully. She had been sneaky and he was probably either going to get angry with her, even though he had promised not to, or think what she was about to tell him was a ridiculous idea.

'You know when you were in hospital and Ethan and I were staying in Brisbane?'

'Yes.'

'Well, I had a fair bit of spare time in between my walks and visiting you.'

'You got a tattoo. No. It can't be that I would have seen

it. I've seen every part of your body and no tattoo. What have you done, Elsie Jackson?'

'Um, well, Peter sent me an email from the company he works for. They're looking for a mature age person. Someone in their twenties or thirties who they can work with and mentor. They're offering a paid internship, a study scholarship type offer and some more bonus rewards.'

He scrunched up his face. 'What's that got to do with me?'

'Peter sent it to me because he thought that you suited the position perfectly.'

He laughed. 'You forgot I didn't even finish school. Are you serious? I guess it's nice of Peter to suggest it but ...'

She blurted the rest of the information out quickly. 'I sent back all your details on your behalf. I told them about your accident and how you had wanted to become a vet but had finished school early. They emailed back and said it sounded like you were a good fit for who they were looking for. They um....'

A horrified look crossed his face and she tried not to stumble over her words. 'They, well, they um, they want to interview you when you're fit enough to travel to Townsville. Peter has given them a character reference highly recommended you, and they're keen to meet and go over what they're offering.'

He blinked but didn't speak. 'Matt, are you listening? They want to interview you.'

He twisted his mouth to the side and she could tell he was thinking. Finally, he spoke. 'Just let me get this right. Without asking me, you put in a job application to a company in a town where I don't even live, for a job I may not even want.'

Her heart sank. 'It's just that I think if you want to do something you should chase it. We know this company is good. They don't offer these sorts of deals very often and they want someone who otherwise would never get to chase their dream.'

Matt's voice was barely audible. 'You did all this behind my back?' She bit her lip and looked down. 'Bloody hell, Elsie. Are you mad?'

Something shifted in her mind and she sat up straight. 'Yeah, maybe I am. But you won't ever do anything about it. You'd just keep fencing for the rest of your life. And that's fine if that's what you want, but deep down I don't think it really is. When are you going to chase your real dream?'

He reached across and took her hand in his. 'I am. I have just got my real dream. You.'

Her spirits lifted for a moment. 'Will you at least take a look at the email they sent? It's got all the details. Please.'

He shook his head. 'You're one stubborn woman. Are you sure they want to interview me? I only went to year ten. I've never studied in my life.' He held out his hands, palms upwards. 'Look at these hands. They're worker's hands. Fencing. Dust. Cattle. That's all I know.'

'Just have a look and give it some thought. It can't hurt.'

***

When she put her laptop in front of him, he looked

over the emails and attachments for a long while. There were some parts that he read out to her and she explained what the conditions meant. Other parts he asked her to read over as well, so everything was clear in his mind. When he closed the laptop he rested his hand on it and stared out the window for a long time. Elsie busied herself in the kitchen, coming back and forth to him with lunch, cups of tea, and eventually a cold beer.

'I think I need that,' he said, as he pulled the tab back and took a sip of the icy cold beverage.

She also opened one and sat next to him, waiting to hear his thoughts.

'There's one problem,' he finally said. 'and it's major.'

'What? If you're worried about the study, Peter will be able to help. He's already told me he's keen to work with you on anything you need. Someone helped him when he started. Studying is a steep learning curve but I know you can do it. I did. Anyone can if they set their mind to it.'

'It's not that.'

'What is it?'

'I'm not leaving you. I want to be with you every day and every night. Townsville is a long way from here.'

She cleared her throat. 'I've been doing a lot of thinking over the last week. If you were, um, if you were, um...'

He squeezed her hand. 'Lay it out. Remember no holding back or any doubts. We're a couple. I need to know what you're thinking.'

'Well, if you were to get this, I could take the job at the college in Townsville. They've emailed me again and said they'd leave the offer open until school starts. The email says they are always after English teachers and there will be a role there for me if I decide to take it.'

'Wow. That throws a different light on everything. You. Me. A different town. And with Ethan.'

'And Peter and Jane,' she added. 'It could be a new start for both of us.'

69

As January rolled by, Matt and Elsie prepared to leave Matfield. Elsie's new contract at Townville College would start on the same date that Matt began in his new role at Davey Veterinary Clinic. There had been teary farewells at the pub when the other teachers returned from holidays to hear the news that Elsie was leaving them. Her friends gathered with them at the pub on Friday night and there had been plenty of laughter and jokes when Elizabeth and Penny retold the story of the night Elsie won Matt as a date.

It all seemed so long ago now, and as Elsie looked around at the group of teachers who had gone out of their way to be her most ardent supporters and work-mates, she felt a warm circle of friendship surrounding her. Everything she had gone through to come to this point in time had been worth it. Even if she needed to navigate the nastiness of Garranto and some of his colleagues, overall the others she worked with had been great and she had formed friendships that would last.

When Matt put his arm around her shoulders and she looked up at him and smiled, she felt like she had won the lotto.

If she hadn't come to Matfield she would never have met Matt. To be honest, as she told Penny earlier that night, 'If it wasn't for Matt I wouldn't be leaving. I would have just stayed and continued here. I like the kids and the teachers. I've had a lot of really good times this year and some funny ones.'

Once Matt had interviewed for the role and checked out that everything was going to suit him, the decision had been an easy one. He was exactly what Davey Veterinarian Clinic was looking for and the contracts had all been completed and signed.

Elsie and Matt had gone through the paperwork and everything else they needed to put into place for the new opportunities to work in Townsville.

'Let's give it a go,' Matt said. 'It's a big step for both of us, but, what does it matter as long as we're together.'

His learning curve would be significantly steeper than hers, but she had confidence in his ability to overcome challenges. Observing him now, walking with a slight limp and his crutches nowhere to be seen, she couldn't help but admire his tenacity. His willingness to embrace something beyond his comfort zone resonated with her. She also would need to make some changes, and although everyone she talked to at the new school had seemed supportive and friendly, there would always be hurdles to navigate and different systems to adjust to. She looked forward to working at a new school and had already put her name down, and been accepted to be a mentor for some of the girls who boarded at the college.

It didn't matter where you were, there were always kids who needed help.

Elizabeth clinked a spoon on her glass. 'Attention everyone.' She threw her most condescending teacher look Paul and Liam's way as they continued to talk. 'Sorry Elizabeth,' they said holding their glasses up high towards her.'

'Thank you, gentlemen,' she said, looking around the group. 'I'd like to make a toast to young Matt and Elsie here.' Elsie smiled and stood up next to Matt where he sat on a stool, his arm wrapping around her waist. 'You might have met here in the outback town of Matfield but now you're on a path to different and exciting times. May you both continue to love, laugh, and enjoy being together as you step forward and aim for your dreams. Enjoy!' She held her wine glass high. 'Here's to a new start for Matt and Elsie.'

Everyone repeated her words and raised their glasses together. Matt stood up and kissed Elsie before clinking his glass against hers. They both spoke at the same time, 'To a new start!'

~~~
~~~

ABOUT THE AUTHOR

Rhonda Forrest is an Australian author who juggles writing and publishing, alongside teaching high school students. She writes captivating contemporary fiction and historical romance about relationships, family life and social issues, set amidst beautiful and uniquely Australian landscapes.

After bringing up three daughters and traversing several careers, Rhonda went on to teach creative writing, English and history. Her passion for literacy, history and travelling around Australia fuels her novels. Along with her husband, she divides her time between Tamborine Mountain and a century-old cottage with a rambling garden overlooking the waters of the Whitsundays.

Recent novels bring to life the remarkable characters and settings that make up the unique Australian heritage and take the reader on a journey from bush to beach, with steamy romances, riveting history and eclectic characters.

Some books are available in audio and large print and you can also find some titles available in Portuguese, Publisher- Leabhar Books Brazil.

If you enjoyed this book or any of Rhonda's other books, you can make a big difference by writing a review, or leaving a star rating. A personal recommendation to family, friends, libraries and book clubs is another great way to share the books with others. You can also follow Rhonda on Facebook, Instagram, Goodreads and Bookbub.

Author's favourite - for your enjoyment, sample chapters from *Elizabeth's Star* are in the back of this book.

Website - https://www.rhondaforrest.com/

ALSO BY RHONDA FORREST

OUTBACK QUEENSLAND ROMANCE SERIES

With a cast of eclectic characters and set amidst the rugged outback of Australia, the **Outback Queensland Romance Series** will introduce you to stories of friendship, resilience, and loving relationships that come together to triumph over obstacles defined by the past.

Two Heartbeats (Book 1) is followed by the sequel, *Time Will Tell* (Book 2)

Turn Left (Book 3), *A New Start* (Book 4), *Outback Magic* (Book 5) and *Echoes of the Outback* (Book 6) are stand-alone books with some links to the other books in this series.

SALTWATER ROMANCE SERIES

SALTWATER ROMANCE SERIES

From the wild freedom of 1970s Australia to the tangled
emotions of the present day, the Saltwater Romance Series
delivers three powerful love stories.

Set against the rainforests of North Queensland, the
Whitsundays, and the golden shores of Stradbroke Island,
these novels explore first love, rebellion, second chances and
the journeys that lead us back to ourselves, and to the ones we
can't forget.

BINDARRA CREEK ROMANCE

Bindarra Creek Romance

BEYOND THE GATE - Mystery Romance at Bindarra Creek

CHRISTMAS AT FORREST GLEN - A Bindarra Creek
Romance

A MAGICAL SUMMER - A Bindarra Creek Small Town
Christmas Romance

A WINTER'S PROMISE - A Bindarra Creek Christmas in July
Romance

ALSO AVAILABLE IN A BOX SET - CLICK HERE!

WHITSUNDAY ROMANCE - YOU MAY NEVER WANT TO LEAVE!

Love by the Jewel Sea - Book 1

Summer by the Jewel Sea - Book 2

The Lure of the Jewel Sea - Book 3

THE SHACK BY THE BAY - Whitsunday Historical Romance

Romantic and purely Australian, *The Shack by the Bay* captures the pristine beauty of the Whitsundays and the wartime memories of older Australians while introducing an eclectic blend of friends and family.

ALL MY HEART - A Tranquil Bay Romance

A small town and school - She only had to last six months.

KICK THE DUST - Contemporary Romance

'If I close my eyes, it's easier to hold onto a memory. When I open them, I think it might really be there in front of me.'

SAMPLE CHAPTERS - ELIZABETH'S STAR (BOOK 1)

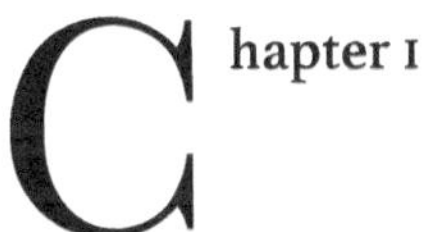 hapter 1

BUNDEEN STATION – Channel Country, Queensland

1929

Michael sat at the kitchen table, running his fingers across the five names carved into the well-worn timber top. His name was in the middle: Michael McTavish, 1916. Two names were written above his; his twin brother, Dan, and elder brother, Rory. Below Michael's name was a star and the year 1918.

'That was the year the Great War ended,' Michael's father, Hamish, said. 'It was the war to end all wars, and Australian men from all over the nation signed up, with sixty thousand never coming back.'

'How many died altogether in the whole world?' Michael asked.

'Millions. Millions and millions. Fifteen, sixteen million they say, but probably more than that.' Hamish grimaced. 'They wouldn't take me because of this bung leg. Let's hope there'll never be anything like it again.'

'Surely, with so many people dying, they've learnt not to start wars.' Anxiety tugged at Michael —the thought of going off to war and dying, never seeing his mother again, stopped him from eating his dinner, just for a moment.

'Let's hope so.' Hamish turned to his wife, Edith. 'Your mother and I are blessed you five boys were born after the war, so we didn't have to suffer the loss of sons like so many others.'

Michael returned to the carvings in the table. Below the star and year 1918 were the names of his two younger brothers, Frank and Lachie. He ran his fingers over the star, the shape familiar, the edges smoothed by the hands that had touched it over the years.

His mother never talked about it, but there had been a baby girl born before he and Dan turned two. Michael often sensed there was something that bothered his mum. Sometimes her eyes dulled, or she stared vacantly across the paddock at nothing in particular. Often, when she sang a lullaby or sat resting in the evening, tears moistened her cheeks. When he asked what she was looking at, she would wipe her face and turn away. 'It's nothing, Mickey. Just something in my eye. Nothing for you to worry about.'

Michael had quizzed his father, but it wasn't until he was older that he found out why his mother was sometimes a bit distant, or sad without reason. Michael would always remember the night their father told the story. It was the night after his and Dan's thirteenth birthday, and they were camped out on the long paddock, the stars filling the night sky above.

Earlier in the afternoon, Michael had ridden ahead to pick the best campsite for the night; by the time the others arrived, the spare horses were hobbled and the damper on the fire. By dusk the cattle were settled, the sun dropping quickly below the low scrub lining the horizon. There were no fences to hold the mob, and Michael chose the camp and fire area carefully, so the smell of preparing dinner wouldn't drift near them. The cattle hated the smell of cooking meat. Even the water used for cooking and drinking was carefully poured out so they wouldn't get wind of it and become unsettled. Camps needed to be tidy and well ordered, with nothing left lying around to be kicked during the night, spooking the cattle and causing a stampede.

The three brothers sat around the fire with their father, the silence of the night settling in. Michael wrapped his heavy coat tighter, warding off the winter chill as he repositioned the billy in the dancing sparks. He watched the fire flicker brightly as slivers of flames licked the dry logs, the branches and twigs crackling in the still of the evening.

Dan placed more logs on the blaze and looked up at the night sky. 'That star to the west is always the brightest and the first one to come out in the evening.'

'That's Elizabeth's star,' Hamish said, casting his eyes upwards.

The three boys waited, looking at each other silently. Michael knew better than to ask questions. His father always thought and paused before he spoke. When he did talk, his Scottish brogue was like music, lilting on the night air.

'You know, your mother and I came here from the home country with only a suitcase each and that old bugle my brother brought back from the Boer War. All the way from Glasgow to Sydney, the two of us, your mother a young lass. We found our way here to Bundeen and it was a lucky day for us, and all of ye, that Bill and Charlotte gave me work and offered for us to buy the hut and block.'

Dan stoked the fire. 'You were going to tell us about Elizabeth.'

'Ah, I was, wasn't I? She was born after you boys.' Hamish nodded towards Michael and Dan. He picked up a stick and stirred the embers of the fire, pausing for a long while before continuing with the story. 'The healthiest chubbiest bairn, with eyes as blue as the sky above Loch Lomond on a clear summer's day.'

The silence hummed with tension as they waited for him to continue. The silhouettes of the cattle in the distance remained motionless, not a swing of a head or bellow of a calf. The dogs lying next to the boys were also silent, two of them lifting their heads and watching Hamish, as if they too were listening to the story. Rory got up and took the billy from the fire, his father holding out his tin mug for a refill.

'Thanks, son.' He took a long sip, his stare fixed on the fire's embers. The glow lit up the boys' faces, the flames throwing flickering shadows across their coats. 'Aye, she was the bonniest baby you ever saw. At six weeks old she was already smiling and reaching up to my face.' Hamish's voice shook, and he pulled his hat lower over his face. 'She'd grab my beard and make those sweet sounds babies make. A wee noise that pulls at ye heart-strings.'

Their father sat upright, wiping his eyes with the back of his leathery hands. 'There's something about a wee girl that affects a man; it's a softness, a love different from that of a son. She held my heart from the moment she was born.'

Michael waited while his father took a deep breath.

'Your mother would never talk about it, not to you boys. Sometimes she and I talked, when it first happened, but after a while she couldn't bear it. I think she always blamed herself.'

'What happened, Dad?' Dan asked.

'It was the middle of winter. You three boys slept in the wee bed together, out near the fireplace to keep you warm. Elizabeth slept right up next to your mother's side of the bed in a crib.' He looked up at the evening star for a long time before continuing, struggling with his words.

'She went to get her from the cot in the morning. I remember lying in bed waiting, because your mother always passed Elizabeth to me after she fed her. It was a morning ritual and it kept us all warm. You know, a special time for the three of us.' A tear rolled down his face and the boys looked at each other, unused to such a show of emotion and unsure what to say.

He placed his cup of tea on the ground, his voice barely audible. 'The wee baby had died. She was dead in your mother's arms.' His hands ran through his hair. 'Your mother screamed my name, yelling at me to wake Elizabeth up. But there was nothing to be done. She was gone.'

Dan's voice was a whisper. 'What made her die, Dad?'

'We never knew. The doctor said sometimes it happens. Babies go to bed healthy and don't ever wake up. Your mother blamed herself. But the bairn had plenty of warmth and it was nobody's fault. Just the will of God, maybe.'

'If that's the will of God, then I don't want anything to do with him!' Michael declared. The thought of his parents' suffering was too much for him to bear.

'I remember her.' Rory spoke up. 'I have a memory of holding a baby in front of the fire. I remember the smell, a soft baby smell.'

'That would be her. You were about four and you used to nurse her. You were only a wee fella yourself.' Hamish's voice broke again. 'She smiled when you talked to her.'

Michael sat by the fire for a long time after his father and Rory turned in for the night. Not far away, Dan played a wistful tune on his harmonica, his silhouette and that of the horse he sat on visible as he rode around the mob. Dan was the night watchman and in charge of the cattle, the tune letting the mob know where he was so they didn't startle. The music, as usual, settled the cattle and, before long, lullabied Hamish and Rory to sleep, their snoring accompanying Dan's tune. Michael's gaze turned towards the evening star, a vivid, winking diamond pointing directly down at him. He stared hard, imagining what his baby sister would have looked like, how her voice might have sounded. A shooting star blazed across the sky. A streak of light, in slow motion, its sparkle fading before it reached the ground.

Chapter 2.

Bundeen Station – 1929

Bundeen Station was situated in the Channel Country of far Western Queensland, the nearest town, Windorah, over one hundred miles to the north. The Diamantina River and several of its tributaries ran through the forty thousand square miles of mostly flat, arid land. In times of high water, the tentacles of braided channels cut through and over the floodplains, leaving in their wake nutritious grasses that were excellent for grazing cattle. The shallow waters, sometimes stretching fifty miles wide, brought moisture and nutrients to the soil, heralding the beginning of plentiful seasons to come.

Michael barely remembered what the plains looked like in flood. The baked, cracked earth and dying trees were a familiar landscape, no matter which direction he travelled, the wet years a distant memory. Bundeen Station was owned by Bill and Charlotte Roberts, who had many years ago sold a one-hundred-acre block to the McTavish family, the small hut on it providing a starting point for the family, who increased its size as their own numbers grew.

It was a harsh environment, but the five boys thrived, all of them loving the lifestyle of working and living among cattle and horses. By the time Michael and Dan were thirteen, and Rory fifteen, they were already skilled stockman. Along with Hamish, who was known as the best ringer in the area, they made a reliable team for moving mobs of cattle.

Bill Roberts was full of praise for them. 'You boys are as good as any of my men. You two,' he nodded towards

Dan and Michael, 'you've got different skills from one another and you make a solid team.'

'Dad says we're like chalk and cheese, both the way we look and the way we are,' Michael said, stretching up tall to look Dan in the eye.

Dan continually reminded Michael, or 'Mickey', as he called him, that he was the eldest. 'Don't forget, I'm older than you by ten minutes—and *way* taller.'

Dan had always been taller, making him an ideal kitchen helper who could reach the tins on top of the hutch. Michael was easy to spot, with a mop of unruly blond hair, unlike Dan's straight, brown hair, always combed back or hidden under a hat. Their facial features were similar: the broad cheeks of their father, the long eyelashes and deep-set eyes of their mother, and a mixture of the two in their full lips and straight white teeth. The fact that the boys all had good teeth was put down to the fact that their pet goats supplied them with plenty of milk, particularly when the boys were little.

Their mother often caught them drinking from the goat or hiding some other stray animal they'd found. 'Lachie, get yourself out from under that goat. You're covered in dust, and not much of that milk is going in your mouth. And Dan, you're squeezing the poor goat dry.' Her eyes missed nothing. 'Mickey, I wasn't born yesterday. What have you got in that box? If it's another lizard or baby bird, you'll have to find food for it—and make sure you use those old rags to keep it warm.'

Lachie and Frank always wanted to help look after the animals, and they followed Michael everywhere, their cries of '*Mickey!*' echoing across the paddocks as they tried to keep up with him. Even the pet parrot had picked up on his name, screeching '*Mickey!*' every afternoon when it wanted feeding.

Michael always made sure to take care with his chores, because although Edith was short in stature, she was in charge of the household. Their father told them that when she first came to Australia at the age of twenty, her waist was tiny, her arms and legs thin and short like a child's. Now, although she had gained a little weight and her face was tanned, she still looked like a youngster, her dark brown eyes and deep dimples an attractive sight.

Edith's wavy hair intrigued Michael, the long blonde tresses hanging down the middle of her back, the colour the same as his and his younger brothers'. At night she sat patiently as Michael plaited it, her eyes closed, talking to him while he braided.

'It's the best feeling in the world, having you boys all together with me.'

Dan often interrupted the tranquillity. 'Ha, Mum, look at Mickey's hair. I plaited it while he was doing yours. He looks like a girl.'

'That's the worst plait I've ever seen.' Rory joined in. 'There's more sticking out than in.'

'Look, everyone, I've tied a pretty ribbon in it. Now he'd pass for a young lass.' Dan tugged hard on the plait, pulling a silly face as he jigged around Michael.

Michael's mother turned around and patted him on the arm. 'Leave him alone, Dan. If only you were all as easy-going. Not through all the years has Michael ever given me a second of grief, unlike the rest of you.'

'What about when he puts the fear of God into you with the tumbles and jumps he does on the horses? You always say the twins give you grey hairs and wrinkles,' Rory said.

'Aw, Mum, you love us.' Dan wrapped his strong arms around her, lifting her off the ground. The boys huddled, hugging her tight, not letting her move, even when she started yelling out to their dad. 'Cheeky bairns, the lot of you. Get out of my way and let me do my work! You're nothing but a bunch of troublemakers and a terrible example to those younger two.'

'Ah, the spoilt ones', Rory said, 'they're the real trouble. Only yesterday Mickey rescued them from the big house. Stealing fruit from right under the nose of Ah Lee. Poor old gardener, with his one ancient tree in the dusty dry paddock and barely a piece of fruit on it. Those two were up it and ready to take what they could.'

MICHAEL's favourite times were when they moved large mobs of cattle across the plains. The days were long and hot, but at night they sat around a campfire, listening to Hamish as he reminisced about life in the old country. It was hard to imagine a country where the landscape was covered in snow for more than half the year and cattle had shaggy coats and long wide horns.

It was a stark contrast to the vast plains of outback Queensland and the robust, short-haired cattle that spent their lives flicking away swarms of flies.

'Was your house like the one we live in?' Michael asked his father.

His father shook his head and wiped the sweat from his forehead. 'Nothing the same at all. It was a thatch-roofed blackhouse, with stone walls on the outside, lined with earth on the inside. The roof was made from rye grass, keeping out the rain and warming your mother and me through the long winter months when the sun hardly shone.'

'Our walls are thick slabs of bark,' Rory said. 'The roof is tin, and Mum says it's hot enough to fry an egg on in summer.'

'Aye, it's a different life. It's hard for ye to believe, but back in the old country our animals slept inside. Us down one end, them down the other. Now we're working with hardened cattle and horses, as well as with men who can tell stories about tracks that are drier and wilder than ours here on Bundeen Station.'

Michael hung on Hamish's every word, his father conjuring exotic images of a different world. 'Are you glad you came here, Dad?'

'Aye, at first it was foreign territory and I had to work hard to earn my place among the cattlemen. Men back home were tough and could withstand the harsh winters and the bleak mountain countryside. But the men here,' he shook his head and stoked the fire, 'when I first arrived, I was in awe of how they'd kill a black snake as thick as your arm, or wrestle with cattle as wild as the devil himself.' He paused for a long while, casting his eyes out into the blackness surrounding them. 'Here the distances are huge, the people are rugged and,' he looked back to the boys, 'this country has everything a man could ever want or need.' He sniffed the air. 'There's nothing better than smelling the cattle nearby, the burning wood there in front of ye, and feeling the isolation that comes from being surrounded by thousands of miles of scrub and desert. Aye, it's a rare country, and it was the best day of our lives when we arrived here.'

*

Although the hut Hamish bought from Bill was small to start with, over the years—as the family grew—several rooms and a long sleepout had been added down one side, and the iron roof extended accordingly.

A new floor with timber boards was a welcome comfort after years of dampening down a dirt floor. The houseproud Edith had turned the hut into a cosy retreat that not only kept them out of the weather, but also had some tender touches of the old country. Straggly sweet peas grew over an arch, welcoming visitors to the house, and there was always a vase full of whatever wildflowers or foliage Edith could lay her hands on.

It was a difficult time in Australia. The Great Depression had begun, and throughout the country—in city and rural areas alike—legions of men were unemployed, having to survive on handouts.

Occasionally a swagman stopped by their hut, his face gaunt, a small bag of belongings hanging from a stick resting on his shoulder. These men were down and out, moving from property to property in search of work. Edith would always find something for them to eat and let them spend a night in one of the sheds, sleeping on the feed bags, or send them on their way with a full belly and perhaps the possibility of work over at the main homestead.

The men were grateful for anything they received, and their gratitude was a reminder that not everyone had food in their belly, or somewhere safe to sleep at night. Michael never wanted to be lonely like they were. Their faces came to him at night when he closed his eyes, and he promised himself to never be in a position where he needed to beg for food or with no family around him.

CHAPTER 3.

Bundeen Station – Winter, 1932

Michael sat warming his hands at the wood-fired stove. He watched the younger two as they helped set the table in readiness for the special dinner tonight for his and Dan's sixteenth birthday. A large pot bubbled and boiled on the stovetop, a delicious aroma filling the room. The availability of sheep on a nearby property catered for the family's traditional meal of haggis, and Michael's mouth watered in anticipation.

'Sit down, the lot of you.' Edith's quiet voice was commanding, and immediately the five boys sat around the table, waiting for their father to join them.

Hamish was a quietly spoken man. He rarely raised his voice but had a canny way of making sure the boys all toed the line. He only needed to tap his finger on the table and someone would be up and getting the milk out of the cold box, or filling the water jug for their mother. Out in the paddocks, a nod of his head or a wave of his hand was enough to command not only his own sons, but any man who was working for him, to ride in the direction he indicated.

Edith was adamant Hamish was the boss and every idea had to be run past him, but Michael and his brothers all knew that the backbone of the family, and the one they needed to heed, was their mother.

For many years, Hamish's work had been out on the stock routes, the droving taking him away from the family for months at a time. He covered countless miles with thousands of head of cattle, mixed with tough men and endured isolation and hardships while battling the heat and cold of the outback. Back at the station, Edith persevered without complaint, continuing to carve out a life for her family. It was a sweet day for the family when Bill offered Hamish the position of homestead stockman, in charge of the activities of the nearby cattle and horses.

'When cattle go astray or I need someone to find water, I can rely on your sons,' Bill said. 'Your boy Michael has an extraordinary gift for finding water. He can track down a steer and find those hidden waterholes that only the Aborigines know about. It's uncanny, like he's one with the land.'

'Maybe he learnt from the Aboriginal kids he played with. They were always out yonder together,' Hamish replied. The two men leaned on the fence, looking over the latest mob of cattle they had brought into the yard.

'I can tell you, that boy would survive in the middle of the desert. His sense of direction is unerring, and his mind is as quick as any.' Bill shook his head. 'Your other boys work as good as any of my older men, but Michael, he's going to be a big asset for you in the future.'

'Aye, he's a grand lad with a heart of gold,' Hamish replied.

Bill chuckled. 'I saw your two boys in the home paddock the other week. It was the day after they brought that big mob in. They were letting off a bit of steam and having a wonderful time doing tricks on their horses.'

Hamish grunted. 'It'll be the death of my poor Edith, watching those two on the horses. I've never seen anyone do what they can.'

'I counted the tumbles in the air and then every time, they landed back squarely on the horse's back. The amazing thing was, the horse never faltered either.'

'They've had their share of falls, but nothing too serious. They've been doing those tricks since they were wee lads.'

'You should be proud of them—and all your boys.'

'Aye, we've been blessed alright. I hope they never have to go through war like our generation did.'

Bill shook his head. 'They say never again will there be a war like that one. It's good times ahead for all of us, once these Depression years roll by. And they will.'

Hamish smiled as he gazed out across the vast expanse stretching in front of them. '*Aye khoi*, never again. They are indeed a lucky generation.'

CHAPTER 4.

Bundeen Station – Spring, 1933

Working with stock in the paddocks was what Michael loved most. The land swarmed with life, and he never tired of watching the many creatures that shared the area where he rode. His keen eyes followed trails of spiky dragon lizards that scuttled through the red dust, their short legs moving at a million miles an hour, seeking safety away from the hooves of horses and cattle. The ambling echidnas were not as fast. Michael would stop and loosen the reins, giving his horse a sniff of the spiked animal that had decided its safest bet was to roll up in a ball and wait until the stock moved on.

The sky was also alive. Enormous flocks of corellas soared overhead, their white bodies stark against the vivid blue sky, their screeches echoing across an emptiness as they flew eastward in search of water. Black kites glided high above, wings spread wide, eyes cast downwards in pursuit of prey. And every so often, thousands of striking blue and yellow budgerigars flicked across the heavens, also seeking to quench their thirst.

At sunset, huge mobs of kangaroos bounded effortlessly in front of the cattle, their bodies partially hidden by clouds of dust stirred up by movement, hazy particles dancing in the glare of the sun. As the sun sank lower, brilliant golds, pinks and reds filled the sky, a few low distant hills the only break in an otherwise flat land. The burning colours of the sky cast their reflected glow back onto land and, for a short while, rich hues of gold and red covered the earth, the cattle and the men who moved across it.

As the sun dipped below the horizon, its last, lingering rays cast long shadows. This signalled the end of the working day, and time to head home and clean up for dinner.

*

The lounge room was a cosy after-dinner retreat, a place and time to reflect on the day now past and what tomorrow might bring. Michael stretched his body out on the long lounge chair, stretching his neck from side to side to relieve the aching and stiffness that had built up during the day. The muscles in his arms were tight, and he rubbed them hard, noticing the hairs on them getting thicker and his once-gangly forearms starting to thicken and look more like a man's. He enjoyed the sight of his body developing, maturing, his limbs now thicker, stronger—no longer those of a boy.

He glanced at Rory and Dan, who lay on cowhide rugs, a serious game of draughts in play. The two younger brothers lay next to them, propped on their elbows, while Hamish watched from his armchair in the corner, a pipe tucked into his mouth, the sweet smell of tobacco wafting through the room.

Edith usually had mending to do, and the golden light from the lamp next to her cast a warm glow over the family as they enjoyed the quiet of the evening. Michael lay on his back, looking at the pictures hanging on the walls. His mother had hung gilded frames, filled with paintings of green pastures and babbling brooks—rural idylls from the old country. There was a carved wooden frame with a photo of Hamish's brother before he went to fight in the Boer War. On the shelf next to the pictures, taking pride of place, was the 'good luck' bugle, brought back from that same war.

Sometimes his father took it down and passed it to Dan, who was the only one of the boys with any musical ability. Dan had inherited his mother's gift for music—he could also play a lively harmonica.

An old drover had given the harmonica to Dan when he was a kid. Edith had invited the drover, who brought a mob of cattle down from way up north, to have a meal with the family. The wiry stockman entertained them for hours on the small verandah, his Scottish tunes a melancholic sound across the plains. For the first time Michael could remember, his mother cried, the music bringing back memories of the people and places that had once been her life.

Hamish passed her a handkerchief and, once she'd composed herself, she sang along, her voice a melodious accompaniment to the drover's music. As the drover was leaving the next day, he gave the small harmonica to Dan, who sat mesmerised at his feet the entire time he played. 'This old tin sandwich belonged to Sid Kidman himself,' he told Dan. 'I'm running out of puff to play, so you learn it now. Your mother knows the tunes. It'll calm the cattle and horses when you're out on the track.'

Dan drove them crazy, the tinny notes shrill to their ears, until he learned to play in tune. His determination paid off and within a few months he mastered every tune his mother could remember. At night Edith's strong voice filled the hut, with the boys joining in, their deep voices blending harmoniously as they sang the haunting lyrics of her favourite songs.

*

Not long after Michael turned sixteen, a mystery load arrived at the hut. Not only was there equipment and supplies for the main house, but hidden behind a cover was a surprise delivery for Edith. It was an upright wooden piano that had made its way on the back of the supply cart all the way from Brisbane.

Hamish grinned like a mischievous boy, laughing loudly when Edith threw herself into his arms. He swung her around like a doll, and his arm stayed around her shoulders as the precious piano was lifted down. The boys manoeuvred it through the front door and positioned it in pride of place in the lounge room, directly below the bugle on the shelf.

After the piano arrived, every night was spent in the lounge, with Edith often playing for hours on end. Her singing was accompanied by the boys, filling the house with music and love. Hamish told them that no man was as lucky as he. Sometimes, he'd lean back in his chair and close his eyes, the only sign that he was awake the smoke that continued to puff from his pipe. Michael knew he was thinking of the tiny baby, Elizabeth. He moved closer to his father and sat on the rug next to him.

'She'll always be with us, Mickey. With us in spirit.' Hamish ruffled Michael's hair. 'Life can be harsh and full of ups and downs. The best day of my life was when I met your mother. Treat a woman well and you'll have a friend for life.'

CHAPTER 5.

The Channel Country – 1933

It was the first night of the New Year, 1933. Edith gazed around the table as the five boys and Hamish devoured every last scrap of the hearty stew she had cooked. She closed her eyes and tried to hold the moment in her heart. The boys were all getting older—sooner or later they'd be wanting to spread their wings.

Only last week she overheard Hamish talking to one of the station managers from further south. The McTavish family had known John O'Donnell for years, and he was well aware of the stockman capabilities of their three older boys.

'You should send those older boys down to work for

me at Durham Station,' he told Hamish. 'I'd give them different work and it would do them good. They could see a bit of town life and mix with other folk in the area. Bill won't mind; it was him who suggested it.'

'I'm not sure my Edith will be wanting to part with any of them.' Hamish pushed tobacco down into the funnel of his pipe, puffing heavily to ensure it caught. He dragged on the pipe, holding it like a treasured friend as he drew it away from his mouth. 'You're right, though. Sometimes they don't talk to anyone outside the family for months.'

'With us being a Kidman property, they'll get to move from one station to the other,' John said. 'There are runs into town for supplies and a special job coming up. I'd be interested in Michael. I'd pay him well.'

'I thought you'd be after my older son, Rory. He's more settled. Michael's only young; he's just turned seventeen.'

'I'll take him and his twin brother, or him and Rory. You're a lucky man, Hamish, having five sons.'

***

Hamish had discussed John's proposal with Edith and now she nodded, indicating that tonight was a good time for a discussion on the matter. No-one would leave while there was still food on the table or left-overs to be scraped from the big pot, warming on the wood fire stove. Besides, no boy or man, would be game to leave the table until she excused them.

Hamish's voice caused them all to stop chattering.

The only sounds were his Scottish brogue and the clinking of cutlery on plates.

'John O'Donnell from Durham Downs came to see me.'

'Aye,' answered Dan. 'That's one in a line of Kidman properties on the Cooper Creek. In full season it can carry more cattle than anywhere else in the area.'

Rory chipped in. 'I've talked to men from there. When it floods, they say the water is like an ocean and deeper than a man is tall.'

'When they had the last big dry, they lost ten thousand head of cattle.' Dan added. 'They also have trouble with wild horses—they eat the good pickings.'

Michael listened with interest. He'd travelled long distances with the cattle, but there were thousands of miles to the south and north he'd never seen. With a trusty horse and a swag, a man could ride the length of the country stretching endlessly in every direction, with ranges to the north, green pastures to the south and, in the east, oceans that rose and fell with the pull of the moon.

He'd only ever seen pictures of the ocean in the geography and history books his mother used for their lessons. She'd tried to be strict with their education, but it was only ever him and the two younger ones left after the first hour passed.

Michael was drawn in by the black-and-white pictures showing cities and villages in other parts of the world, as well as oceans with waves that were high and curled at the top. He plied his mother with questions, his finger running over a page showing mountains covered in snow.

'Life can't stay the same forever. One day you boys will move on, maybe marry and build a life somewhere for yourselves.' Edith patted Michael's hair down, flattening the unruly curls and pushing a few stray strands from his face. He looked up from the book, the dark brown of her eyes similar to his own.

'The younger two will be around for a while,' Michael said. 'Frank told me he wants to get married and have ten children, and Lachie said he's going build a house for himself right next to you and Dad.'

Edith laughed. 'Wouldn't that be grand. All those little ones running around and you boys close by. Mind you, you'll all have to become a bit more social for any of that to happen.'

'I want to see other places, Mum, but I'll always come back here to you and Dad. This is my home and where I belong.'

'There's a big world out there, Mickey, but we'll always be here for ye to come back to.'

*

Now Michael waited for his father to continue. He looked to his mother for clues, but she shook her head, not giving anything away.

Hamish sat back in his chair, his arms crossed as he looked at the boys. 'John O'Donnell has asked if ye would like to go and work for him. He's willing to pay good money, and you'd be on the properties as well as droving cattle to stockyards further south.'

Frank and Lachie sat upright, their faces taut, their eyes wide, as if they were soldiers at attention in the army.

'He is, of course, only after ye older boys.'

The younger boys' faces fell. They scowled at each other across the table.

Rory was the first to break the silence. He lay his knife and fork down and pushed his plate to the side. 'I'm not wanting to leave this place. I'm happy here.'

'I'm not forcing any of you to go, but your mother and I have talked about it and it would be good to see what's on the other side of these paddocks.'

Michael looked out the window. Out there were places and people he could only imagine.

He looked towards his mother. 'What do you think?'

She hesitated then spoke softly. 'You'd learn new things, and John O'Donnell is a good man.'

Michael held his mother's gaze. 'I wouldn't want to leave this place or any of you,' he cast his eyes around the table, his hands clasped and resting on his lap, 'but if it's for a short while, it would be fine.' He paused and looked at Dan. 'But I understand if Dan is the one to go.'

Dan sat upright. 'I've wanted to do something different for a while and,' he grinned at Michael, 'there aren't too many girls around here.'

Edith smiled. 'It's okay, Dan, to admit missing the company of women your own age. You're young men now.'

Michael's shoulders slouched. He may have to wait his turn. Dan was bigger and stronger, and full of confidence.

*

Edith listened with interest as she poured Hamish a cup of tea, the steam wisping up in spirals before disappearing into the rafters of the hut. Silence drew down upon them again as Hamish methodically placed three teaspoons of sugar into his cup and began to stir. It was a habit of his, and no one would dare hurry him when he was stirring his tea. He stirred it for what seemed an eternity before tapping the spoon on the side of the cup. Initially this was to rid the spoon of any drops of tea threatening to blot Edith's clean tablecloth. But they all knew that the number of times he tapped the spoon signified the seriousness of whatever conversation was taking place.

The tapping went on and on as Hamish concentrated, his eyes fixed on the spoon. After a while it was too much for Edith, who leaned over and gently stilled his hand. He lay the spoon down on the table.

'John said he'd take two of you. Are ye sure, Rory, you don't want to go?'

'I'm sure, Father. I'm nineteen, but I want another couple of years here. I want to teach these youngest boys a thing or two.'

It would be a different stage for the family without the twins, but it had to happen sooner or later. Dan needed to spread his wings, he was restless, itching for adventure. Edith's gaze lingered on Michael; her kindred spirit, the most soft-hearted, caring and kind son a mother could ever wish for. She would miss them, but they weren't boys any longer, rather two young men on the cusp of a new adventure.

Far to the west a dingo howled; another, nearer the small hut, took up the mournful cry. Edith looked around the table in the golden glow of the kerosene lantern. The dingoes howled again, and a shiver ran down her spine.

A spider running over my grave, she thought. Was this a premonition of what lay ahead, or was it normal anxiety for a mother experiencing the impending separation of her family for the first time? It would take her a long time to find out and, when she did, she would think back to this night so many years earlier, when they had all sat together as a family, looking forward to a bright future.

~~~

ELIZABETH'S STAR is Book 1 in a series of 3 books - We'll Meet Again Trilogy

~~~